Book Two in 'The Corrupted Trilogy'

Afflicted

R E Harper

ISBN:978-1-80068-368-6

Dedicated to anyone who has ever struggled with loving themselves because it can be one of the hardest things we learn.

'It is good for me that I have been afflicted.'

- Mary Rowlandson

Prologue

I wish I could help her; I know she's struggling, but there is not much I can do for her until she accepts help. I wish I could tell her why I'm so intrigued and inspired by her, but I know I can't; there are rules. Besides, I don't want to add my own issues on to what she is already dealing with…I'm the psychiatrist after all, not the patient. My mind is still trying to process what happened and I feel guilty that I didn't do more to protect her. If she ever found out the truth, I'm not sure she'd ever forgive me, and she's been through so much already.

Chapter 1: Call me Daniel

Robertson sat behind his desk in the office and glanced at his watch anxiously. Lucy was running late for their appointment, which wouldn't be as much of a concern if she hadn't skipped the previous five. Deciding this time that he needed to take action, Robertson stood up and walked out of his office towards the cafeteria to search for Lucy. Just before he got there, he walked into nurse Elaine.

"Ahh Hi Elaine," he greeted, "have you seen Lucy? She's late for our appointment." Elaine grimaced and shrugged her shoulders apologetically.

"I think she is in the gym again," she said sadly. Robertson ran a hand through his hair and stared ahead without really seeing, lost in thought. Why couldn't Lucy just try to hear him out? He knew she'd needed time to process, and he thought he'd been helping her to look the other way over the missed sessions. However, now it was starting to dawn on him that perhaps it had not been the best decision, because instead of processing, Lucy seemed to be avoiding the issue entirely. Elaine suddenly cleared her throat reminding him that she was still there.

"She's not doing so well, is she?" he said, trying to sound casual. Elaine shook her head sadly.

"The fact she thought she was innocent was the only thing she had going for her." Robertson did not have a response to this because he knew it was the truth. Instead, he looked down at the floor, while putting both his hands in his pockets. He couldn't help but feeling somewhat responsible for Lucy's condition despite knowing that it was what had needed to happen. When he looked back up, Elaine was still there and opened her mouth as if she was struggling to say something. Robertson nodded at her in encouragement. "I know I'm not supposed to know," acknowledged Elaine hesitantly, "but I heard the other doctor talking about Remy." Robertson frowned at her, he already felt so bad knowing he should have done more, but he hardly felt like discussing all that with a work colleague.

"Inquiries are still ongoing at this stage," affirmed Robertson politely, "but she clearly had mental health issues that we weren't aware of. I'm sure things will be out in the open before too long." He shuffled nervously on his feet wondering how to make a swift exit.

"Does Lucy know about the inquiry?" asked Elaine anxiously. Robertson shook his head.

"I thought it best not tell her unless it pulls anything up," he replied, "She's already dealing with so much." Elaine nodded and looked as though she wanted to ask more questions. However, sensing that the doctor was becoming increasingly uncomfortable with the conversation, she merely nodded at him and walked down the corridor. Robertson tried not to dwell on what Elaine had said as he walked to the institute gym. His thoughts turned to Lucy and how it might be a good thing if she was pouring her stress into exercise.

Opening the single door to the gym he couldn't help but notice it was smaller than he remembered, only having seen it once before when he was given a tour upon beginning his job. He nodded at the security guard stood to the right just inside the door and the security guard politely nodded back after laying his eyes on Robertson's staff lanyard.

Robertson looked around the small, long room, filled with various types of exercise machines, to find Lucy working out on a cross trainer. He sighed as he took a moment to watch her, she clearly had a lot of frustration as she was frantically working the machine with a fierce look of determination etched on her face. She definitely looked as though she had something to prove. Eventually he walked towards her put his hand on hers. "Lucy," said Robertson and Lucy gasped, as she turned her head towards him.

"Oh, I'm late for our appointment, aren't I?" She glanced at the clock on the wall, but she did not sound sincere. Robertson shrugged his shoulders casually, though he was more annoyed with her lack of care then he would allow her to see.

"Not to worry. You've only missed the first ten minutes," he said kindly, "it's a good job I've found you. We can go back to the office from here." Lucy stopped moving on the machine and jumped off it. She grabbed her bottle of water from off the floor and took a sip as Robertson gestured for her to follow him.

"What? Now?" asked Lucy, looking down at herself. Robertson nodded at her in response. "But I'm all sweaty and smelly!" protested Lucy beseechingly. She was wearing grey workout bottoms, an oversized t-shirt, and cheap trainers. Robertson put a hand under his chin and observed her for a moment or two before he grinned.

"You'll do," he stated, and Lucy's mouth dropped open in surprise. Roberson did not wait for her to reply, instead he gestured with his head for her to follow him. Then he turned around and began to head for the door. Lucy watched him for a moment debating whether to follow. Eventually she sighed and headed in the direction of his office.

Once they had arrived in his office, he gestured for her to sit down, but Lucy had already had her fill of following his instructions especially after he had interrupted her workout session, so she crossed her arms and tilted her head to the side waiting for him to speak. Robertson sighed and sat down in his chair. "You do know that avoiding our sessions won't do you any good, don't you?"

"Who says I'm avoiding them?" she answered defensively.

"Who says I'm that stupid?" retorted Robertson, "Our last session, apparently you had food poisoning, the session before that it was a highly contagious cough and I think the time before that you said you'd overslept." He did not look angry but held up his hand as if encouraging her to explain herself. Finally, Lucy sighed.

"I'm still processing everything," she said honestly. Robertson nodded.

"I'm aware. I don't expect you to have figured things out overnight." Lucy flung her arms into the air in frustration.

“Then how do you expect me to talk about them?” Robertson looked at her sympathetically but offered no explanation. Lucy gave up and flung herself in the chair in front of his desk.

“Well trying would be a very good start don’t you think?” he suggested, but Lucy forcibly shook her head.

“I’m worried, that if I start talking, I’ll lose it completely,” she admitted sadly, “I can barely deal with my own dark thoughts about what I did. I can’t even begin to tell them to somebody else.” Robertson leaned forward and propped his elbows up on the desk.

“I’m not for a minute saying it’s going to be easy,” he stated, “but I can promise you it will help.” Lucy opened her mouth to tell him to mind his own business or something along those lines, but then she closed it again. She knew he was only trying to help, but she had given up hope and there was nothing he could do to change that. Instead, she decided to go for a different approach.

“I might end up shouting at you, crying or worse.” She looked at him pointedly. Robertson studied her expression for a moment before he continued.

“I don’t care about that,” he replied, “In fact go for it; shout at me, insult me...heck, slap me again if it helps, but anything is better than you going through this alone.” Lucy just stared at him in response hardly knowing what to say. She had never met anyone so willing to help her before, so unwilling to not allow her to deal with the darkness alone, yet she was also so unwilling to be helped.

“Taking to you would be like admitting I need help,” she admitted quietly. She wrapped her arms around herself and nervously drummed her fingers against her arms.

“I think we both agree that you do need help.” Lucy nodded at him but did nothing to indicate that she was now willing to cooperate.

“But it’s more than that,” she explained anxiously, “It would be like admitting I’m deserving of help, when I feel like anything but.” Robertson nodded, then gave her a sad smile.

"You don't think you deserve anything much, do you?" he asked quietly. He leaned back in his chair and tentatively awaited her answer.

"Not after what I did. I don't just feel guilty. I feel ashamed, disgusted with myself. Lower than the lowest creature who walks the earth. I could try to blame what I've been through, all the crap I had to put up with, but the unavoidable truth is I did it; I made that choice, and I can't ever take it back." Robertson opened and closed his mouth several times trying to decide the right thing to say.

"But what led you to make that choice?" he asked, "That's what we need to explore. Do you honestly think people are born with the desire to kill others?" Lucy looked horrified at the very suggestion and shook her head quickly.

"Of course not, "she replied "but I don't believe there is any excuse for killing either." Robertson put a hand to his chin as though deep in thought.

"Have you heard of the Trolley Dilemma?" he asked, and Lucy shrugged her shoulders feeling perplexed. "Imagine a trolley cart is heading down a track, it's out of control and there is no way of stopping it, but you can divert it to one of two tracks." Lucy sighed wondering where he was going with all of this. "The first track has two family members on it who will surely be killed if the train goes that way," said Robertson, "but on the other track is ten complete strangers who you don't know who would also be killed if you diverted it that way." Lucy raised her eyebrows at him, she almost appreciated the point he was trying to make, but she knew it was not the same thing "You may have made a choice Lucy," said Robertson earnestly, "and yes it was probably the worse choice you ever made and feeling guilty is understandable. However, that impossible choice was forced upon you by bad experiences and a lack of support, which led you to sleeping on the streets and fearing for your life." Lucy almost admired the passion in his voice as he spoke. She desperately wanted to believe him; to have the strength to fight, but it was no use.

“I could have walked away.” As much as she respected him, she was unwilling to allow anyone to sway her from the notion that she had taken someone’s life, even if it had not been intentional.

“So could he.” Lucy scoffed at this.

“Doesn’t mean he deserved to die,” she responded angrily.

“It doesn’t mean you don’t deserve to live.”

A silence descended among them as they both felt the tension of sharing very different perspectives. Lucy wanted to be angry with him for trying to defend her, to defend in any part what she had done, but she didn’t have the energy for it. She didn’t have the energy for anything much lately, apart from religiously going to the gym because it helped her to know that she could still feel something. Eventually after five minutes of silence, Robertson spoke. “Lucy? Can I tell you something? Promise you won’t get upset?” Lucy looked at him wondering what secret he was about to divulge.

“What?” she asked curiously.

“You’ve just been talking about it,” he said quietly, and he watched her carefully for a reaction. Lucy blinked at him as she realised, he was right, and it infuriated her.

“You’re an arsehole you know.” she said.

“I’ve been told,” he replied sincerely. Lucy sighed and stood up from the chair feeling the need to walk around the office. Robertson watched her curiously, appearing unconcerned. “Your lawyer is coming to see you this afternoon, right?” he asked, making an attempt to change the subject. Lucy scowled at the question.

“Yes! I kind of wish I could represent myself. I don’t trust many people; that last one tried to make me plead not guilty.”

“You might like this one,” he replied, “I have heard he is very good at his job.” Lucy chose not to respond to this, preferring to make up her own mind once she had met him.

"Will you be there?" she asked curiously, "At the meeting with my lawyer?" Robertson shook his head.

"No, it wouldn't be appropriate," he stated, "You could ask me there as your support, but I don't think it's a good idea. I might have to give testimony in court." Lucy's mouth dropped open, but she closed it again quickly. Of course, it should come as no surprise to her that the doc might be asked to testify in her court case, but she hadn't given it much thought.

"What would you say if you are?" she asked curiously. Robertson held up his hands as if the answer was obvious.

"The truth," he stated. Then he smiled at her to offer some reassurance. Lucy wanted to smile back at him, to show that she appreciated it, but she couldn't bring herself to so instead she nodded.

"Good. So what do you think my chances are Doc?" Robertson smiled at her then stood up and came around the desk to see in front of her on the edge of it.

"Not that I'm opposed to my delightful nickname," he stated, "but do you ever get bored of calling me Doc?" Lucy raised her eyebrows in surprised and she couldn't help but notice he had ignored her question.

"Not really. Doctor Robertson is a bit long winded. Why?" Robertson looked extremely amused as he crossed his arms.

"You can call me Daniel," he offered. Lucy suddenly burst out laughing and then caught herself. She hadn't laughed in a long time, and she felt guilty for doing so. Robertson gaped at her seemingly offended at her response to his gesture. "What?" he asked irritated, "It's my name!" Lucy smiled at him slightly.

"I know," she acknowledged, "It just seems strange. It could take some getting used to." Robertson nodded and smiled.

"Why?" he asked sarcastically. "Are you going anywhere?" Lucy was about to snap at him when she looked up at his face and realised that he was teasing her. Caught in the moment, she decided to play along with his little game.

“As a matter of fact ,I was thinking of nipping to the theatre this afternoon,” she replied, “Would you care to join?” Robertson’s smile grew wider, delighted that Lucy was reverting back to her old habits of teasing him.

“Sure!” he stated enthusiastically, “I like theatre. What we would be watching?” Lucy put a finger under her chin as if the decision was a deep thought provoking one.

“I’ve never seen Wicked. That’s supposed to be good.” Robertson suddenly grinned as if enjoying a private joke.

“About a person who’s gravely misunderstood by many around her,” he offered “Sometimes even misunderstood by herself; I think you’d like it.” Lucy face palmed herself, trust the doc to relate everything back to psychoanalysing her.

“Maybe one day,” she said hopefully. She couldn’t help but think what her life might be like now if she’d taken a different path, made different choices, would she be a person who regularly went to theatre? Would she be a wife? A mother? A successful woman? “What do you do?” she asked suddenly, and Robertson blinked at her unsure as to the meaning of her question.

“At the theatre?” he asked bemused, causing Lucy to shake her head.

“No; in your free time. Do you hang out at the local pub? Shoot some hoops with the guys?” Robertson laughed.

“Do I even look like I’ve shot a hoop in my life?” he questioned, “Basketball really isn’t my sport.” Lucy grinned sheepishly, she liked that he was able to make fun of himself.

“The pub then?” she asked. Robertson shook his head at her.

“I’m not much of a drinker,” he stated honestly. Lucy sighed; she wanted to get an idea of what was happening in the outside world, but it didn't look like she would get them from Robertson, who didn't sound like he ever went anywhere or did anything.

"Do you ever have any fun?" she asked earnestly. Robertson grimaced and put a hand to the back of his head.

"I like to travel, explore culture, art, theatre, the museum, eat nice food," he offered, "You know the boring stuff." Lucy shook her head.

"It all sounds amazing!" she said, and she really meant it, but then anything outside of these four walls sounded like heaven compared to what she had been used to the past two years. Suddenly Robertson looked at his watch and stood up from the desk.

"Well I won't keep you," he noted, "I don't want you to be late for your first appointment with your new lawyer." He held out his hand to help her up out of the chair, Lucy considered it an odd gesture because it was not something he had done before, but she took it anyway and pulled herself up. "Things will get better," he stated, "Please try to come to your next appointment." Lucy realised that they were still holding hands and looked down at hers in his curiously. Robertson seemed to realise this too, for he suddenly looked down and let go of her hand quickly. To avoid any awkwardness, she quickly headed for the door and opened it.

"Well see you tomorrow…Daniel." Robertson laughed as she closed the door behind her.

Chapter 2: Your Mind Can Convict You

Lucy took a deep breath trying to steal herself before she entered the room to meet her second lawyer. She really didn't see the point of having one; she remembered killing someone, so she was guilty, and it was as simple as that. However, for some reason, formality and the Doc had dictated or rather advised that she was to participate in a circus show with a judge and jury.

When she entered the room, she saw a tall well-built handsome black man with short black hair and piercing brown eyes. He was dressed in a sharp navy suit paired with a light blue tie, and he was sat behind a rectangular wooden table. He smiled and stood up when he saw her come in.

"Hello," he said, holding out his hand, "you must be Lucy." Lucy took his hand somewhat bemused. "My name is Elijah James," he added politely. "I'm looking forward to working with you." Lucy rolled her eyes. She got that he was trying to make a good impression, but that didn't mean he had to be so over the top.

"Are you really?" she asked curiously, and he looked at her surprise. "Why would you be looking forward to working with a murderer?" She questioned bluntly, "what does that say about you?" Elijah did not look offended by her questions; instead, he paused thoughtfully to consider them.

"It says that it is not my job to judge," he replied, "instead it's my job to ensure the jury has the clearest picture possible of why you did what you did to be able to make their decision." Lucy shrugged her shoulders. He could try to over complicate matters as much as he wanted, but the bottom line was that it didn't matter why it had happened. The point was it had happened, and by her hands. She took a seat on the chair at the table in front of him and crossed her arms, determined not to allow him to give her any pardons. However, Elijah smiled at her and sat down too, almost as if he had mistaken her taking a seat for some form of cooperation. "I believe your last lawyer quit," he offered, "Care to tell me why?" Lucy rolled her eyes as she noted the file on the table in front of him.

"I'm sure you already know!" she responded. She was extremely guarded, unsure whether she could even begin to trust the person who would be representing her in the justice system. Then again, it didn't really matter; he would only be her lawyer until the plea hearing.

"You refused to work with him because you feel so much guilt about what you did. Apparently the last straw was when he suggested you plead not guilty." Lucy scowled in disgust; why didn't people understand? She didn't deserve to be treated like a normal human being; she was a murderer! They should not be so quick to try and defend her actions!

"He treated me like I was innocent," she said bitterly, "I didn't deserve that." Elijah put a hand to his chin thoughtfully.

"It's the job of a lawyer though," he stated simply, "I must admit I was surprised when Dan…Dr Robertson phoned me." Lucy suddenly sat up in her chair surprised.

"Wait?" she said cautiously, "He recommended you for me? Are you two friends or something?" Elijah looked surprised that she had not been made aware of this information. "We went to college together," he answered honestly, "He seems to think we will make a good team you and I."

"Does he indeed?" replied Lucy, making a mental note to have words with 'Daniel' next time she saw him. Elijah looked at her curiously and it irked Lucy. It was the same kind of expression that the doc wore when he was trying to psychoanalyse her.

"I can tell you are a hard person to win over," said Elijah finally. He crossed his arms and leaned back in his chair. Lucy sighed in frustration, she didn't care whether she gained his approval or not! In fact, she would prefer it if he hated her, at least then she could feel more confident about his character.

“Murderers can’t afford to be picky,” she stated sarcastically. Elijah smiled, which made Lucy’s mouth drop open slightly. She was not used to people being so casual to her defensive attitude, well apart from the Doc, but even he was rattled every now and again.

“Please don’t say anything like that in court,” he suggested seriously, but he looked amused at her comment.

“I thought they had to hear the truth.” she replied. She placed her elbow on the table and leaned on her hand while tapping her other one on the table. Elijah sighed, quietly wondering just how much he had taken on with this new client.

“They do need to hear the truth, but the truth can be painted with many different colours,” he finally answered. Lucy scoffed and held up her hands.

“Isn’t that the same as lying?” she queried. Elijah shook his head slowly.

“Not at all, it’s not like we’re making up evidence,” he protested, “We’re just telling our side of the story the way we see it.” Lucy took a moment to think about what he was saying, but eventually she sank further back in her chair realising it didn’t matter either way.

“How do you see it?” she asked curiously, “Cause the way I see it, I killed someone.” Elijah raised his eyebrows.

“Is it just that black and white?” he inquired inquisitively, “You saw someone in the street? Said hey have some of this and stabbed them with a knife cause you felt like it?” Lucy shuddered at the malice in his words.

“No, who does that?” she answered. Elijah looked at her pointedly while adjusting his suit jacket.

“Other murderers,” he said bluntly, “See that’s what we’re doing Lucy, we’re trying to make it clear that your intent that night was not to end someone’s life but merely to defend yourself.” Lucy was torn, she knew there was a difference between what she had done and someone who actually intended and planned to commit murder, but she was so wrapped up in her guilt that all she could think about was getting the worst possible punishment. Finally, she decided that she did not have to commit to anything for now and just needed information about what was to come.

"So what are we going to do?" she asked, "Say that my mental health was a factor? We've got to be careful otherwise they'll just keep me in somewhere like here." Elijah looked mildly impressed by her comment, but this annoyed Lucy, making her wonder if he thought she was mentally challenged.

"The point is Lucy, I really think I can get you off on self- defence at a push," he noted seriously, "but you need to decide how much you want this, how much your life is worth fighting for. I think the biggest thing you're struggling with right now is accepting you made a mistake…yes it was a horrible mistake with drastic consequences, but it wasn't calculated. You're not evil; you were scared and lashed out. Unless you decide you want to defend yourself in this trial, then what is there to look forward to in life? Rotting in some jail cell for the next ten years?" Lucy wrapped her arms around her shoulders, she knew he was right, and it was not like she wanted to waste the next ten years of her life in jail, but what else was there? How could she ever move passed what she had done?

Elijah stood up and opened his briefcase to put her file back into it. Lucy casually gazed at its contents and saw a small bible tucked into a side pocket. "Are you a Christian?" blurted Lucy looking up at him. Elijah raised his eyebrows in surprise but nodded. "My best friend was a Christian," explained Lucy honestly "but then she died." Elijah closed his briefcase, straightened his tie, and put a hand on Lucy's shoulder. She looked at it in distain but said nothing.

"Then she'll be with God," He reassured, but Lucy found his statement far from satisfactory. In fact, she found it outrageous; how could he imply that her friend was now happily chatting away in heaven with the same God who had given her cancer? The same God who if he existed had done nothing to prevent Lucy from becoming a murderer?

"You must meet lots of people like me," she stated "murderers, thieves…how can you think there is a God when there is so much evil in the world?" Elijah did not seem the least bit offended by her questions, instead he smiled at her slightly.

"It's because of all the evil in the world that I know there is a God." Lucy stared at him in confusion.

"How can any God forgive such evil?" she protested. Elijah smiled slightly.

"If God only forgave the people who deserved it then none of us would be going to heaven," answered Elijah coolly. His calm demeanour annoyed Lucy, she wished he could give her more conclusive answers, so instead she decided to try enticing him into an argument.

"I don't believe there is a God or a heaven," she stated forcefully. Elijah casually shrugged his shoulders but continued to smile at her.

"Then we agree to disagree," he said "I'm up to speed with your case but will go through the proper details the day after tomorrow. I'm expecting the plea hearing to be next week but will let you know when I know. Have a think about what we've said today; your mind can convict you more than they can in that courtroom." He casually walked over to the door and knocked on it to be let out by security.

"Maybe God can intervene on my behalf," replied Lucy sarcastically. However, this only caused Elijah to chuckle.

"Well, I'll certainly be praying."

Then the door opened, and he was gone, leaving Lucy alone with her troubling thoughts. She couldn't believe she was surrounded by so many people who put their faith in a God who would allow all this to happen; was it because their lives were so much better than hers? She wanted more than anything to feel there was a God out there, that there was a purpose to all this. However, accepting that would not only mean accepting that she might just be heading to a dark place when she died, but that God allowed everything that she had been through to come to pass. Even allowed Father Graham into his church, had he known he would make that decision to hurt Lucy? She remembered something Bella said about God giving people choices, was God hoping Father Graham would make the right choice. If he had made the right choice, would she even be here right now?

Chapter 3: What if he were a Good Man…

I smile at Father Graham as he stands talking behind the pulpit. He really has been such a strong role model for me in my walk with God, ever since he started babysitting me occasionally on a Sunday after church, while my brother was taken to football practice. Of course, I'm 17 now and I don't need a babysitter, but I'm still glad he is in my life. He was really there for me when I lost Bella 6 months ago. "We don't just need God, we need to be Godly," he says, "May God bless you as you leave here today." Then the congregation gets up to leave and I stay seated. I know that Father Graham wants to talk to me. I watch as he makes his usual rounds asking how people are and then finally, he comes and sits beside me.

"Have you continued to pray about continuing your studies in America?" he asks curiously, and I sigh. I should have known that's why he wanted to talk to me, I haven't made up my mind yet, and I know he wants me to stay to help out within the church in some way. Probably partly so he can continue to keep an eye on me; he can be quite protective. He's even trying to convince me to become head of the children's group here, but I just don't feel it's where I'm meant to be.

"I have," I reply honestly, "but I feel like God isn't answering." Father Graham smiles knowingly.

"God always answers," he states, "but sometimes we're not prepared to listen and other times he's trying to teach us something in the waiting." I sigh, I know he is right, and that God is not a genie who merely grants wishes. Yet it's still frustrating to hope for something and yet not know if it's meant for me.

"I guess I'm just impatient." I admit and Father Graham nods at me as if he completely understands what it's like to ask for things and not be given them. Then my thoughts turn to college and how at the moment, it's being made more difficult by a man child named Jeremy Oakley.

"That guy is still harassing me," I continue, "Even though I told him I won't date him because he's not a Christian." Father Graham places a hand on my shoulder and looks at me in concern.

"I hope that is not the reason you are considering going to America?" he asks. I shake my head truthfully, although I am less than impressed with Jeremy's stalker tendencies, its more because I want to travel and see what more the USA has to offer. I can't explain it, but I feel like I belong there somehow.

"No, I just feel like I want to go somewhere completely new," I say, "especially now that my dad and Bella are gone." Father Graham nods and frowns at me.

"Yes, you've been through a lot in such a short time." he admits "That's why you must pray for God to take away your hurt and suffering. It can do things to a person if left unchecked." I nod, although I am unsure whether my hurt over Bella or my dad can ever be taken away; I'm not even sure if I want it to be taken away because who would I be without it?

"What if who we are is because of that hurt and anger?" I ask curiously and Father Graham shakes his head at me quickly.

"I really don't believe that," he says calmly, "God uses hurt and anger to shape us, but that doesn't mean we have to keep it." I study Father Graham's face carefully, I've always believed him to be a wise man, but this time he sounds like he is speaking from experience.

"Has he taken your hurt and anger away?" I ask. Then I immediately regret saying it; it's a personal question and not one that I should be asking my priest. However, Father Graham looks at me thoughtfully, it would seem the question hasn't offended.

"Yes, but it wasn't easy. I had a rather horrific childhood; my dad was a monster to put it frankly."

"Oh wow," I reply, "I'm sorry." I cannot think of anything else to say, my parents have always had their moments, but I would certainly not describe either of them as having been a monster.

That's quite a strong opinion to make especially coming from a priest, so I know whatever his dad did then it must have been pretty terrible.

"Don't be sorry," insists Father Graham, "God taught me something through it, he taught me that I could live a life full of fear, anger and hurt or I could allow God to work in me and turn it into something I could help others with. It's why I volunteer to help damaged youths at the local community centre." My respect for Father Graham has just gone up tenfold, it's one thing to survive suffering and pain, but to turn it into something that can actually benefit somebody else is inspiring and I hope one day I get to be that selfless.

"What do you think would have happened if God hadn't taken your hurt and anger?" I question in wonder. Father Graham shivers and I realise that he must ponder the question a lot himself.

"I dread to think," he answers truthfully "I probably would have become a monster too. Not by choice, but indirectly by allowing that pain and anger to manifest inside of me. Pain and anger are tools that the enemy can use to motivate you into doing evil." I nod, I know he's right, so I make a mental note to say a prayer tonight for God to at least ensure that my sadness and anger over Bella and my dad does not go unchecked.

"Thank you, Father Graham," I say gratefully, "I don't know what I would do right now without your council or Gods. I know he has a plan for me I'm just not sure what at the moment." I stand up to leave as I said I would help my mum make Sunday lunch.

"I'm sure he has an amazing plan for you," acknowledges Father Graham in a reassuring tone. Then he too stands up and begins to make his way back to his office at the back of the church.

I smile as I exit thinking about how my life is full of endless possibilities and wondering which one, I will choose.

Predicted Verdict: Guilty

Chapter 4: Too Busy Surviving

Once again Robertson was alone in his office when Lucy should have been there for their appointment. He had tried to be kind and considerate with her, but now he saw that he might have to take a firmer approach, so he picked up the phone. "Nicoletta, can you get security to escort Lucy to her appointment please?" he said politely.

Ten minutes later, there was a knock on the door. Robertson stood up to answer it, but before he could get there. Lucy burst in looking furious and Robertson had to try extremely hard not to laugh as he took stock of the unicorn pyjamas bottoms she was wearing with a baby pink t-shirt.

"What an earth are you playing at?" she stated furiously. Robertson shrugged and security looked at him as if they were unsure if they should leave Lucy alone with him, but he simply nodded and gestured for them to close the door.

"I like the unicorns," he noted, as he sat back down in his chair. Lucy looked torn between amusement and annoyance.

"I've seen you wear worse ties," she replied, and Robertson chuckled once more. They sat there in silence for a few moments, before Robertson sighed and decided to cut to the chase.

"It's a long and drawn-out process Lucy," he stated seriously "It's not just about accepting what you did, it's about understanding why you did what you did and putting coping strategies in place, so it doesn't happen again. Not that it would because I would hope you wouldn't be in the same position, but these things take time, it's not unusual for people who have had dissociative amnesia to suffer from PTSD, depression or to even regress after the things they've been through." Robertson leaned back in his chair after he spoke, observing her to see if his words had made any impact. Lucy sat up in her chair with a look of outrage.

"Where do you get off on such bullshit?" she snapped, "Your psychoanalysing skills are way off the mark and this whole fucking professor vibe you've got going on is unbelievably creepy. So don't try and sing your merry song to me pal cause I don't give a shit!" She sat back in the chair, crossed her arms, and waited for his reaction. Robertson glared at her in frustration, in some ways he and Lucy had made a lot of progress since he had started working with her and in other ways, he felt they had not made much progress at all. However, he knew he needed to be patient, he knew that with his patients it was always two steps forward and one step back.

"You finished?" he asked trying to keep his tone light. Lucy smiled at him slightly.

"Yeah, I think I am," she confirmed casually "How was your day?" Robertson grinned at her in amusement.

"Boring…uneventful until now," he admitted honestly, "How was yours?" Lucy grimaced at his question; she couldn't lie to him.

"Same as every other day really," she retorted, "really fucking shit! Every time I close my eyes…every time I breathe…every time I move…I see it happening all over again, I see myself plunging that knife through his chest and I'm screaming at myself to stop, but I never do." When she had finished, she looked at him to see if he would be looking at her any differently, but he wasn't.

"The important thing is that you're screaming at yourself to stop." Lucy was halfway through rolling her eyes at him when she suddenly stopped and looked away.

"My new lawyer thinks I should plead not guilty to manslaughter," she relayed. Robertson nodded seemingly unsurprised.

"Well, he's a good lawyer. I'd listen to him." This time Lucy did roll her eyes.

"Of course you would think he's a good lawyer," she said, "when were you going to tell me you'd recommended him, you went to college together." Robertson studied Lucy's expression carefully, trying to gauge if she was annoyed, but it was more curiosity, he recognised on her face, than anything.

“Is that a problem?” he asked. Lucy ignored the question because she was not sure how to answer it.

“How can I stand up there though and claim not to be guilty of manslaughter when I feel like I deserve so much worse?” said Lucy sadly. She put her head down and looked at the floor. Robertson blinked trying very hard to control the conflicting emotions he was feeling.

“You think you deserve to be prosecuted for murder?” he asked quietly. Lucy nodded and Robertson felt his heart sink into his stomach. He wished more than anything he could ease some of her guilt, but he knew she had to do that for herself. Instead, he tried to appeal to her reasoning.

“But it wasn’t premeditated,” he offered, “and it wasn’t done with malice.” Lucy scowled, brushing off his comments as if they were a personal attack.

“What different does it make?” she protested. “He’s still dead.” Robertson wanted to tell her that it made all the difference in the world, but he knew that would get them nowhere so instead he kept quiet. “He thinks he can get me off on self-defence,” said Lucy miserably, sinking lower into her chair.

“I’m guessing you are not so happy about that,” sighed Robertson. She looked at him in disgust, before her expression softened realising that it was not him, she was angry and disgusted with; it was herself.

“It would mean I’d get off completely. How can that even be an outcome? I took away somebody’s life, whether it was to protect myself or not; he’s still dead!” Robertson said nothing for a moment, as he contemplated what he could say to ease her suffering. He knew what he wanted to say, but it might make things worse. Instead, he decided that he would try a different approach and encourage her to follow her own reasoning.

“What do you deserve?” he asked, leaning his elbows on the desk and propping his head on his hands. Lucy frowned and avoided his eye contact.

“I deserve to be locked up and never let out.” It was not the answer the Robertson had been hoping for, but at least she was being honest.

“You think you are a danger to society?” he asked. This time Lucy looked up at him sadly.

“A few months ago didn’t think I was a murderer,” she acknowledged miserably, “but I am! Who knows what else I’m capable of?” Robertson had to prevent himself from groaning out loud, instead he stood up and walked over to his bookshelf causing Lucy to look at him curiously.

“I’d like you to read something for me,” he suggested. Lucy scowled.

“Oh great!” she said sarcastically, “homework!” Robertson took a small paperback book off the shelf and shook his head in response to her comment.

“No,” he replied honestly, “I’d just like your thoughts on something.” He then opened the book, skimmed through a few pages before suddenly tearing a page out and handing it to her. Lucy gapped at him in disbelief as she took the page.

“You should probably stay away from libraries you know,” she commented, and Robertson grinned at her sheepishly. He sat back down in his chair and looked at her expectantly.

“You want me to read it now?” she asked. Robertson nodded.

“Why? Do you have more pressing plans?”

Lucy sighed and leaned back in her chair as she read the words contained on the small page she held in her hand. It was about a woman called Isabel White, she had been married to a guy who had soon developed a bad temper and physically abused her over the course of their five-year marriage. Eventually, she’d had enough and when he was in the process of beating her, she had taken a carving knife and ran him through with it. Once she had finished reading the page Lucy looked up at Robertson.

"She served 10 years in jail," he stated, and Lucy's mouth fell open. She sat up in the chair and threw her hands up in the air.

"That's bullshit!" she retorted, "After all the things he did to her…tortured her…humiliated her...all she did was put an end to her suffering by sticking up for herself...it wasn't her fault!" Robertson smiled and looked at her pointedly. Lucy blinked as she suddenly realised what he was getting at. "Oh!" she exclaimed, as she sank back in her chair, "I know what you did there, but she had no way out…she'd suffered for years…been tortured…" Lucy trailed off as she realised that she couldn't quite put into words what she really wanted to say. Robertson stood up from his chair, came around the desk and perched on the end of it.

"Do you think it's only self-defence if you're subjected to torture?" he remarked. Then he crossed his arms observing her carefully while awaiting a response.

"No," said Lucy cautiously, "but that guy deserved it; he hurt her!" Robertson rubbed his chin thoughtfully with his hand.

"So it's only self-Defence if someone deserves it?" he further inquired. Lucy groaned loudly feeling conflicted.

"No," said Lucy exasperated, "but he had hurt her again and again year after year." She looked at him beseechingly, almost as if pleading for him not to continue, but Robertson knew that his questions were having some impact, so he persevered regardless.

"You'd been hurt again and again, year after year," he stated, but Lucy shook her head.

"Not by the person I killed!" she said firmly. Robertson could tell that she was beginning to get rather irritated by the way her hands balled into fists, but he couldn't miss out on this opportunity to get through to her. So he moved off the edge off the desk and came to crouch in front of her so that she could not avoid eye contact with him.

Yes," he said sternly, "but you thought he was trying to hurt you."

"It doesn't mean he would have," protested Lucy quietly.

"It doesn't mean he wouldn't have either." He noticed that Lucy was trying to avoid his eye contact and he couldn't blame her. He knew it was hard to face someone's kindness when you thought so little of yourself.

"Why are you so determined to make me see myself as just a victim in this?" she inquired. Robertson placed a hand over hers and she looked down at it, before making eye contact with him again.

"I'm not. I'm trying to encourage you to be kind to yourself. Something I don't think you ever learnt to do because you're too busy surviving." Lucy felt tears begin to form in her eyes at the truth in his words.

"I'm just fucked up," said Lucy finally and she turned her hand around so that they were now holding hands. Robertson looked at her for a few moments and he could tell they were both wondering the same thing; whether she had crossed a line? Yet deep down, he knew that they had crossed and blurred so many lines, that it was becoming more difficult to see them. He knew he had to maintain professional boundaries, but there was also a battle raging inside of him, about whether to tell her a secret he had been keeping or to just hold his silence. He knew that Lucy thought of him as this 'well put together psychiatrist', who didn't know what it was to suffer, but it was a misconception, one that he actively encouraged.

"Maybe I'm as fucked up too," he admitted, "Maybe I'm just better at hiding it. Humans have this fucked up idea of pain; that you deal with it, and it makes you stronger, but it's still there, festering…we just learn to accept it as a part of ourselves, It never goes away, it does fade in time, but it doesn't make us stronger…surviving makes us stronger." Lucy felt a tear roll down her cheek at his confession, Robertson considered wiping her tear away, but suddenly realised how inappropriate that would be, so he let go off her hand, stood up and retrieved the box of tissues from his desk.

"I don't want to spend my life just surviving," said Lucy miserably as she took a tissue from the box, he held out to her.

"Then you need to fight for something better." Lucy looked at him bewildered.

"What though?" she asked desperately. Suddenly Robertson smiled at her.

"I was hoping you'd ask," he replied, and Lucy sighed. Robertson could tell that she was less than enthusiastic, but he also knew that no matter what Lucy thought of herself, he would not give up on her.

Chapter 5: She'd think I was a fraud

I nearly told her today; I nearly let it all come spilling out. The only thing that stopped me is that I'm a complete coward. I don't want to see her crumble as she learns the truth about everything; about me, about what I've done! I know she thinks I'm better than her, but if only she knew what kind of man I really am, she'd think I was a fraud, and the truth is she'd be right. I am a fraud; I sit behind that desk everyday trying to keep my professional head on. Trying to help people with their problems, but it's all an act, because inside, I'm just as messed up as the rest of them. I didn't mean for any of this to happen and now I'm in far over my head. It's all going to come out eventually; it's inevitable, but for now I just can't bear to destroy the trust that I've built up with her. I still don't know everything for myself, there is still more to find out, so for that reason all of it must remain a secret.

Chapter 6: Everybody has Secrets

The next day, Lucy found herself sat in the meeting room sat opposite Elijah. They had already said their hello, but now they both seemed intent on playing a long game of awkward silence each hoping the other might have something to say first. Finally, Elijah sighed and sat up slightly in his chair.

"We finally have…" he began. However, suddenly there was a gentle knock at the door and as it opened slightly, Robertson put his head through it.

"Ahh sorry to interrupt," said Robertson, looking slightly sheepish, "Elijah I was just wondering if you could run by my office before you leave." Elijah nodded in response. Robertson smiled at Lucy who seemed rather bemused at his appearance.

"Either come in or go away," she said finally, though she grinned at him slightly. Robertson seemed to take it as a begrudging invitation and entered the room. Elijah quickly looked between them both as if he was trying to figure out what had just happened.

"We finally have a date for the plea hearing," he stated bewildered, "its next week." Lucy shrugged as if she was not interested in the slightest. Elijah looked at Robertson with a pained expression.

"Do you think it will take long from the plea hearing to go to the main trial?" asked Robertson. Lucy rolled her eyes, because she already knew the answer; besides she wasn't planning on going to trail anyway, but instead of chiming in with a sarcastic comment, she decided to let Elijah answer.

"Not really," explained Elijah "Not in cases such as these."

"Do you think Remy might show up?" blurted out Lucy suddenly. Elijah exchanged puzzled glances with Robertson as if he was unsure how to answer the question.

"Why would she?" asked Robertson quietly. He crossed his arms and leaned against the wall.

"Well, it's her brother, isn't it?" replied Lucy, "She'll probably want to see what happens." Elijah looked pained as if such questions were a waste of his time and Robertson seemed quite unwilling to speak.

"I don't think she will be, not after what she did," offered Elijah finally, "The police still want to question her about what happened." Lucy was about to reply with 'she had deserved what she got' when Robertson cut in before her.

"Lucy, can you give me and Elijah a minute please?" he asked. Lucy looked at him dumbfound before she grinned slightly wondering if he was just trying to tease her.

"Oh sure," she stated politely, "Why don't you plan my trial without me…are you kidding?" She waited for him to break out into a grin or laugh to show he was not being serious, but his face remained stern and weary looking. Feeling perplexed Lucy jumped up from the table, "Fine," she exclaimed. She looked between Robertson and Elijah giving them each an annoyed look before heading for the door and closing it behind her. Once she was outside, she resolved to listen in on the conversation because if they thought she would just allow them to speak about her trial without her; they had another thing coming. Usually there were security guards waiting outside the door, but this time they were thankfully absent. Lucy wondered if it was because Robertson or Elijah had told them she was not considered a significant threat. Crouching down so she couldn't be seen through the panel of glass, she cupped her hand against the door next to her ear. At first, she thought that she might not be able to hear, but then sure enough, although their voices were muffled by the thick wooden door, she could still make out what they were saying.

"You must tell her," said Elijah, "it's not right that she doesn't know." Lucy heard Robertson groan in response.

“Don’t you think I know that?” he said wearily, “I want to tell her…believe me!” Lucy felt her breath hitch in her throat; what was it that Robertson was keeping a secret from her?

“She’ll find out sooner or later with the investigation,” explained Elijah, “and I’ve no doubt they will use it in her trial.”

“You’re not saying anything I don’t already know,” Replied Robertson bitterly, “but I’m afraid the impact it would have on her, especially considering my job is on the line.” Lucy put a hand to her mouth in shock and had to stop herself from nearly falling into the door. Robertson could lose his job? What had he done that was so bad? What was there an investigation into? Then it suddenly hit Lucy, the only thing that they logically would be investigating was how Remy had managed to get hold of a knife and also escape from the institute. Lucy felt her stomach sink as she realised that maybe it meant Robertson had something to do with it? Why else would his job be on the line? She suddenly felt angry; he was always expecting her to confide in him yet always kept his own cards close to his chest. She wanted to storm into the room and tell them she had overheard what they had been saying, but she decided to wait and see if they revealed anything else they were keeping from her.

“Have you looked into any more into it?” said Elijah suddenly. There was a long pause and Lucy wondered whether they knew she was listening in as the anticipation was killing her.

“I’m trying to,” retorted Robertson finally, “but I’m afraid of what I might find. Besides the whole thing is already so messed up, I can’t even begin to imagine what she might do or say if I told her.”

“Be careful!” warned Elijah, “you’ve never been one to let your emotions dictate your professionalism.”

“How can I not be emotional over this? Think of the implications!”

“Delaying it won’t change the truth.” Lucy heard Robertson sigh deeply.

“I know you’re right,” he replied, “but until I know more, then I don’t want her to know anything.”

Lucy suddenly moved away from her position on the floor to lean against the wall. She felt sick with anger and frustration. For a brief time, she had considered that Robertson actually cared about her as a person and then to find out he might be keeping something from her, something which was about what had happened to her.

Suddenly, the door of the meeting room opened, and Robertson nearly walked straight into her. "Oh, sorry Lucy," he said, but quickly hurried away without a second glance at her. Never had Lucy felt so unimportant. Begrudgingly she went back into the meeting room with Elijah and wondered whether to try and get any useful information from him, but then she decided against it. She didn't know him that well yet and from the sounds of the conversation, it had been Robertson with the secret, not Elijah.

"Have you thought how you might plead during the plea hearing?" asked Elijah. Lucy sighed in response, she knew he was basically asking her if she thought she was worthy of being saved, but the truth of the matter is she had made a bad choice and people had to pay for bad choices. However, she knew Elijah wouldn't be happy with her decision, so she decided to opt for a more diplomatic answer.

"I have, but I still have a lot to think about." Elijah nodded his head, he almost seemed encouraged by her answer.

"If we do go to trial, would you like to attend jury selection?" he offered, but Lucy shook her head quickly.

"And watch as the people who could decide my fate are selected and rejected?" she exclaimed, "No thanks!" Elijah shrugged his shoulders acknowledging that it made little difference to him.

"Right then," he said, "Let's go over what happened one more time." Lucy sighed and slumped further down in her chair wanting their meeting to be over as quickly as possible.

Later that day, Lucy was sat in Robertson's office sat on the chair with her arms folded and a scowl upon her face. Robertson stroked his chin anxiously with his hand wondering what an earth he had done wrong within the first thirty seconds of their meeting to warrant such treatment.

“So, your meeting with Elijah we went well?” he asked suddenly. Lucy rolled her eyes knowing he was trying to engage her in conversation, but at the same time she knew they couldn’t sit for an hour in complete silence, so she decided to cut to the chase.

“Do you keep secrets?” she questioned. Robertson raised his eyebrows.

“Everyone has secrets Lucy,” he explained seriously, “My job requires me to keep many secrets.” Lucy scowled at him, which only served to confuse him more.

“From me?” she snapped. Robertson suddenly looked quite worried, as well as confused, at what she was getting at.

“I can’t quite go telling you about other people’s conditions,” he stated nervously. This did nothing to appease Lucy’s temperament.

“Even if the secret is about me?” she snapped, glaring at him. Robertson went slightly red and suddenly looked quite flustered. He attempted to shuffle through the papers on his desk and avoided Lucy’s discerning gaze.

“What are you talking about?” he replied. Lucy, seeing how nervous he was, for a moment felt sorry for him and she wondered why nothing was ever straight forward between them.

“Nothing!” she sighed, “I just thought we could trust each other” Robertson looked pained at her statement.

“We can…” he began, but Lucy cut him off.

“Are you in trouble?” she asked fiercely, “Are you going to lose your job?” Robertson’s mouth dropped open in surprise, it was not what he had expected.

“Where did you hear that?”

"That's not important," said Lucy, as she waved her hand. There was a moment or two of silence between them before Robertson took a deep breath, almost as if he was stealing himself to say something.

"My job is fine," he affirmed, "Please don't worry." Lucy snarled at him, knowing that he was lying to her face.

"It's something to do with Remy isn't it?" she spat. Robertson groaned and slumped down in his chair as though he had been defeated.

"I might have known you would be eavesdropping into the conversation," he confirmed in annoyance, "I almost feel stupid for expecting you not to. What did you hear?" Lucy sat up and crossed her arms in defiance, she wasn't going to allow him to make her feel bad for listening in, not when he was hiding something from her.

"All of it!" said Lucy, "Why are they holding you responsible?" Robertson put a hand to his forehead.

"They are not; not exactly," he said wearily "but you are my patient, and I had a duty of care." Lucy rolled her eyes thinking if people cared about her why did they lie? Robertson for his part looked slightly offended at Lucy's reaction to his answer.

"What about this investigation?" noted Lucy undeterred, "I had a right to know it was happening; it does involve me after all." Robertson sighed; it was the sigh of a man who was quickly losing sight of his own convictions and was now staring into the abyss. He slowly sat up in his chair and held his head down.

"I know," he admitted earnestly "You're right; I'm sorry." Lucy was so shocked by his sincere apology that she didn't respond straight away, but then she remembered she still didn't have any of the answers to her questions.

"Ok so tell me." Lucy sat back in her chair and crossed her legs.

"I can't," he stated sadly, "It could compromise the investigation." Lucy jumped up out of her chair outraged.

"Bullshit!!" she roared, "You've watched me drive myself mad for months trying to figure out how she managed to trick all these professionals; I deserve to know how she did it." Robertson opened his mouth to speak but then closed his eyes and put his head in his hands for a few moments. Lucy watched him trying to work out what was actually going on in his head. Suddenly, he groaned and sat up straightening his tie.

"Ok," he stated cautiously, "but try not to…" Lucy looked at him accusingly.

"What?" she retorted. Robertson grinned sheepishly.

"Slap me or throw something at me," he pleaded. Lucy's mouth dropped open as she wondered for a split second if she actually did want to know the truth? From the sounds of it, it was really bad, and she was not sure if she could handle it. Nevertheless, curiosity always got the best of her.

"What did you do?" enquired Lucy seriously. Robertson stood up from his chair, moved around the desk and sat on the edge of it while crossing his arms.

"I withheld information about Remy," he explained, "but I was under strict instructions." Lucy bunched her fists in frustration; he wasn't telling her anything she didn't already know.

"What information?" snapped Lucy impatiently. Robertson looked pained as if he wanted to tell her anything, but the truth. It was a few long moments before he answered and if it wasn't for the fact that Lucy respected him so much, she would have raged, slapped him, or walked out.

"Remy was never a patient here," he revealed. Lucy's mouth dropped open as she found not a single coherent thought crossed her mind; her brain refused to process the information.

"What the fuck?" she exclaimed. Robertson lowered his eyes to stare at the floor; he could not look at her as he finally told her the truth.

"She was…is a psychologist," he confessed, "She was meant to be doing research here at the institute as part of her postgrad studies." Lucy's vision clouded over as she was beginning to see red; what had she been? Some lab rat who was some kind of fucking experiment?

"So they willingly let her in?" spat Lucy, "How the fuck did she get the ethical approval for that?"

"Well, it wasn't known about her brother obviously. Honestly, she was very convincing as a professional. I thought she was a good person." *Well, that makes it ok then,* thought Lucy angrily, then another thought occurred to her.

"And you knew," retorted Lucy "and you…you…encouraged me to be friends with her!!" Robertson threw his hands up in frustration, this time meeting her eyes as he tried to explain.

"Oh come on Lucy. Do you think I knew she was going to attack you?" he asked, "That she holds you responsible for her brother? That she even has a brother? What kind of person do you think I am?" Lucy had heard enough; she stood up quickly from the chair in fury, but when she spoke her tone was calm and measured.

"A liar!" said Lucy, "I think you're a liar, who tries to get others to tell the truth, which also makes you a hypocrite." Robertson's face fell and Lucy had never seen him look so ashamed, but that didn't matter. She turned around to flee the room, unable to stand for his excuses any longer. Robertson jumped up from the desk and quickly followed her.

"Lucy," he begged pleadingly, "Please, don't just leave." Lucy stopped walking and rounded on him.

"Why not? So I can sit here and be lied to some more? No thanks." She went to open the door, but Robertson put his hand on it, only allowing her to open it so far, certainly not far enough to walk out.

"I wanted to tell you!" he insisted, "I was told not to." His voice was thick with emotion, something which Lucy had never heard before and any other time she would have been genuinely touched by it, but now it only made her even angrier.

“Good on you Daniel,” she said sarcastically, “Always doing what you’re told; I guess that’s why you’re sat behind that desk, and I’m stuck in here.” Robertson looked as if he had been kicked in the stomach, he opened his mouth to say more, but then closed it as he removed his hand from the door and watched her leave the room, slamming the door behind her.

Chapter 7: Don't Plead Guilty

The night before her plea hearing, Lucy could not sleep; it was close to midnight and her mind was a whirlwind of emotions. She had skipped out on the last few sessions with Robertson, she knew she would have to go back eventually, but she needed time to process everything first. Her thoughts also turned to that of the hearing tomorrow; she still hadn't told Elijah what she was going to do, but she was 99% sure that she would be pleading guilty. She had only avoided telling him, because she knew he would try to talk her out of it.

It was just her luck to get a lawyer who was another God loving holier than thou person. It was almost as if God was playing some kind of joke on her by putting people in her life who loved him when all she did was hate him. First of all, he'd given her Father Graham and then Bella. Her stomach sank at the thought of Bella; she hadn't thought of her in so long because it hurt to know what she would think of her, especially now Lucy knew the truth about what happened.

She was just beginning to drift off to sleep when suddenly she saw a shadow in the corner of the room, she blinked thinking it would disappear, but then she saw the shadow had a face and she sat bolt upright.

She quickly fumbled for the lamp switch on the wall next to her, but when the light came on the figure had not disappeared and instead looked extremely familiar. Lucy gasped as she rubbed her eyes waiting for the image of Bella in front of her to disappear, but when it didn't, she began to panic. Lucy realised that there must be two explanations for what she was seeing; either she had completely lost it and was hallucinating, or she was having some kind of messed up nightmare. Bella did not speak, she only smiled at Lucy as though waiting for something.

"You're dead" stated Lucy bluntly. Then immediately, she felt stupid; there was no point talking to something that you knew wasn't real; it just made you even crazier.

"Am I?" replied Bella calmly, "Ahhh that explains why I still look 16 then? I was wondering about that." Lucy blinked; it was exactly the same voice that she remembered from all those years ago and she didn't realise that her imagination could be quite so vivid. Deciding to partake in this bizarre episode for now, Lucy decided that she would engage in conversation with her dead best friend.

"So you…you're a ghost?" asked Lucy. She tried to make it sound as casual as possible, but she wasn't sure why. After all, if Bella was a ghost, then it's not like it would come as a shock to her. However, Bella just smiled appearing not fazed by her question.

"I guess I must be," answered Bella. Lucy waited for her to elaborate, but when she said nothing further, she began to get frustrated. If this was her imagination, then why would it make her wait so long to find out what was happening.

"Why haven't you visited me before?" enquired Lucy, crossing her arms. She knew it was ridiculous, because how could she be annoyed with a hallucination or a nightmare.

"I've been busy." Lucy suddenly wondered what she had been doing, forgetting her resolve that what she was seeing was not real.

"Are you in heaven?" asked Lucy curiously. Bella smiled.

"Let's keep the focus on you," said Bella calmly. Lucy almost groaned in disappointment, it would have been nice to have a conclusive answer to the question, but then she suddenly remembered that this wasn't real, so it didn't even matter. Since this was a nightmare or a hallucination, Lucy realised that she could be as honest as she wished without really having to worry about the consequences.

"I bet you didn't think your best friend would turn out to be a murderer ey?" stated Lucy bitterly. She looked up at Bella to see if what she'd said had affected her, but Bella simply shook her head.

"My best friend isn't a murderer. She was scared and made a rash decision. A horrible decision: she didn't intend to kill anyone." Lucy felt mixed emotions at Bella's words; hearing that Bella didn't think of her in a horrible way was a relief, but a part of her also felt angry because of it too.

"Someone is still dead because of me," insisted Lucy, determined to not let anyone absolve her of her guilt.

"I know," replied Bella sadly, "but have you never questioned why he approached you in the street that night?" Lucy's mouth dropped open at the question; what an earth was Bella trying to insinuate? That the poor guy had some kind of death wish?

"I ran straight into him," protested Lucy. She was more convinced than ever now that Bella was just a figment of her own imagination trying to ease her guilt, she lowered her head feeling ashamed.

"But you were distressed and clearly scared of him. Why didn't he just let you go?" Lucy sighed; it wasn't that simple, and it had nothing to do with the matter at hand; that she had killed someone.

"I don't know," sighed Lucy sadly, "He was probably trying to help." Lucy decided her brain must really be doing a number on her; Bella would have cared about someone who had died, even if it had been the very thing that had caused Lucy to end up in this place.

"Do you think he made a good choice in trying to grab that knife from you?" asked Bella undeterred. Lucy scoffed and held her hands up; what difference did it make now?

"Well he'd probably say no now, wouldn't he?" snapped Lucy, "Oh wait…nope he can't; he's dead!" Bella rolled her eyes although she remained calm.

"So you're saying he made a bad decision?" said Bella pointedly. Lucy sighed; why did everyone think that one bad decision was enough to condemn a man to death and then something suddenly hit her like a bolt of lightning. If one wrong decision was not enough to condemn a man to death, did that mean that one bad decision was not enough to condemn her? Lucy quickly brushed the thought off.

Everyone has to deal with the consequences of their own actions, including her.

"Yes, but that doesn't mean he deserved to die." She didn't care if Bella was a hallucination; she had no right to try and make Lucy feel better or try to convince her that she didn't deserve to be punished.

"Nobody deserves to die Lucy, but it happens anyway," replied Bella, "All that matters is where you go from here." Bella's words stung Lucy as she realised that of course Bella could be angry over the deserving to die thing.

"To jail probably," answered Lucy bitterly, "Manslaughter carries a good 10 years." Suddenly Bella moved towards Lucy on the bed. She stopped and engulfed Lucy's hands with her own. Lucy gasped as she felt how cold Bella's hands were.

"That's why I'm here," explained Bella, "Don't plead guilty to manslaughter." Lucy blinked.

"Not you as well. Why is everybody so determined for me not to deal with the consequences of what I did?"

"You are already punishing yourself with your guilt," insisted Bella, "There is no point spending 10 years in jail on top of that."

"Why not? What would I be doing otherwise? My life is already over." Bella shook her head.

"You made me a promise," she said sweetly. Lucy didn't have to ask what Bella was talking about because she already knew. It was something that had played on her mind for the past twenty years.

"I've already broken it," said Lucy sadly. She lowered her head, but then felt Bella squeeze her hands and she could not help but smile, it was something that Bella used to do to reassure her.

"There are things you don't know and things I can't tell you. Your life will be meaningless if you plead guilty tomorrow. Just promise me you'll think about it." Lucy sighed, she didn't want to make Bella yet another promise she couldn't keep. Instead, she decided to ask her a question that would either confirm her insanity or go along with it.

“Are you real or are you my conscience trying to do a number on me?” asked Lucy seriously. Bella shrugged her shoulders as if the answer was unimportant, but when she caught sight of Lucy’s desperate expression, she decided to vocalise her answer.

“Either way, you need to listen,” she replied. Then she let go of Lucy’s hands, stood up and took a step back.

“I miss you.” Bella gave her a sad smile.

“I miss you too,” replied Bella “You have no idea what’s to come.” Lucy gaped at her in shock.

“When I die or in court?” she asked, secretly dreading the answer.

Bella did not respond. She gave Lucy one more small smile before she suddenly disappeared. Lucy sat on the edge of her bed for a very long time after, mulling over what Bella had said, eventually she lay her head back down on the pillow and fell into a deep sleep with the bedside lamp still flooding the room with light.

The next morning Lucy woke and decided that Bella had been a dream manifesting her own subconscious and it made her feel sick, because it meant a small part of her wanted to get away with it. Determined not to allow that to happen Lucy was not even more sure that she would plead guilty today.

She was sat in the cafeteria eating breakfast alone, when she spotted Robertson heading for her table. She jumped up and picked up her stuff to leave, but he increased his pace determined to catch up to her.

“Lucy,” he began, “I just wanted to say good luck at your hearing today.” Lucy merely looked at him with an unreadable expression before starting to walk away, but he grabbed her by the shoulder and turned her round to face him. “You can hate me all you want,” acknowledged Robertson, "but I've only ever tried to do what's best for you." Lucy sighed; how could she forgive him for being so deceitful, but then he was his psychiatrist and did have to follow orders.

"I don't hate you," she said sincerely, I just don't like you very much right now." Once again Robertson looked like he had been kicked in the stomach, so much so that Lucy actually felt a small pang of sympathy for him. "We'll talk," she added curtly, before turning and walking away. It was the kindest comment she could give him under the circumstances.

Lucy took a deep breathe before the car door open and she was escorted into the courthouse. She blinked as several lightbulbs went off in her face from waiting photographers, all screaming at her to answer their questions. The armed guard accompanying her seemed to take it all in his stride as he pushed them all out of the way so she could get passed. Lucy thought she would have had to be the dumbest person on the planet to try anything on the way to a plea hearing, but she understood why he was there. After all, she didn't even trust herself right now.

The courtroom was a lot larger than any that Lucy remembered; having been in only a few as a paralegal. The isle was narrow with rows of benches either side for spectators to sit on. At the front of the benches were two tables; once which she knew was for the prosecutor and the other for the defender, which was Elijah. The judge's podium was tall so as to be clearly visible from all angles of the courtroom and the Jury benches to the right-hand side were of course empty. Juries were not required at plea hearings. Elijah led her to the table on the left and gestured for her to take a seat in the empty chair. Lucy did as she was told, looking around at a handful of people around the room. Her eyes fell upon that of a tall muscular blond man wearing a smart suit, he was laughing with another smartly dressed man, before they both walked up to the front and placed their things on the desk on the right-hand side of the court room. Lucy realised that one of them must be her prosecutor. A silence descended across the courtroom, as Lucy saw a man wearing a smart uniform walk and stand in front of the judge's podium.

"All rise," said the bailiff. Lucy stood and to her relief looked and saw that there were only a handful of people in the room. Knowing it would be different if she actually had a full trial, it made her feel all the more grateful that she was steeled in her resolve to plead guilty. The front court room door opened and in walked the judge who Lucy was pleasantly surprised to see was a middle-aged woman with short hair and glasses.

"You may be seated," she instructed. "This hearing for Lucy Boragas is now in session. Before we begin, prosecutor I believe you offered a plea deal to the defendant?" Lucy looked to see the muscular middle-aged man on the right-hand side table stand up.

"Yes, your honour we have," he stated. He had a thick southern accent and a distinct air of confidence. "We did offer seven and a half years for a guilty plea," he continued, "but we have yet to hear any sort of response, so we assumed they won't be taking any deal."

"Mr James?" said the judge. Elijah looked at Lucy wearily and then stood up.

"Yes, your honour." The judge leaned forward and gazed at him over her black rimmed glasses.

"Has the defendant heard the plea deal and had adequate time to make a decision?" she inquired. Elijah looked down at Lucy who had the decency to cringe at him in an apologetic manner.

"Unfortunately, the defendant refused to hear it," explained Elijah.

"Excuse me?" replied the judge. She looked unimpressed and was clearly the sort of person who felt that everyone and everything had its proper place. Suddenly the prosecutor stepped out from behind his desk, he smiled as he walked forward towards the front of the courtroom. Lucy thought he looked far too happy for a man who was involved in a potential murder trial.

"Your honour if I may," he said brashly.

"Why not?" stated the judge firmly, "It seems like Mr James may need some assistance." Lucy scowled; it had not been her intention to embarrass her lawyer and she felt the judge was being extremely rude. The prosecutor walked to the desk in front of Lucy, he smiled at her, but Lucy did not return his smile. She hated the way he was looking at her; like a predator studying its prey. She knew she deserved it, but the fact that he thought she deserved it too made her outraged for some unknown reason.

"I'd think very carefully about what you want to come out of this case," he noted pointedly, "Your lawyer can advise you but ultimately it's your decision. We're offering you seven and half years in jail if you plead guilty here and now. Heck you'll be out and about in no time at all." *'He made it sound so easy'* thought Lucy, but she wanted no deals. She only wanted what she deserved and that was to be fairly punished without any hint of mercy.

"Do you accept the plea deal Miss Boragas?" asked the Judge. Elijah turned towards Lucy; he didn't seem remotely concerned that he had just been pulled up in front of the whole courtroom. "It's a fair deal so I wouldn't blame you if you wanted to take it." he said quietly, "but I still think I can get you off on self-defence. Ultimately it's up to you." Lucy looked around the room; first at the judge and then at the prosecutor; this was her moment of truth! She could be a coward and accept a lesser verdict or she could be brave and face the jury. Lucy stood up; she didn't know if she was supposed to, but it seemed appropriate.

"No, your honour," she answered, "I won't be accepting their plea deal." She deliberately stared defiantly at the prosecutor as she sat down slowly. He looked momentarily shocked. Then he smiled, held his hands up and calmy walked back to his seat. Lucy turned towards Elijah who smiled at her, and she couldn't understand why, until she suddenly realised that he thought this meant she had decided to defend herself when it was the furthest possible thing from the truth. She felt a smell pang of quilt as she imagined what his face would look like once she actually pleaded guilty.

"Very well," said the Judge, "Miss Boragas, would you please take the stand so we could hear your plea." Elijah looked inquisitively at

Lucy, and she thought maybe she ought to tell him what she was planning to do. However, then Lucy caught sight of the judge glaring at her and decided she had better get it over with. She walked over and sat in the witness stand then looked around, waiting nervously for what would come next.

"Miss Borogas," began the judge, "do you confirm you are about to enter a plea under your own free will, with a sound mind and after seeking counsel from a professional?" Lucy nodded and then remembered that this was a courtroom, and she would be required to vocalise her answer.

"Yes, your honour," she replied nervously.

"Very well. Lucy Boragas on the charge of voluntary manslaughter how do you plead?" Lucy opened her mouth to say 'Guilty' only no words came out. It was like the back of her throat had seized up and she could not do anything except look around in horror. *'This is ridiculous'* she thought, *'this is what I came here to do; to plead guilty so why can't I say the actual words.'*

"Excuse me young lady," stated the judge harshly, "you do know you refusing to speak will go on record as not guilty, don't you? You can't just stand there looking cute." Her tone was stern, and Lucy flushed red; this is not how things were supposed to go.

"Erm…yes. Sorry," said Lucy nervously.

"Right then, I shall repeat, how do you plead to the charge of voluntary Manslaughter?" Lucy looked over at Elijah who nodded at her firmly expecting her to plead not guilty, but she still couldn't do it. As nice as Elijah was, all she had to do was plead guilty and all this would be over. She opened her mouth to speak again, but then suddenly she looked at the back of the courtroom and could have sworn she saw Bella. She took a sharp intake of breath and did a double take, before realising that it was not Bella, only someone who looked like her. It was a woman with a blonde bob wearing a smart suit and holding a notebook poised with a pen. The image of Bella from last night came back to her along with the words 'You made me a promise', and then she thought of what Elijah had said, 'Your intent that night was not to end someone's life but merely defend yourself'. Did she owe it to herself to give herself a fighting chance? What would she say to someone else in her position? She turned her attention back to the judge before she suddenly looked at the floor deeply ashamed. "Not guilty," she said clearly, but quietly. There was a few moments of silence and Lucy looked at the back of the room to see a lot of journalists, including the woman with the blonde bob, scribbling furiously in their notebooks. She knew this would be a big story for them and she was already regretting her decision.

"Now normally at this point I would set the bail amount," said the judge, "but I have been informed that it is your psychiatrist's medical opinion that you should continue to live at the Charwood institute while receiving treatment due to the risk of danger to self. Are you aware of this Miss Boragas?" Lucy did not speak, but only nodded in reply. She was still in shock about what she had actually done. "Miss Boragas, this is a court of law, and you will answer yes or no!" barked the judge, finally losing her patience. Lucy finally lifted her head thinking that she might as well just go with it now that she had blurted out the wrong choice. After all, a jury would probably still find her guilty, so it was not that she was likely to get off anyway. Perhaps a long-drawn-out trial, not knowing what would happen, was no more than she deserved.

"Sorry, your honour," she began, trying to sound professional, "Yes, I am aware that I am to remain at the institute throughout my court case." The judge's eyes seemed to soften slightly as she seemed to recognise Lucy's change in attitude.

"Good, now given the public interest in this case I would like to move forward as quickly as possible. Do we need a preliminary hearing?" She looked over at Elijah who shook his head slowly.

"No, your honour," he replied, "Given the evidence against my client, we would just like to move forward with the formal trial." The judge nodded, agreeing with the decision.

"Well that makes things a little easier," she stated, "do you have anything to add prosecutor?" The prosecutor stood up and Lucy couldn't help but notice he seemed even happier than he had been before; perhaps he was one of those lawyers who thrived off big cases.

“No mam,” he replied, “We look forward to bringing the full force of the law in a full trial.” He smiled maliciously at Lucy, before he sat down causing Lucy to roll her eyes. Did he really think she was scared of anything he could do? She’d already resigned herself to the fact she was guilty and there was no worse punishment than that.

“Very well,” said the judge, bringing Lucy out of her thoughts. “The trial will be organised at the earliest convenience,” she continued, “which I expect will be next week or the week after. Someone will be in touch with both of you to arrange the details.” She gestured at Elijah and the prosecutor. “Miss Borogas you are free to return to the institute,” said the judge. Lucy did not need telling twice; she could not wait to leave this place. She jumped up from the chair and was getting out of the stand when she saw Elijah jump to his feet.

“Your honour, before we leave here today,” he began, “I wanted to ask about press access to the courtroom given my clients sensitive condition. I know it’s highly unorthodox, but could a special dispensation be made?” Lucy suddenly felt a new found respect for Elijah as she saw the disapproving faces of the press glaring from the back of the room. However, as she looked towards the judge, she already knew what the answer would be because she looked extremely unimpressed.

“We are in the United States of America Mr James,” She answered sternly, “The full extent of the law includes the people the right to transparency and scepticism. I will not be allowing a special dispensation in this case. Your client should discuss any concerns with press intrusion with her psychiatrist. We are done here.” Once the judge had turned and left the room, Lucy walked over to Elijah who shrugged his shoulders and grinned slightly.

“I knew there was not a chance,” acknowledge Elijah, “but I thought I’d try anyway.” Lucy grinned at him, but then suddenly stopped as the realisation of what had happened began to weigh heavy on her. She was now going to have to go through a full trial, with the press, judge, and a jury to contend with. Everything would be dragged out;

why an earth had she not just pleaded guilty. “I can tell you are feeling overwhelmed,” Noted Elijah, “Perhaps we should get out of here.” Lucy nodded and offered no further comment. She definitely needed to get of here and go somewhere quiet where she could hear her own thoughts again. They were just about to start heading out of the courtroom when the prosecutor walked up to them; Lucy glared at him, but he did not seem to notice as he held out his hand to Elijah.

“I don’t believe we’ve been properly introduced,” he said assuredly, “I’m Mitch Jacobson.” Elijah did not return his smile, but he did reach forward to take his hand. Then Mitch turned his attention to Lucy. “I do hope you feel ready for this trial.” offered Mitch, “I dread to think of how awful it’s been for you being in the institute for so long.” Elijah opened his mouth to speak, but Lucy raised her hand to stop him.

“Careful Mr Jacobson,” warned Lucy sternly, “you wouldn’t want anyone suggesting that you are capable of prosecutorial misconduct. Have a good day.” Mitch’s mouth dropped open in shock as Lucy smiled and gestured to Elijah they should leave. Elijah walked alongside Lucy looking begrudgingly amused by the exchange.

As they exited the courtroom, light bulbs started flashing in Lucy’s face again and there was clearly more press here than there had been when she entered. They were like a pack of wild vultures all hounding her with questions she could barely make out because they were all shouting at once.

“Did you do it Lucy?” she heard someone shout. She was about to turn around and tell them to mind their own business when she felt Elijah pushing her firmly towards the waiting car.

Once they were inside Elijah smiled at her. “I must admit,” he began “I thought for a moment there you were going to plead guilty.” Lucy looked at him sheepishly.

“That was actually the plan.” Elijah raised his eyebrows in surprise.

“What made you change your mind?” he asked curiously. Lucy did not reply, she wasn’t even sure she had an answer herself. Had the hallucination or ghost of Bella really had that much impact? Was it just another way of Lucy's subconscious trying to punish her by prolonging the agony that a trial would bring? Or had Bella actually been trying to look out for Lucy? She had been such a good friend in Lucy's life, was it possible that she was trying to remain so even now? Would she love her no matter what? Was she still deserving of Bella's kindness?

Chapter 8: What if We Were Still Friends…

Today is Wednesday the 4th of October and I will remember today for the rest of my life, because today is the day that my best friend has just been given the all clear from cancer. It's the most amazing miracle, the doctors are stumped, they were expecting her to die, everybody was, including her and she hasn't, it's the best thing that's ever happened in my entire life. I feel free and happy and like I could take on the world, because my best friend is still here, where she belongs, right by my side. We are in the waiting room while Bella's mum is finishing talking to the doctors. Bella is sat down, but I am stood up because I am restless from the good news.

"I told you that praying works," says Bella happily.

"It would certainly seem that way," I offer and Bella sighs. I know what she is thinking; how much more would it take for me to believe that there is a God? I prayed to him to cure Bella and he did. What more could I ask for?

"The doctors say it's a miracle Lucy. You can't get much more Godly than that." I know that everything she is saying is true, but I'm still not ready to put my faith in a God that allowed Father Graham into my life.

"I know," I reply, "I want to believe in him. I know I should, but it's just hard because it would be putting my trust in something that allows bad things to happen as well as good." Bella opens her mouth to continue her case, but then she seems to have a change of heart. Instead, she smiles at me. Then I suddenly remember there is something I wanted to tell her, but I am worried what she might think of what I did.

"Would you love me even if I sinned?" I ask suddenly. Bella's mouth drops open in surprise and she stands up to walk over to me. Then she places a hand on my shoulder and looks me in the eyes.

“Of course I would,” she answers, “You’re my best friend and I love you no matter what.” I sigh as Bella looks at me expectantly. Of course she knows there is a reason why I am asking the question.

“So, I finally got up the courage to dump Jeremy,” I explain. Bella smiles at me as if she is proud, but she hasn’t heard the rest of it yet. “I did it in a public place, but he still tried to intimidate me,” I confess, “and he grabbed me to stop me from leaving.” Bella’s calm and happy disposition suddenly evaporates, and she suddenly looks quite angry.

“Lucy that’s…” she begins, but I shake my head and smile.

“It’s ok,” I interrupt, “What I wanted to tell you is that you inspired me. With how brave you have been throughout all of this, and I thought if you can be that brave so can I. I punched him in the face.” Bella’s mouth drops open and then she looks torn between laughter and horror.

“Oh Lucy,” she exclaims, “I don’t condone violence, but do you think maybe he got the message?” Then we both burst into hysterical laughter. We are still laughing when Bella’s mum comes out of the doctor’s office and she watches us with a bemused, but cheery expression.

“Let’s head home, shall we?” says Bella’s mum, “We’ve got some celebrating to do.” She gestures for us to follow her out of the hospital, but we walk a few paces behind her still eager to talk amongst ourselves.

“You make me a better person you know,” I admit honestly. Bella links her arm through mine and smiles.

“You do the same for me. Thanks for being with me through all of this.” I cannot help, but feel delighted with her compliment, but then what else could I have done?

“You don’t need to thank me; you’re my best friend. How could I have done anything else except be right by your side?” This makes Bella smile even more and I’m not sure how anything can make today much better.

“Everyone should have at least one person who makes them better because it makes the world seem less cruel somehow,” says Bella happily, but I stop walking at her words because she’s right, the world can be quite a dark and cruel place at times. Bella stops and looks at me curiously, while her mum carries on walking unaware that we are lagging behind.

“Why does God allow such cruelty in the world?” I ask curiously. I know it’s a big question and there is no straight answer, but it’s the one thing that stops me from truly believing in him, so I have to ask it. Bella does not look intimidated by my question, instead she pauses to give it some thought. Eventually she puts a hand on my shoulder encouragingly.

“Because God loves his people, but his people are born with the capacity to be cruel,” says Bella passionately, “But God is the one who makes everybody better.” I don’t respond to her answer because I’m not sure how to. It’s a difficult thing to get my head around and I think maybe I’ll think about it some more later, but for now I just want to celebrate with my best friend. Bella seems to understand this because she takes my hand and pulls me along to where her mum is waiting at the exit of the hospital.

“Mum, Lucy and I are going to go for ice cream.” I smile at her because it sounds like such a nice idea.

“Ice cream makes everything better too,” I confirm. Then we head to the ice cream van just outside the park across from the hospital.

Predicted Verdict: Guilty

Chapter 9: Answers

The next day Lucy was debating whether to attend her appointment that afternoon with Robertson so they could actually discuss the whole Remy business, when Elaine approach her just as she was leaving the cafeteria.

"Lucy I've been asked to inform you that you will attend a meeting with an independent panel today," she said quietly, "so they can ask you some questions about Remy." Lucy groaned; it was not something that she wanted to do with her day.

"Do I have a choice?" asked Lucy. Elaine smiled slightly in response.

"Of course," she replied, "I can tell them to get lost if it will make you feel better." Lucy laughed at that and wondered for a moment whether she should actually take Elaine up on the offer. However, she knew that the sooner she answered questions about Remy then the quicker this whole thing could be put to rest.

"No, it's fine Elaine," she stated, "I'll go. What time is it?" Elaine looked at the watch on her wrist.

"It's at 11am," she said, "So you've got a bit of time before your meeting with Doctor Robertson." Elaine gave her a rather pointed look and Lucy realised that Elaine probably knew quite a lot about what went on at the institute, including the fact that Lucy had not been attending her daily meetings with the Doc. Lucy sighed as Elaine walked away, thinking that today would probably be a good day to talk with Daniel about what had happened in their previous meeting.

At ten minutes before 11, Lucy headed towards the big meeting room near the director's office. Despite Elaine not mentioning where the meeting would be held, Lucy knowing it was a panel figured it would be in there, because it was really the only room that was logically big enough. She hesitated outside, wondering what kind of questions they might ask her and then she knocked on the door. She heard a voice from inside shout, “Enter,” so she took a deep breath and opened the door. As she walked in, she noted there was a long table on the other side of the room which six people sat behind. Behind them was a long panel window, which appeared to bring very little light into the room despite it being a bright day. In the middle of the room there was an empty chair, which she guessed must be for her. Without waiting for an invitation, she slowly walked across the room and sat in the chair.

The six people around the table all kept their eyes focused on Lucy, as if they found her fascinating. Lucy didn’t like it at all. All of them were smartly dressed and not one of them must have been below fifty years of age. Lucy guessed they all must be from some kind of investigative body and that you didn’t get onto panels like these without having a wealth of experience. A man wearing a smart suit with very little hair towards the middle of the table stood up and looked around at the other panel members before setting his eyes on Lucy.

“This meeting is being recorded,” he stated, “could you please state your name for the record.” Lucy had to reframe from rolling her eyes; it’s not like she would have sent along someone to impersonate her.

“Lucy Maria Boragas,” she replied. The man on the panel nodded at her and then sat down. Lucy tried not to make a snap judgement about his character, but he seemed to have an air of arrogance about him, which made him instantly dislikeable.

“Thank you, Miss Boragas,” he replied, “My name is Simon Banks. I am the lead investigator in this case. Can you first tell us how you met the patient known as Remy?” Lucy blinked thinking; it was rather strange to refer to someone as ‘a patient known as…’ but then suddenly the truth dawned on her.

“What do you mean known as?” said Lucy in surprise, “she used a fake name? What was her real name?” As soon as the question left her lips, she knew she had been incredibly stupid. Of course Remy wouldn’t give a real name to anyone because then they might have been able to work out what her real intentions had been. The lead investigator 'Simon Banks' looked towards the fellow members cautiously before answering her question.

"I'm unable to share that information at this time. Can you tell us how you came to know Remy?" Lucy scoffed. So, they expected her to answer their questions without giving her anything?

"I'm unable to share that information at this time," replied Lucy coolly. Simon Banks' facial expression quickly changed to reflect his anger. He was clearly a man more used to having people comply when he yielded his authority, as opposed to being challenged. Simon turned and whispered something to his colleague next to him, a blonde glamorous looking woman in her early fifties. Then he painted a discerning smile on his face before turning to face Lucy once more.

"Miss Boragas," he stated sternly, "I hope you understand the seriousness of this meeting." Lucy crossed her arms; she knew she was guilty of murder, but she certainly knew in this case she had done nothing wrong. It was them who had decided to let a person hell bent on revenge into a mental facility, so she wasn't about to allow them to make her feel guilty about that too.

"As I understand it, I'm here because somebody made a huge fuck up and allowed someone who was clearly dangerous to enter this facility under false pretences," she stated calmly, "please could you clarify for me if I'm wrong." Simon looked like he had been slapped but remained silent. Instead, he looked up and down the long table to see if anyone else could put together a reasonable answer. "Just as I thought," insisted Lucy, "Remy approached me one day and introduced herself. I warned her off at first because I don't like to hang out with people; not at an institute." Lucy saw that most of the panel members had taken to making notes on their papers in front of them on the table. However, Simon Banks did not take any such notes, instead he nodded at Lucy almost as if he appreciated her cooperating with them. Lucy scowled at him; she had not answered the question to be polite; she had answered it because she wanted to get out of this place as quickly as possible.

"So you tried to warn her off," stated Simon, "did she take offence to this?" Lucy rolled her eyes at his question.

"How should I know?" she retorted, "I didn't hang around to find out." Simon flushed slightly red as he became increasingly frustrated with Lucy's answers, but she didn't care less. She didn't even understand why there had to be an investigation; Remy or whoever she was, she'd had the chance to kill her, and she hadn't…end of story.

The glamorous blonde woman next to Simon cleared her throat politely, indicating she wanted to speak. She was wearing ruby red lipstick which seem to perfectly match her neatly painted round nails.

"Margaret Westchester. So what made you become friends with her?" she asked. Lucy thought she looked extremely professional, but she did note that the woman's tone was at least friendly and less conceded than Simons.

"Da…" began Lucy, but then she caught herself. It wouldn't look great for the Doc if the panel knew they were on first name terms. "Doctor Robertson advised it," she said honestly. Margaret exchanged a curious look with Simon, who then turned his attention back to Lucy.

"How exactly did he make this recommendation?" he asked. Lucy blinked, why did it even matter? So she put on the best impression of Robertson she could muster including the American accent.

"Lucy, make yourself a friend," she said. A few of the panel members laughed and exchanged amused glances. However, Simon quickly glared at them each in turn, which quickly put an end to their enjoyment.

"Please try to be cooperative," warned Simon wearily. Lucy was not sure if he was speaking to her or the other panel members. She sighed and decided she might as well play ball and make it less painful for all involved.

“I was telling him that I didn’t like Remy,” she explained, “and he suggested I try to pursue…make friends with her…bond.” She knew she wasn’t being very good at giving coherent answers, but she was doing the best she could under the circumstances. Then an uneasy feeling came over her; was this what being on a trial in a courtroom would be like?

“Why do you think he asked you to do this?” asked Simon. Lucy scowled back at him, wondering if they were trying to get her to say things that would lead Daniel to getting in trouble.

“He thought I’d make a good study project I suppose,” she said coolly, “I am pretty compelling.” Simon smiled at her in response, but it was not a friendly smile, it was the smile of someone who was part way through executing a well thought out plan.

“Did he make any other comments about Remy?” asked Margaret. Lucy shook her head straight away, resolving to be much more careful in the answers she gave.

“No, it was always me who brought her up.” Simon leaned towards Margaret and whispered something in her ear. This irritated Lucy as it was them who had wanted her to be there, not the other way around.

“Excuse me, Mr Banks,” she began politely, “have you got something you would like to share with the rest of the class? Only it’s awfully rude to whisper in the presence of company considering the circumstances. One might come to the conclusion that you are up to something.” Simon glared at her, but Margaret looked slightly amused. For a moment Lucy thought he was going to throw her out of the meeting room, which wouldn’t have bothered her in the slightest, but sadly he didn’t. Instead, he straightened his jacket as though preparing for battle.

“Did you inform Doctor Robertson of your plans to escape the institute with Remy and your fellow patient Max?” he asked. Once again Lucy found herself rolling her eyes at him and wondered who an earth had written the investigative questions, they seemed to be a waste of time.

"That would have been incredibly stupid," replied Lucy. Simon opened his mouth to speak but an older looking gentleman wearing glasses at the end of the long table on the right-hand side banged his fist on the table as if to gain people's attention. He had a full head of white hair and a neatly trimmed white moustache. He smiled at Lucy before he began speaking.

"Dr Roger Snide. Did you discuss what had happened afterwards with Doctor Robertson?" he asked. Lucy nodded thinking that it could not possibly get Daniel in trouble to tell them something like that.

"Yes," she replied.

"What did he say?" asked Roger. Lucy noted he had a kinder face than Simon, but that didn't mean she was about to trust him.

"He was a bit pissed off to tell you the truth," she admitted, wondering if it was the right thing to say.

"And he showed this to you?" said Roger. He was not even looking at Lucy as he asked the question but scribbling some notes down on the paper in front of him.

"Well, he didn't scold me if that's what you're getting at. He just said he wished I hadn't attempted it." Roger nodded and gestured with his hand as if to say he was finished, usually Lucy might have found this rude, but she liked how he was a man of few words.

"Does Doctor Robertson usually give unsolicited advice?" asked Simon, drawing Lucy's attention back towards him.

"Isn't that his job as a psychiatrist?" offered Lucy in amusement. Margaret seemed to agree with Lucy as she nodded her head slightly, but Simon looked undeterred.

"No, it's his job to give his medical opinions to you." Lucy was becoming increasingly frustrated, wondering who he thought he was and how somebody like him could asked to be the lead investigator of anything. It was like her mum had always told her as a child 'you catch more flies with honey than with vinegar', but Simon seemed to be nothing but sour.

"He only gives me advice when I ask for it," stated Lucy defiantly, feeling pretty pleased with herself. *'Let them put that on record'* she thought.

"Were you aware of Remy's brother?" asked Simon. Lucy's eyebrows shot up in surprise at the question.

"What kind of a stupid question is that?" she snapped, "of course not." Simon did not seem to be fazed by Lucy's anger and raised voice. Instead, he smiled as though his strategy was working; did he expect her to crack?

"Did Remy tell you anything in the confrontation that might indicate where she was going?" he inquired. Lucy nearly laughed out loud.

"Yeah," replied Lucy sarcastically, "as she held a knife to my throat she said and if anybody needs me, I'll be at 62 Sycamore Avenue." Simon smiled sinisterly, before responding.

"Can you spell that for me?" he retorted. Lucy had heard enough, she stood up from her chair intending to leave.

"You dickhead!" she exclaimed, "look, this is pointless. I have no idea where she is and if I did, I'm not sure I'd tell you. The point is I killed her brother and she chose not to kill me. I hardly think that's a crime." Simon Banks stood up and looked around at his colleagues. Lucy saw the two security guards from either side of the room move forward, but Simon gestured for them to stay back. Lucy scoffed at the drama of it all, all she had done was stand up in her chair, it's not like she had picked it up and thrown it at the panel members.

"Miss Boragas," warned Simon wearily, "it's not up to you to establish the reason for this meeting. Just to cooperate with its proceedings." He fidgeted slightly, as though he was becoming increasingly nervous by this turn of events, and Lucy had to wonder if he was afraid of her. Then she realised this could well be the case, after all she was on trial for manslaughter. This thought more than anything sobered her, and she slowly walked back and sat back down in the empty chair.

“I think I’ve been perfectly reasonable given the circumstances,” she offered calmy, “I’d be well within my rights to sue the institute for negligence, so let’s at least keep it civil, shall we?” This time Simon’s mouth fell open and he looked around at the other panel members who all suddenly looked very uncomfortable, and for one shining moment Lucy thought that perhaps she might have made a good lawyer had her life not changed so drastically. However, then she figured that no good lawyer would call someone a dickhead in a courtroom either.

“Can you at least answer us one last question?” asked Simon. Lucy merely nodded in response. "Why do you think Doctor Robertson took it upon himself to inform you of Remy’s research project at this facility?” continued Simon curiously. Lucy stood up enraged once more, were they actually angry with Daniel for telling her? At what point had they been planning to inform her of the whole thing?

“Because unlike most of you here,” she stated angrily, “he’s actually a decent human being. This meeting is over.” Lucy then calmy got up out of her chair and walked out the room without glancing back.

Once she had eaten a quick lunch in the cafeteria, she made her way to Daniel’s office wondering whether she ought to mention to him what had happened in the panel meeting.

Once she arrived at his door, she knocked softly almost hoping that he wouldn’t hear her, but when he said, “come in,” from the other side, she hesitated feeling a little awkward. Finally, Lucy took a deep breath and steeled herself before she opened the door. After all the questioning over Remy, she was in no mood for an argument. However, she knew that it was inevitable considering how annoyed she was at him, and she knew they couldn’t just sit there in silence again. She slowly opened the door and walked into see Robertson look up from his place behind the desk. His expression was a mixture of relief and concern when he saw Lucy enter.

“Oh good,” he said enthusiastically, “thanks for coming.” He stood up and came around the desk to meet her.

“You’re welcome,” she said curtly, then sat down in the chair, without waiting for an invitation. Daniel studied her for a moment as if he was trying to work out the right thing to say. This made Lucy feel very self-conscious and she started to tap her foot nervously on the floor.

“How has your day been?” he asked politely. Lucy nearly rolled her eyes at his cautious attitude towards her, though she understood where it was coming from.

“Ok,” she replied in a formal tone and Robertson cringed.

“Lucy please,” he said pleadingly, “I thought we were making some real progress recently.” Lucy crossed her arms and sat back in the chair glaring at him.

“We were,” she stated bluntly, “before I found out you were keeping something so big from me.” Daniel sighed and put his hands in his pockets.

“You don’t think I felt awful over that,” he replied honestly, “Do you not think I wanted to tell you?” Lucy did not have a reply to his question, because it didn’t matter how much he had wanted to, the fact was he hadn’t, and she felt betrayed. “Would it make you feel better to slap me?” he offered.

“Don’t temp me,” retorted Lucy. Daniel jumped off his desk and came over to lean on the side of Lucy’s armchair so that they were next to each other. Lucy wondered for a moment whether he was testing her to see if she really would slap him when he was in such close proximity.

“Lucy, I hate it when you’re so mad at me,” he stated sadly, “when you just shut yourself off like this, it drives me insane.” Lucy’s mouth dropped open, wondering why it would affect him so much.

“Why?” she asked curiously. For a moment she completely forgot that she was meant to be furious with him over Remy.

"When I first got to know you, you were so defensive," he began, "and then I got to know the real you and I…well the real you…you're…" Robertson trailed off as if it was something that he could not convey in words. However, when he saw Lucy still looking at him expectantly, he tried again. "I know I deserve your anger." He put his head down, "I did have some concerns about Remy that I didn't flag up." Lucy stood up from her chair finding that she no longer wanted to sit down with how annoyed she was feeling.

"What kind of concerns?" she asked, crossing her arms. Daniel also stood up and placed his hands in his pocket as he faced her.

"Just stuff you mentioned to me," he explained, "and then the whole escape plan fiasco which hardly anybody knew was going to happen." Lucy scowled because she felt so stupid. He'd seen a few red flags over Remy, whereas Lucy had only ever seen her as a friend. However, then Lucy reminded herself that Daniel knew a whole lot more than she had.

"Why didn't you raise your concerns then?" enquired Lucy, "Have her kicked out?" Daniel suddenly looked rather uncomfortable, he started shifting his body slightly from side to side, shuffling his feet and Lucy thought it was maybe because he realised how stupid he had been.

"Because then she came into my office and accused me…us of having feelings for each other and to be careful," he stated nervously, "then it seemed a really stupid thing to do." Lucy's mouth dropped open in shock. It almost sounded like he had been blackmailed by Remy and she couldn't help but feel somewhat responsible. Perhaps she had accidently shared something with Remy that had led her to believe that there was something more between her and Daniel. Lucy opened her mouth to say something, but before she could, Daniel threw his hands into the air suddenly looking like a man deranged. "I FUCKED UP OK!" he yelled. "You always tell me that I act like I'm on some kind of pedestal; well this is me. I'm a normal human being and I make mistakes. I fucked up!!" Lucy took a step back in shock, she had never seen Daniel lose control like that before, but strangely she kind of liked it. Once she had recovered, she took a few steps towards him and placed her hand on his shoulder. He looked at her hand curiously before meeting her gaze.

"Lucy," she said, putting on her best American accent, "you're not fucked up! No more than the rest of us, except me of course; I'm one big fuck up!" Daniel's mouth twitched, oddly amused at her impersonation, but he also looked slightly angry too.

"Point taken," he said, through gritted teeth, but then suddenly Lucy burst out laughing. Daniel looked at her surprised, but then found himself laughing slightly too. Finally, Lucy perched herself on the edge of his desk.

"Well, what are we going to do?" she asked curiously. "We're just two fucks up stuck in this hellhole…oh wait…they've not actually committed you yet." Daniel put a hand to his face wearily as he sank back down in his chair behind the desk.

"Give them time," he admitted, "it'll happen." Lucy grinned at him then sighed as she sat back down. She was still angry and annoyed with him over the whole Remy situation, but at least for now, she was happy to let the issue lie.

"So do you want to know what happened in my plea hearing?" she offered. Daniel grinned and leaned forward on the desk.

"Sorry," he stated, "Elijah beat you to it."

"Dammit!" replied Lucy amused.

"He said you wiped the smug smile off your prosecutors face," Daniel stated happily.

"Yeah, I don't know why but I instantly disliked him," she said surprised, "You think I'd like the bloke who's trying to prove my guilt, but he's just such an arsehole." Daniel shrugged his shoulders.

"Well sadly there are many arseholes in the world. I'm just trying to prove I'm not one of them." He looked at Lucy waiting for her to answer a question he had not asked. Lucy smiled slightly, before deciding to put him out of his misery.

“There are two types of arseholes,” she began, “arseholes who are just bad people and then there are good people who are sometimes arseholes.” Daniel put his hand to his chin for a moment before shrugging his shoulders and grinning sheepishly.

“Dare I ask which one you think I am?” he enquired, and Lucy was genuinely touched by the nervous tone she heard in his voice.

“You’ve done more for me then I ever could have expected,” she admitted honestly, “ever should have expected with being my psychiatrist. I’m still angry with you over the whole Remy thing, but I know why you did it.” Daniel’s mouth dropped open in astonishment, but then he closed it again just as quickly.

“Thank you,” he replied finally. However, he did not seem to look like a man who had been appeased by her answer. There was still a haunting look behind Daniel’s eyes that Lucy just couldn’t fathom. Perhaps he was worried about the investigation?

“You’re welcome,” said Lucy politely, “are you in a lot of trouble? They know you told me; I didn’t tell them.”

“No, I told them.” Lucy’s mouth dropped open as she wondered whether she had misheard him. “I’m not really in more trouble than I already was,” he continued, “They would have had to tell you eventually. I just think they’re a bit pissed they didn’t have longer to come up with a plan to save their own arses.” Lucy sniggered despite her surprise and Daniel also looked amused.

“My trial should start next week or the week after,” said Lucy suddenly, “I can’t even believe I’ve done this. That I’m actually going to have to go through a trial.”

“I know, but I’m glad you did. I was really worried that you would plead guilty without giving yourself a chance.”

“I’m still debating if I’m worth that chance,” admitted Lucy quietly. For a moment, she wondered if she ought to tell him about the imaginary conversation she'd had with her best friend and that was the reason she had changed her mind, but she decided some things are best left unsaid. *'Besides'* she thought *'it would be nice, to leave him to think that he'd had something to do with it, not that he'd be completely wrong'.*

"I wish I could be in court to support you," said Daniel suddenly. Lucy blinked, despite all the progress they had made together, she still could not figure him out.

"Why?" she asked suspiciously, "have you ever been there for any other patient's trial?" Daniel groaned and put his head in his hands.

"Why do you always take kindness as something to cross examine?" he questioned. Lucy crossed her arms.

"In my experience people rarely treat you with kindness unless they want something." Daniel grimaced. For a few moments an awkward silence passed between them, eventually he sighed.

"I don't want anything from you, Lucy," said Daniel quietly. The way he said it made Lucy feel bad that she had ever doubted his intentions. Despite him making some bad choices, he had still always tried to help her.

"I'm sorry. I'm just struggling to accept that people can just choose to be kind without reason." Once again Daniel grimaced, caught off guard by her brash statement.

"I really wish you would. There are genuinely decent people in this world, as hard as that is to believe." Lucy knew what he was saying was true, but the sad fact was, that she felt the world was more cruel than kind and thus produced more non-decent people than good people. However, she knew if she actually said this to Daniel then it would just start an argument between them. Instead, she pursued another line of enquiry.

"Why do you want to come to court to support me?" she asked. She knew that Daniel was a kind man, much kinder than many other people she had met, but she knew it was not normal procedure for psychiatrists to do that sort of thing for their patients.

"Is it that hard to believe that I care?" he asked. He held Lucy's gaze as he asked the question, almost willing her to believe it. However, Lucy had no idea why a man such as Daniel would want anything to do with someone like her, let alone actually care about her, so she lowered her head to stare at the floor.

"Yes," she replied quietly. She looked back up to see that Daniel looked truly upset at her response; he opened his mouth to speak when suddenly there was a knock at the door. It opened and in walked Elijah.

"I apologise for the interruption," he began, "but I charge the state per the hour and Lucy is like twenty minutes late for our meeting." Daniel's mouth dropped open and he looked at his watch.

"Sorry about that Elijah." Elijah did not look angry with his friend, instead he smiled at him.

"You're slipping Daniel," said Elijah. Lucy laughed at Elijah's comment, causing Elijah to look at her in surprise. "Wow, I didn't know you could laugh." Lucy shrugged her shoulders and bounced up from the armchair.

"Well, see you later Daniel. Come on, Elijah. I've got a few ideas that might help to piss off the prosecutor." Elijah looked extremely shocked as he glanced at Daniel for a moment. Daniel shrugged his shoulders grinning sheepishly. Then he laughed as Elijah followed Lucy out the room with a bemused expression on his face.

Chapter 10: That Fighting Spirit

A week later found Lucy sat in the meeting room with Elijah running over the details of her trial, which would begin in three days' time. Lucy was feeling extremely nervous as despite feeling slightly more optimistic in general, she still knew that she was probably heading to jail unless Elijah could pull off a miracle. Not that she wanted him to, but she was not looking forward to spending the next ten years of her life locked up either.

"So how are you feeling about Monday?" he asked cautiously. Lucy and Elijah felt like they had gotten to know each other quite a lot over the past week. She sensed over the week he had started to understand her more.

"I wish it would just go away," admitted Lucy, shrugging her shoulders.

"That's not a great start. I'm going to need some more of that fighting spirit." Lucy rolled her eyes wondering why it was he couldn't realise that she had no fighting spirit; not anymore, but then a small part inside of her knew that just wasn't true. She had stood up to the prosecutor well enough. Stood up to the panel well enough. This was different though; this was literally about life and death.

"So, on Monday there will be opening statements," said Lucy, in a matter-of-fact tone, "Who are the witnesses being called?" Elijah couldn't help, but notice she had side stepped his comment.

"The ones you'd expect," said Elijah, "the victim's friends, but then they will call on the professionals, before you." Lucy sighed; she was hoping that she wouldn't have to testify, but then deep down she knew that was stupid.

"Shame I don't have any reliable witness eh?" she stated sadly.

"Well Daniel is giving you a medical testimony," affirmed Elijah reassuringly, "I'm sorry Lucy but considering the evidence in this case I would recommend you testify." Lucy was not reassured by this, because as nice as it was of Daniel to do that for her, she had too much legal knowledge to know that his testimony would not sway the jury into a not guilty verdict. Then she mentally scolded herself, she didn't want to be found not guilty; did she?

"As touched as I am by that," admitted Lucy, "I doubt it will be enough to get me off on self-defence." Elijah said nothing in response to this and Lucy thought that spoke for itself because no good lawyer would think that a doctor's testimony alone would be enough.

"How long has Daniel been working with you?" asked Elijah suddenly. Lucy took a moment to think about this, as it seemed like her and Daniel had been on such a long journey together that she had known him for a while, but she suddenly realised it was not that long at all.

"Since last year, so about six months," she replied, "why?" Lucy wondered how it was that Elijah did not know this, wasn't it his job as a lawyer to know this kind of stuff. Suddenly, Lucy realised that it was probably just a polite way of stirring the topic of conversation; something which Elijah confirmed when he spoke next.

"Have you noticed a change in his behaviour?" he asked curiously. Lucy groaned in response.

"Don't you start. You sound like that bloody Simon guy on the investigation panel. They were all asking questions about him as well. I don't understand why he's in so much trouble over this. I know I'm his patient, but Remy wasn't." Elijah shrugged his shoulders as if he too was unsure of the reason.

"I think they think he should have spotted the warning signs earlier," guessed Elijah. Lucy scowled because how could somebody be in trouble just for not realising that another person was deceitful.

"What does it matter either way?" stated Lucy adamantly, "She didn't kill me, just roughed me up a bit. I actually wonder if her doing that made me remember." Elijah raised his eyebrows at her in surprise.

“What do you mean?” he asked. Lucy sighed because it was difficult to make others understand what she had been going through.

“Everybody keeps saying that it was in self-defence and yeah I suppose that’s true in a way,” began Lucy, “but most of it… I think it was because of all the rage, pain, and sadness I’d been carrying around inside of me. It just came out at the wrong time in the wrong way. Remy was obviously in pain, sad and angry too because I’d killed her brother, but she still managed to make the right choice.” Elijah put a hand to his chin looking thoughtful before he shook his head in disagreement.

“The circumstances were completely different,” he stated, “Remy was not fighting for her life; she intended to kill you. At no point did you intend to kill someone.” Lucy blinked, how could anybody else know exactly what she was thinking at that time? Heck she wasn’t sure if she even knew.

“I don’t know though,” admitted Lucy nervously, “I mean yes I was terrified. I’d just been attacked and just wanted to be alone, but in the heat of the moment maybe all the rage I’d been keeping bottled up, maybe it came out and maybe I in some part wanted to kill him.” She looked at Elijah expecting him to look slightly panicked that his client had just confessed she didn’t know if she had committed manslaughter, but instead he looked thoughtful.

“That’s something that still bothers me about this case,” Elijah said pointedly.

“You worry that I wanted to kill him as well?” asked Lucy. She didn’t know how she should feel about it, but she at least needed her lawyer to know one way or the other considering the trial was tomorrow.

“Oh no no!” said Elijah quickly, “I am 99.9% sure that you didn’t want to kill him, that’s not what’s bothering me.” Lucy wondered whether she should ask Elijah how he knew that she hadn’t wanted to kill someone, but she was worried about the answer he would give her, and curiosity got the best of her.

“What is bothering you?” she enquired. Elijah’s gaze was far away and distant.

“The man who attacked you,” Elijah replied, “There’s no sign of him.” Lucy exhaled quickly, because she knew if that man could be found he could confirm her story but considering he might have been homeless himself then he would be near impossible to track. Then suddenly Lucy had a thought about what Elijah might mean with bringing it up.

“You think I made it up?” asked Lucy. She could not blame him if that was the conclusion he had come to, but Elijah looked a little amused by her question.

“If you were going to make something up,” suggested Elijah, “I would hope you would be a tad cleverer than saying someone attacked you beforehand.” Lucy didn’t know if he was paying her a compliment or an insult.

“Well, it’s probably near impossible to track him down,” she said sadly.

“Yes, you’re right,” admitted Elijah, “but it would certainly help our case.” Suddenly Elijah looked down at this watch. “Well, it’s almost lunch time, I don’t want to keep you. I’m sure you must be hungry.” Lucy shook her head.

“I don’t know if I’m going to be able to eat anything before this trial is over,” admitted Lucy, but she still stood up from the table, taking the hint. Lucy could not fathom why she might be so nervous about her trial might go when she knew and wanted the most likely outcome. However, it was one thing to accept something was going to happen, and another to stand by while it actually happened.

“I’ll see you at eight on Monday,” said Elijah “Try not to worry too much. Tell Daniel I said hi.” Lucy left, feeling oddly amused by the fact they were all on first name terms now.

After lunch, Lucy made her way to Daniel's office and was about to knock on the door when she heard him speaking on the other side. "Please call me…" he said, and Lucy realised that he was obviously on the phone. She waited another minute before knocking, then Daniel came and opened the door.

"Hi," he said, grinning, "So I heard it on the down low that you were quite complimentary of me at the investigation panel." Lucy's mouth dropped open before she realised that Robertson was teasing her. She grinned and went to sit on the armchair.

"I wouldn't go that far," she said amused, "I only stated you were better than the rest of them." Robertson sat back behind his desk and smiled.

"Yeah, but coming from you that is quite a compliment," he replied. Lucy could feel herself flushing red slightly, she wasn't used to being told that her opinions mattered all that much.

"Yeah, well be careful won't you. Don't let your head get too big that it won't fit through the office door." Robertson laughed and then shrugged his shoulders, knowing there was little chance of it happening.

"I'll try not to," he replied earnestly. Then he held her gaze just a bit longer than normal and Lucy suddenly felt an uneasy feeling growing in the pit of her stomach. Unable to stand it any longer, Lucy broke eye contact with him.

"I'm nervous for Monday," she admitted as she looked at the floor.

"Don't be," said Robertson reassuringly, "Elijah will be there; he'll make sure you're ok." Suddenly a thought occurred to Lucy with Daniel and Elijah being friends and she debated whether to ask him something before deciding to bite the bullet.

"You've not…" she began hesitantly, then she trailed off. Robertson studied her curiously wondering what she might ask.

"What?" he enquired. Lucy grinned at him sheepishly.

“You wouldn’t have happened to tell Elijah to keep an eye on me, would you?” she asked. She was almost flushed red as she said it, and she wondered why that was, after all Daniel was her psychiatrist and it would be a reasonable request for him to make of Elijah. Daniel grinned sheepishly.

“Elijah’s good at his job,” he stated, “he doesn’t need me to tell him what to do.” However, Lucy couldn’t help, but notice he had not exactly answered her question. Knowing that it was not worth a potential argument, Lucy’s thought turned to that of how Elijah and Daniel could have become friends; they were so different.

“What was he like at college?” asked Lucy. Robertson chuckled as the distant memory came back to him of his meeting with Elijah.

“The same,” he replied. Lucy rolled her eyes thinking that he was obviously going to make things difficult for her.

“Boring. How did you guys become friends? Let me guess? Church?” Robertson blinked, but then smiled.

“It was Elijah who led me to my faith actually,” stated Daniel. Lucy had to refrain for rolling her eyes as she knew it would be disrespectful.

“Let me guess,” she began, “You were a naive young man from a small town, he was a confident young Christian man from a big city…you never really stood a chance.” Robertson raised his eyebrows in surprise but then laughed.

“Something like that. When you spend enough time with Elijah you find that he is a very kind and interesting guy. You cannot help but wonder what makes him tick.” Lucy considered his comments thoughtfully.

“What makes you tick?” she asked. Then she realised that the question might be considered too personal, and she knew Daniel didn’t do personal. However, she was surprised to see that Daniel cocked an eyebrow at her in response.

“You really want to know?” he asked. Lucy noted there was almost a flirtatious tone to his question and her mouth suddenly went very dry. The way Daniel was looking at her. as he asked the question, was something that she could not reconcile herself with. Then she suddenly snapped out of it; there is no way that a man like Daniel would ever be interested in someone like her. What an earth did she have to offer him besides jail visits and a bad attitude? So, she decided to turn the conversation in the direction of their usual friendly banter.

“Maybe I can guess,” she said grinning then realised that she was actually unintentionally being a little flirtatious herself. He did not respond to her comment, only looked at her expectantly waiting for her to guess. “Coffee?” she asked half- jokingly. Daniel rolled his eyes at her, much to Lucy’s amusement.

“Come on Lucy,” he said challengingly, “You hate it when I psychoanalyse you, now is the time to get your own back.”

“Something happened!” blurted Lucy suddenly, “something happened to you that made you want to be a psychiatrist. Don’t get me wrong, I think you enjoy the job, but it seems like something you got pushed towards.” Daniel blinked at her and stood up from his chair.

“What makes you think I got pushed towards it?” he asked surprised. He made his way around the desk and Lucy presumed he was going to sit in his usual place on the edge of it. Instead, he sat on the arm of the armchair next to her and look at her, waiting for her to answer his question. Lucy turned herself towards him, determined to get her point across in a clear manner.

“The passion you have for it,” explained Lucy simply, “Most people don’t usually have passion like that unless it comes from an experience or sense of injustice. It’s like Charles Dickens, he wrote about the poor because he had first-hand experience of seeing their suffering. He wanted others to see it too.” Daniel suddenly grew restless sitting on the side of the armchair; he shuffled his feet and itched the back of one hand. Lucy noticed this and reached out to place a hand on his arm. “You don’t have to tell me,” she said kindly, "I mean you can if you want to, but I won't press you on it." Lucy smiled at him in what she hoped was a reassuring manner, but Daniel said nothing. Instead, he leaned forward towards her and brushed a strand of hair that had fell in front of her face. Lucy opened her mouth to speak but found no words would form. Abruptly, he jumped up causing Lucy to lean away quickly and then he moved back round to his own chair.

"I do like a good detective series," he offered, as he sat down, "Figuring out puzzles, the occasional game of Cluedo."

"Am I a puzzle?" asked Lucy curiously. Daniel did not respond and for a moment, they just looked at each other in silence. Finally, Daniel sighed, sat up a little straighter and unconsciously straightened his tie.

"Now about Monday," he began, "Elijah said you might get called to testify, so let's discuss how you might handle that." Lucy sighed and leaned back in the armchair. *'Same old Daniel'* she thought, but then deep down she knew that it was far from the truth. Something had been shifting between them for a while now, but the real question was whether they would at some point address it or continue to ignore it.

Chapter 11: The Unexpected Witness

Monday morning came round all too quickly, and Lucy woke up extremely nervous for her trial. It was only 7am so she got dressed and not feeling hungry, she decided to take the chance to see if Daniel was in his office to steady her nerves.

When she got there, she raised her hand to knock when she became aware of two voices talking on the other side, recognising one of them as Daniel, she quickly realised that the other voice belonged to Elijah. Lucy froze wondering what they could be talking about. Then she felt silly; they were good friends, why wouldn't they be having a casual conversation. She also knew she shouldn't be listening in, but once again, as it always did, curiosity got the best of her.

"She's a remarkable woman, Daniel," said Elijah. Lucy edged closer to the door and her first thought was that he might have got a girlfriend and she was extremely surprised to find that her stomach dropped at the thought.

"I agree," replied Daniel. Lucy listened intently, wondering who they could be talking about and why Daniel had not mentioned this someone in his life, but then he never really shared much anyway.

"Hmmm," offered Elijah.

"What's that noise about?"

"Forgive me for overstepping my friend," began Elijah, "but you two seem more like good friends than doctor and patient." Lucy's stomach did a flip as she realised that they must be talking about her, unless of course Daniel had other female patients who he got along well with. Once again, seeds of jealousy reared their ugly heads and Lucy scowled angrily; who an earth did she think she was?

"Well, there is a reason for that." There were a few moments of silence before Elijah finally responded.

"Care to share." Lucy listened with bated breath; it was something she had always wondered herself.

"She hates anyone in authority; particularly anyone in authority over her," stated Daniel, "it all stems back to a traumatic childhood. Therefore I had to be a little less formal to break down some of her barriers." Lucy's heart was in her mouth, had his kindness and friendship really been an act so that she would trust him?

"It's not her barriers I'm worried about," warned Elijah bluntly. Lucy's mouth dropped open.

"What are you trying to suggest?" replied Daniel. Lucy suddenly found that her throat was dry, also wondering exactly what Elijah was trying to suggest, but secretly wishing that Daniel might suggest it too.

"I'm suggesting she has gotten under your skin," Noted Elijah, "Don't get me wrong; I can completely understand why. After, well…it's only natural you would gravitate towards her but be careful my friend." Lucy realised that breathing was becoming difficult, as she tried to digest what Elijah was saying. Was he merely accusing Daniel of being too unprofessional or was there something more behind it?

"Every time I try to be more professional and put some distance between us, she regresses or bottles it all up again," offered Daniel in a calm and measured tone. Lucy lowered her head to the floor sadly; it did sound like her to be fair.

"And you follow her further and further down the rabbit hole trying bring her back." There was silence for a few moments and Lucy was debating whether to simply walk away. She had already heard more than she should have heard or wanted to hear. Then she heard Daniel speak again and found that, even if she wanted to, she could not tear herself away.

"What do you think I should do?" he asked. Lucy heard Elijah laugh slightly and thought he was being rude.

“You are going to be annoyed with me, but I think you should pray on it,” he offered, “Things are already looking difficult for you here, perhaps God is telling you to move on.” Lucy found herself shaking her head though she knew it was stupid since nobody could see her, surely Daniel wouldn’t just up and leave?

“I don’t feel that’s what he’s saying though Elijah,” sighed Daniel, “particularly in regard to Lucy.” Lucy suddenly felt that she needed some air as everything had become overwhelming. She already had the trial to contend with and now this, what this was she wasn’t sure, but she knew it could only be dangerous for both of them.

She rushed down the corridor and back towards the courtyard she had walked through at the way there. Once outside, she found a small bench to sit on and began to contemplate what she had heard. Surrounded by the colourful flowerbeds and the large rectangular patch of grass, she found that she could think much better. Besides the bench she sat on, was a tall, large willow tree, which usually gave her much needed shelter on hot sunny days. It also partially obscured the view from one of two long double-glazed window panels on either side of the courtyard. She had often come here over the last two years, it was almost a form of escape, where she could forget all the things she didn’t want to think about. She found, however, that she couldn’t stop herself thinking of what Daniel had said. She had been glad that he had confirmed that it had been her they were talking about although it had been fairly obvious, but what did it all mean? She didn’t want her friendship with Daniel to get him in trouble or to force him to leave. So, resolving to try to and maintain more of a professional distance in the next meeting with Daniel, Lucy’s thoughts turned to the beginning of her trial.

Lucy stepped through the entrance of the courthouse and groaned loudly; she hated the press with a passion, all shouting questions at her hoping to get some kind of response. She had tried her best to ignore them, but it wasn’t easy, not when they were all making assumptions about her and what she had done, as if it was them that had experienced it and not her.

This time when Lucy walked into the courtroom there were a lot more people, which of course was to be expected. Many of them turned to look at her as she and Elijah made their way to the front. Lucy looked at Elijah to see if he was fazed by any of it, but he seemed to be holding his cards close to his chest as his face was expressionless. Once they were seated at the table ready for things to begin, Lucy took a deep breath and looked at the faces of her probable executioners.

There were six women and six men on the jury, which she had expected. Elijah had warned her that things may not go there way if there were more men than women on the jury, because a woman was more likely to understand her fear and vulnerability of living on the streets. Lucy wasn't sure if he was correct, but she concluded that he had made sure it was the case at the jury selection. The six women on the jury all varied in age, with the youngest looking about twenty-seven and the oldest looking in their early sixties. Lucy was surprised to see a man on there who looked exceptionally young, far too young for jury duty; he can't have been older than twenty. What right did he have to judge someone when he had such little life experience? Yet, as a murderer she couldn't argue that she was entitled to anything much anyway, so what did it matter? It was impossible to make out anything further about the jury, as they all say with stony serious faces waiting for the trial to begin. None of them dared look in her direction.

Lucy looked over to the prosecutor's table to see Mitch Jacobson was looking right at her curiously. Lucy guessed that he was thinking about the last time they spoke and her brazen comment suggesting he might be capable of prosecutorial misconduct. She smiled at him shyly just to show that she was intimidated and then suddenly the court bailiff stepped forward at the front. "All rise."

Lucy took a deep breath as she and everyone else stood up. She quickly looked around the courtroom and then suddenly her heart caught in her throat. At the very back, entering the courtroom was the last person she'd ever expected to see. A person she hadn't seen for almost 3 years, not since they had cruelly rejected her; her birth mother Amanda Wilshire!

Lucy almost collapsed back into her chair in shock, what an earth would her birth mother be doing here? For one moment Lucy wondered if she had been brought in by the prosecution to testify against her, but then that was ridiculous. Her birth mother didn't know anything about her and therefore couldn't possibly be part of this case. Then Amanda caught her eye, looked slightly worried, but smiled at Lucy nervously. Lucy did not know what to do in return because smiling back at the woman, who had rejected her, seemed wrong on many levels. However, this did not stop Lucy from hoping that, maybe just maybe, her birth mother was here to support her. Then again it might be too much to ask from a woman who had never wanted her. Amanda looked around the courtroom, presumably looking for somewhere to sit, but then suddenly a look of horror crossed her face, and she began to slowly walk backwards. Lucy wanted to shout after her, tell her not to leave, but then the judge said, "All be seated," so she slowly sat down and watched Amanda exit the courtroom. Lucy knew that she should feel nothing for the woman, but she had not been expected to see her today of all days. A day which was already emotional for her, but she could not stop the few tears that fell down her cheeks. Elijah mistook her tears for feelings of fear.

"It's going to be ok," he offered. Lucy wanted so much to believe him, but the tight knot she had felt in her stomach when she awoke that morning had suddenly become a whole lot tighter.

"The case of Miss Boragas vs the state in the case of the manslaughter of Alex Pembrokeshire is officially in session," stated the judge.

She hit her gavel down in front of her before looking over at Mitch Jacobson. "Prosecutor are you ready to make your opening statement?" she asked. Mitch Jacobson stood up, gave a quick glance at Lucy, and then nodded at the judge.

"Yes, your honour." The judge gestured for him to take the floor. Mitch Jacobson strolled towards the front with an air of total confidence and control.

"Let me be clear, we are not here today to prosecute Miss Boragas for murder," he began, "We know she did not plan to commit murder that night, nor do we underestimate the suffering she faced on the streets when she was made homeless. That being said we cannot allow Miss Boragas to think that her circumstances made it acceptable to end someone else's life. We all have to deal with the hand we are dealt in life and the victim did nothing to warrant such violence from Miss Boragas. She acted impulsively and in the heat of the moment, showing a complete disregard for human life, therefore legally she committed involuntary manslaughter and should serve time in jail. That's what we will be attempting to prove in this trial."

Lucy scowled at Mitch as he made his way back to his seat. He didn't know her; he had no idea what she had been through, and she certainly didn't think it was acceptable to take someone's life. Elijah then stood up and Lucy wondered what he might say about her, especially since Mitch had made her out to be so horrible.

"Miss Boragas does not deny that she took someone's life that night, an action that she feels great remorse over, but her intention was not to kill anyone; merely to protect herself," said Elijah, "Wouldn't you feel threatened if you'd spent months living on the street, having to fend for yourself, then someone attacks you and you try to run. While you are trying to run away from danger out of nowhere some random stranger approaches and tries to take your only means of survival…what would you make of it? Why did the random stranger take it upon himself to grab and intimidate Miss Boragas instead of simply allowing her to leave? If he had done so, my client would not have felt the need to act in self-defence. This is what we aim to prove to the jury." Elijah walked back to his chair and sat down. Lucy was admittedly a little impressed by his speech as she pondered the answers to some of the questions he had asked. However, there was no time for her to dwell in thought, because then, Mitch Jacobson stood up once more.

"We, the prosecution, would like to call our first witness," he said "Mark Somerville." Lucy watched as a smartly dressed gentleman made his way down the courtroom aisle. She knew he must have been one of the victim's friends, but she did not recognise his face. He was a clean-shaven man except for a neatly trimmed moustache, which she thought made him look rather devious. He stepped into the witness box and looked straight at Lucy; Lucy stared back wondering what he was about to say.

The court bailiff stepped next to the witness box and then raised his right hand. "Do you swear to tell the truth, the whole truth and nothing, but the truth so help you God?" he asked. Mark Somerville appeared calm and collected as he nodded.

"I do," he stated, as he also raised his right hand. Mitch Jacobson then walked towards the witness box but turned around so that he could still be seen by the court. Lucy thought this made him look more like some kind of showman than a lawyer, but then she realised that perhaps it was part of a lawyer's job to put on a good show. Glancing at Elijah next to her, she wondered how he might perform because he didn't seem at all like Jacobson. Mitch surveyed the room as if taking in the atmosphere before he spoke.

"Mr Somerville," he began "can you tell me how you knew the deceased?" Mark Somerville straightened his tie before he spoke, and Lucy was suddenly reminded of Daniel. How he straightened his tie when he was nervous or trying to appear more professional.

"He was one of my best mates," said Mark sadly. Mitch nodded at him encouragingly.

"And where were you on the night when Mr Pembrokeshire was killed?" asked Mitch.

"I was there. I saw the whole thing." He glanced at Lucy coldly as he spoke and Lucy for the first time, felt angry. If he had been there, he would have known that she was terrified and fighting for her life. Then something suddenly washed over Lucy like an icy bucket of water had been poured over her head; *'I didn't intend to kill'*. She thought, '*I just wanted to survive*'. Perhaps Daniel had been right? She was brought back from this profound revelation by Mitch Jacobson speaking.

"So, in your own words please can you tell us what happened?" instructed Jacobson. Mark took a deep breath, which Lucy knew must be part of an act because nobody needed to breathe that loudly.

"We had been out having a few drinks to celebrate my mate just landing a big promotion at work. We had just left a club and we were walking to flag down a taxi when this girl just appears from out of nowhere. She seemed distressed, so Alex was trying to calm her down. She was really defensive, and Alex was saying he wasn't going to hurt her, when suddenly she just pulled a knife. Alex backed off a bit, but he didn't want her to hurt her, so he asked her to give him the knife, then she just stabbed him." Lucy scowled at him; Alex hadn't backed off at all! He had continued to try and grab the knife from her and that was the very thing that had caused her instincts to take over.

"Was the girl that stabbed him," replied Mitch, "the girl here at court today named Lucy Boragas?" Mark nodded and once again shot Lucy an icy glare.

"100%," retorted Mark, "I mean it was dark, but while we were trying to hold her, waiting for the police, we were standing by the light of the shop window. It's her alright." Mitch nodded and then pointedly looked at the jury. Lucy found her hate for Jacobson growing stronger with each passing sentence and expression he gave. He seemed too confident and sure of himself, sure that he was right, and Lucy was a horrible being, but then she remembered that despite how it happened, she had still ended someone's life. That one fact made Mitch Jacobson a far better person than her, as much as she didn't like to admit it.

"And Alex did nothing to provoke her?" queried Jacobson, "He didn't attack her or grab her?" Once again Mark shook his head.

"No, he wasn't like that," said Mark. Lucy nearly laughed aloud; of course, this man would say that about someone who had been one of his best friends. It was just amazing how easily he could lie to a room full of people, unless that was honestly what he had thought had happened. After all, Lucy had thought she wasn't the type of person to kill someone yet here they were.

“No further questions,” said Mitch, as he coolly walked back to his seat.

“Mr James would you like to cross examine the witness?” asked the judge. Elijah stood up and nodded. Lucy looked at him curiously, eager to see him at work. She had grown to like Elijah as a good man, despite knowing he believed in an imaginary god.

“Yes, your honour.” Elijah stepped forward and rather than turn around and address the court, he spoke to Mark directly. “Mark, you said you and your friends had gone out for a few drinks to celebrate a big promotion,” he started, “Had Alex been drinking?” Mark put a hand to his neck fidgeting nervously.

“He had about 3 beers,” admitted Mark. Elijah nodded, then looked around to ensure that he still commanded the attention of the room. Lucy thought he was more natural than Jacobson, but then perhaps she was biased.

“Would you say this might have limited his ability to act rationally when confronting Miss Boragas?” questioned Elijah. Jacobson stood up quickly looking enraged.

“I object,” he said firmly, “He’s asking a leading question.” Elijah held his hands up before the judge could respond.

“I’ll rephrase,” he replied coolly, “Was three beers enough to affect Mr Pembrokeshire’s reasonable thought process?” Lucy grinned, Elijah came across as so smooth; nothing fazed him, Lucy wished she could be half as confident as he was.

“No, it didn’t even touch him,” answered Mark, shaking his head. “He could hold his drink.” Elijah nodded.

“I understand. You also said that you can identify Miss Boragas because you held her by the light of a shop window until the police arrived. Does this mean you could not see the confrontation clearly between Miss Boragas and the victim?” Mark suddenly looked like he had been forced to swallow something quite unpleasant.

“I mean it was dark and we didn’t have the clearest view,” said Mark nervously, “but we could still see what was going on.” Elijah turned towards the jury as he spoke next.

“Yet you could not see Miss Boragas’ face to make out exactly what her intentions were or that of your friend?” asked Elijah coolly. Mark scowled at the question, but then seemed to remember himself, as his face took on a more neutral expression.

“Well…I…I mean yeah,” he began, “but you can tell a lot by body language.” Elijah put his hand on his chin thoughtfully.

“What body language would you say indicates that somebody intends to end somebody’s life?” he asked. Once again Mark looked increasingly nervous and agitated, Lucy almost felt sorry for him, but at the same time she was willing Elijah on.

“I dunno,” said Mark quietly, “Lashing out quickly without hesitation.”

“So, the same body language that is used when acting in self-defence then?” offered Elijah, Mark looked like somebody had slapped him across the face.

“I…I,” stuttered Mark, but Elijah cut across him.

“Mr Somerville, I’ve done a bit of digging on your friend,” he began, “and despite by all accounts being a seemingly decent guy he was in fact a frequent drug user was he not? Had he taken any drugs that night?” Lucy’s mouth fell open as she contemplated why Elijah had not shared that information with her. Though, she had been a drug user at one point in her life too, so it was not her job to judge someone else who had been. Mark’s face flushed a deep shade of red, as he looked as though he would rather by anywhere else then in the witness stand.

“What? I…look he doesn’t…I mean he didn’t do hardcore drugs,” he state quickly, “just the occasional harmless pills for personal use. He hadn’t taken any that night.” Elijah shrugged his shoulders casually.

"That you are aware of," he added. Then he returned to the desk and retrieved a brown wallet lying on it. He opened it as he walked back to the front. "Alex Pembrokeshire spent two months in Georgia at a drug addiction facility, eight months before he died. Now no one here is suggesting that being a frequent drug user means you should lose your life. As we have stated, his death is indeed regrettable, but it must be questioned what kind of state of mind he was in that night to continue to confront someone who was obviously scared and intimidated. No further questions." Mark frowned before opening his mouth to reply, but then decided to think better of it and quickly made his way out of the witness box.

Elijah walked calmly back to the desk and sat down. Lucy felt the sudden urge to hug him for defending her so vigorously. All eyes turned to the judge for the next point of proceedings, but the judge removed her glasses.

"I propose we take a recess," she stated wearily, "it's now 12:15. We will resume at 1:30pm." She banged her gavel, stood up and left the courtroom hastily. Lucy watched her leave in dismay wondering why they couldn't just go straight through.

"Come on," said Elijah, "The courthouse restaurant has very decent sandwiches." Lucy stood up miserably thinking that there is no way she could attempt to eat anything, at least not until today was over.

Forty-five minutes later, Elijah and Lucy were sat back in the courtroom waiting for the trial to resume. Elijah had managed to encourage Lucy to eat three bites of a cheese sandwich, but she was now regretting it because her stomach was in bits. The bailiff walked to the front and Lucy tried to steel herself once more. "All rise." The courtroom stood up as the judge walked in and sat back down.

"You may be seated. The court is now back in session." She banged her gavel back down and Lucy knew she would grow to hate the sound by the end of her trial. "Prosecutor, would you like to present your next witness?" she added. Jacobson stood up and flashed the jury a smile.

"Yes, your honour," he said confidently, "We call Laura Tisgard, medical examiner to the stand." A woman walked into the courtroom wearing a smart expensive looking suit. Lucy looked pointedly at Elijah. He had told her that part of Jacobson's strategy usually involved calling upon so called experts to overload the jury with facts, even when the charges did not rely on the facts in question. "Can you confirm that you were the first medical officer to examine the body, Miss Tisgard?" asked Jacobson. Laura nodded and surveyed the room. Lucy was given the distinct impression that Laura thought a lot of herself and her career choice, but Lucy couldn't imagine anything worse than examining dead bodies.

"Yes, I was," she stated confidently. Jacobson nodded, then turned around to face the rest of the court, as if he were entertaining an audience.

"How many stab wounds was there on the body, Miss Tisgard?" he asked. Laura ran a hand through her strawberry blonde hair checking to see if it was still immaculate. Lucy could tell she took a lot of pride in her appearance.

"Just the one," replied Laura, "it went in 3 inches deep and was about 1.5 inches wide straight into the heart." She looked around, as if she expected people to be impressed with her findings, but Lucy cringed thinking about the damage she had inflicted upon another human being. Mitch Jacobson nodded at Laura and his face looked solemn, but Lucy knew that he had no real care for the victim, all he cared about was a guilty verdict.

"In your medical opinion," began Mitch, "would a person who was acting in self-defence go for the heart?" Elijah turned to Lucy and rolled his eyes, causing Lucy to grin, because she had never seen him do it before.

"It would be unusual," acknowledged Laura, "as they would usually go for the hand or the arms." Lucy scowled, she had gone for his arms at first, but he still hadn't left her alone.

"For the knife to go in 3 inches deep would you say reasonable force was used?" enquired Jacobson. Lucy was pleased to see that the medical examiner shook her head to this question. She then licked her deep red lipstick-stained lips, preparing herself to offer further information.

"Not necessarily. I mean that could well be the case, but I would say the knife used was pretty sharp, probably a meat cleaver type which would mean it would slice right through skin and organs very easily." Lucy shivered thinking that was not the reason she'd had chosen the knife.

"Thank you for your time, Miss Tisgard. No further questions." He casually strolled back to his seat straightening his tie. Elijah rose out of his chair to address the judge.

"We don't wish to cross examine the Medical examiner," he said, "Thank you." Lucy couldn't blame him for that decision because nothing the medical examiner had said had really been of any relevance. Jacobson looked amused by the choice, before he stood up once more.

"For our next witness we would like to call the forensic scientist Dr Stephen Lankin to the stand," he said. Lucy had to laugh because Elijah put a hand to his face and groaned. It was frustrating as all Jacobson seemed to be doing was playing for time presenting nothing of real relevance. Having said that, Lucy also felt slightly relieved that there were other witnesses, as it delayed her having to testify, though she knew she would have to eventually.

Stephen Lankin was a tall nervous looking man with short spiky hair and glasses. He seemed to be fighting an inner urge to run as he stumbled into the witness box. Jacobson seemed oblivious to the scientist's nervous disposition as he gazed at him in a matter-of-fact fashion.

"Could you describe what you found when you arrived at the scene of the crime?" he asked. Stephen nervously adjusted his glasses as he surveyed the room.

"I arrived on the scene at about 11:52pm to find the victim deceased on his back with a pool of blood around him." A shiver went down Lucy's spine as she lowered her head in shame, She had done that;

she was the reason there was one less person in the world. She was brought out of her tragic haunting thoughts by the feeling of Elijah's hand on her shoulder trying to offer some form of comfort. Though she did not feel comforted, she appreciated the gesture.

"Was there any other evidence to suggest it was something other than the knife that killed him?" asked Jacobson. Lucy rolled her eyes, thinking Jacobson was definitely more showman than a good lawyer, but maybe that's what it was all about; who could put on the best performance?

"No, it was definitely the knife," answered Stephen anxiously, "It went straight through his chest and hit a vital artery above his heart. He was dead within a minute; two at the most." Lucy felt the cheese sandwich she'd had threaten to leave her stomach, as a wave of guilt driven nausea hit her. It had been a rash action she had taken, but that action had led to a man losing his life in the space of a very short amount of time.

"Almost as if the person who stabbed him was aiming for it?" questioned Jacobson. Elijah jumped to his feet extremely quickly.

"Objection," he stated calmly, "that's argumentative!" The judge nodded at Elijah and looked sternly at Jacobson.

"I'm inclined to agree with Mr James; objection sustained," she said, "Prosecutor, please refrain from drawing your own conclusion without a factual basis." Jacobson did not look the slightest bit embarrassed by his error. He smiled sheepishly, as he held up his hands in surrender.

"Yes, your honour," he said sweetly, "Sorry, I forgot myself." Lucy rolled her eyes and leaned closer to Elijah.

"Kiss arse!" she whispered. To Lucy's surprise, Elijah snickered at her comment. She thought he would think it was below the belt.

"So did you find a set of fingerprints on the knife?" asked Jacobson. Stephen coughed into his hand, before answering.

"Yes," he replied, "there were three sets of fingerprints we managed to procure from the knife." Lucy looked at Elijah questioningly wondering where Jacobson was going with his questioning. There was no denying she had been there or that she had stabbed him with the knife so what was the point. Elijah looked equally perplexed.

"Who did the fingerprints belong to?" inquired Jacobson. Elijah tensed next to Lucy, and she could tell he was becoming increasingly frustrated, and she couldn't blame him.

"The victim, Miss Boragas and a local take-out owner," said Stephen meekly, "The take-out owner's prints were there because we established the knife was taken from there some months before." Lucy shivered as she had a flashback to the day, she had stolen the knife. She was down to her last $20 and had decided to buy some cheap food from some local take out. The guy running the place was rushed off his feet trying to serve his customers and it had been so easy to lean over the counter and remove the knife from its place on the chopping board. She had taken it because some mean drunk had basically thrown her out of her sleeping place the night before because he had wanted it for himself. It made her realise that on the streets you have to fend for yourself, because nobody else cared.

"In what position was the victim found?" asked Jacobson, drawing Lucy from her memory. Suddenly Elijah jumped up beside her.

"Objection, your honour," he said exasperated. The judge nodded at him appreciatively as if she too had been waiting for him to take this action.

"On what grounds?" she asked, but Lucy had a feeling the judge already knew the answer and was just following procedure.

"Lack of relevance?" stated Elijah wearily, "Miss Boragas does not deny she was there, nor does she deny she stabbed someone in the heat of the moment. The point of this case is whether my client committed manslaughter or self-defence, not whether she committed the act itself; this is a waste of the court's time." The judge remained expressionless as she turned towards the prosecutor.

"Mr Jacobson, how do you respond?" she asked. Jacobson shrugged his shoulders as if he was clueless about the interruption. Lucy scowled at him knowing it was all an act.

"I'm simply trying to allow the jury to build up a picture of the facts of that night, so it is clear in their minds what happened," stated Mitch, "before we actually establish Miss Boragas' intentions." The judge's face fell for a moment before she took on a more composed expression and Lucy suddenly thought that being a judge must be a frustrating job.

"Overruled," noted the judge sourly. Elijah sat back down looking thoroughly annoyed and Lucy watched him for a few moments. Angry Elijah was not something she was used to seeing, almost like seeing Daniel lose his temper.

"Thank you, your honour," said Jacobson arrogantly, "So, before I was rudely interrupted, what position was the victim found in?" Stephen looked at the judge in confusion. Lucy had the feeling that he wasn't sure of the relevance of the question either, but regardless of this he still answered it.

"On his back," said Stephen, "which clearly indicated that he was stabbed and fell backwards."

"In your medical opinion," began Mitch, "do you think given the position of the stab wound and the way in which the victim's body was found, is there anything that indicates it was done in self-defence?" Stephen sighed and shook his head.

"No," he said. This caused Mitch to smile and look pointedly at the jury. "However," added Stephen, as he glanced at Lucy. He studied her as if she were a fascinating experiment. Lucy found it rather unnerving. "There is nothing to indicate that the intention was manslaughter either," he continued, "These things are rarely established based on forensic evidence." Lucy smiled as Jacobson suddenly lost his calm composure and scowled, but then in an instant the scowl was gone, and he calmly nodded at Stephen.

"Thank you for your time, Mr Lankin," he said through gritted teeth.

"Do you wish to cross examine the forensic scientist Mr James?" asked the judge. Elijah stood up and smiled slightly.

"No, your honour." said Elijah "I think he has made things relatively clear." The judge nodded and then glanced at the watch on her wrist.

"Thank you, Mr James. The time is now 4:10. I propose we end for today and reconvene at 9am tomorrow morning. Any objections to this?" Lucy looked over at Jacobson expecting him to protest, but he simply nodded and so did Elijah. The judge brought down her gavel, then stood up and left the courtroom. Lucy felt an overwhelming feeling of relief that at least for now, it was over.

As Elijah led her back to the car, through the persistently loud reporters eager to get her story, Lucy felt emotionally exhausted When they were finally in the car and heading back to the institute, Elijah spoke.

"Well half of today was almost a waste of time," sighed Elijah, "Almost as if there was no point us being there at all." Lucy nodded but offered nothing further in response. "It started well but went redundant very fast." Lucy nodded again thinking of how she had felt at the start of today in the courtroom. Then she remembered the fact that her birth mother had been there and the emotions she had been keeping at bay over it began to slowly make their way to the surface. Elijah patted her on the shoulder thinking Lucy was quiet because she was overwhelmed with the first day of her trial. He obviously had no idea that her birth mother had been there, how could he? She had not expected it herself and then for her to leave just as quickly: was it just an attempt to torment Lucy? Had she come to make amends? Suddenly Lucy began to think about what would have happened if that woman who seemed to have no regard for real human emotion, would have raised her. Would it have changed her being a murderer? Or would it have changed the woman?

Chapter 12: What if She'd been a Mother…

"Give it to me," I yell angrily. I am caught in a tug of war with the girl down the road over a hula hoop. Maggie has had it for a whole ten minutes now and it doesn't seem fair, not when I haven't had a turn. I'm the one who asked my friend if we could borrow it while she visits her cousins down south. An adult who walks past with their shopping rolls her eyes at us and tuts. She probably thinks fighting over a hula hoop is stupid, but my mum has always taught me to fight for the things I want in life. The other girl is strong too so instead of trying to be stronger, I try to be smarter; I allow some slack on the hula hoop and Maggie falls backwards slightly in shock, then I quickly pull hard, and the hula hoop comes out of her hand. I grin at her and hold the hula hoop up proudly, while Maggie looks at me angrily. My victory is short lived though as I suddenly see my mum walking down the street and I wonder how much she saw.

"I hope you're being kind Lucy," she warns. I look at Maggie as if daring her to say anything, but she stays quiet.

"I'm always kind, mom," I say sweetly. Mom laughs slightly.

"I'm not sure I believe that one." I shrug my shoulders to pretend I don't know what she's talking about, but we both know the truth; I'm no angel.

"Is Tom home from work yet?" I ask. Tom is mum's new boyfriend. He works at the advertising agency with mom; I really like him.

"Yes," replies mom, "come and say hi." I turn to Maggie, wave, and walk towards the house taking the hula hoop with me. We live in a quiet house in the suburbs, just outside of New York city. We used to live in England but when I was about three, we moved here, and I like it a lot. I can't really remember what life was like in England, but mom tells me that it always rained a lot and people are more miserable there.

I walk into the house and see Tom sitting on the sofa, I smile at him.

“Hey kiddo,” he says, “How's it going?” I shrug my shoulders and reply with the response we have come to answer with as our own little tradition.

“It’s going,” I say grinning. Mom suddenly puts her hand on my shoulder.

“Sit down Lucy,” she says kindly, “We have some news.” I look between them both in wonder, then I smile. Maybe the news is that Tom and mom are going to get married, they’ve been living together for almost a month now so it seems only right that it should be the next step. Besides, I want them to get married because then I know that Tom is going to stick around. Once I am seated on the sofa, I look up at mom. Tom gets up off the sofa and goes to stand next to her. They are both smiling so I know that it’s good news; I wonder if I will be a bridesmaid?

“I’m pregnant,” says my mom in excitement, but I just stare at her confused.

“What?” I ask. Mom and Tom just continue to smile at me.

“You’re going to have a brother or sister,” continues mom, “and it’s going to be lovely.” This time my mouth drops open; this isn’t how it’s supposed to go, they are not even married. How can they have a baby? I shiver as I remember mom giving me the talk on where babies come from; I gagged the entire time.

“But...you and Tom,” I begin nervously, “you’ve only been together like 3 months.” Can my mom not see that they shouldn’t be having a baby right now? It’s not right! It doesn’t make any sense! Anyway, what’s going to happen to me? I was just getting used to us as a three, now I’ve got to get used to a fourth person; it’s not fair!

“That doesn’t matter,” states mom, “he’s going to make a great father and he’s going to be there for me, you and the baby.” I look at Tom scowling he’s not the man who could be my dad, because he’s now going to be somebody else’s dad and they are actually going to be related.

"How do you know?" I ask quietly. She can't know that Tom is going to stick around forever, because they are not married, and my dad didn't stick around either. Mom comes and sits next to me on the sofa. She puts an arm around me, and I bury my head into her side.

"I'm going to tell you the truth," she says kindly, "When I was pregnant with you, I didn't know if I could do it." I lift my head up to look at her wondering what she could mean.

"Do what?" I ask. My mom strokes my face with her hand, and I am surprised because mom isn't usually like this.

"Be your mum," she replies, "I considered allowing someone else to be your mum. Be your parents." My mouth drops open; does that mean she didn't want me? Did she think I was a mistake?

"Why?" I ask quietly, but I have knots in my tummy. I'm not sure I want to hear the answer she is about to give me.

"Because you reminded me of your dad, and he was a horrible person." I nod at her feeling a little relieved it wasn't my fault, but then how could I have reminded her of my dad? I've never even met him. We've not spoken about my dad much, but from what my mum has told me he is not a nice man; she hasn't exactly said that, but she did say I am better off not knowing him which says a lot.

"Where is my dad?" I ask. I decide I want to know more; I know mom says he is horrible, but I need more than that. She doesn't answer so I ask again; I want to know where he is. Maybe someday I can meet him. "Where is my dad?" I repeat and this time my mom looks up at Tom who nods at her. Wait, does Tom know where my dad is? Why does he get to know before me?

"He's in jail," states my mum and my heart falls through my tummy because he can't be in jail. Only really bad people go to jail, but then maybe it was a mistake. I remember we learnt about a man who got wrongly jailed in second grade.

"Why?" I ask. Hoping that she'll tell me that it was a big misunderstanding and he's already working on getting out. My mom doesn't look at me when she speaks next.

"Because of something very bad he did." I want to know what he did, but I also don't want to know, because I'm worried that the more I know, the more I could end up like him and mom thinks he is horrible. Instead, I ask her a question that I hope will lead to a better answer.

"Why did you decide to keep me?" I whisper. Mom looks at me with tears in her eyes. She chokes up a little and has to cough.

"I was determined to give you up," she begins, "but then I saw you right after you were born. You were so small and so helpless, and I just knew that it wasn't your fault of how you came into this world, but I could possibly make it a better one for you." I almost breathe a sigh of relief as I hug her, because I now know that despite my father being a horrible person; my mum loved me from the very beginning. Tom then moves forward and sits beside me on the other side of the sofa. He rubs my back and I turn my face towards him and give him a small smile. I may not trust him completely, but at least he's already a better dad than mine was or will be.

Predicted Verdict: Guilty

Chapter 13: You are my Patient

As soon as they got back from the courthouse, Lucy made a beeline for Daniel's office. She knew that it was probably after his usual working hours, but she figured these were special circumstances. She felt that if she did not talk to someone then her emotions would overwhelm her. She didn't even bother to knock on the office door, instead she threw it open and walked straight in. Daniel who was sitting behind his desk looked up at her, he did not seem surprised, and Lucy wondered for a moment whether he had been expecting her. Her suspicions were confirmed when Daniel looked at his watch and gestured for her to sit down.

"Rough day?" he enquired. It took all of her strength not to burst out crying, instead she nodded and sat down in the chair.

"You're still here?" she asked, looking at him inquisitively. Daniel tilted his head and smiled sheepishly.

"Something told me it would be best to stick around," he offered. This time Lucy began to sob, she couldn't take his kindness, not on top of everything else she had endured today. Daniel stood up and came around the desk, offering her a box of tissues. "The first day of trial was always bound to be difficult," he said. Lucy shrugged her shoulder as she wiped her face with the tissues.

"The trial itself went alright," she said emotionally, "Elijah did well." Daniel raised his eyebrows at her in confusion.

"Then what else happened?" he asked. Lucy did not answer at first, instead she tried to get her sobs under control, telling herself the woman was not worth her tears.

"My mum showed up," said Lucy quietly. Daniel looked even more confused at Lucy's statement.

"Well that's unsurprising," he stated, "I thought she had told you she was trying to make it over for the trial." Lucy shook her head and scoffed; of course Daniel would think she was referring to her adoptive mum; this woman was mother in name only.

"No, I mean my birth mom," she replied. This time Daniel's mouth fell open.

"You mean the birth mom who rejected you when you sought her out?" he asked. Lucy nodded at him avoiding his eye contact, she almost felt embarrassed about it.

"Yes," said Lucy bitterly, "The very same."

"Why?" asked Daniel. Lucy sighed and shrugged her shoulders; how was she supposed to know?

"I don't know," she said sadly, "she just took one look at me and fled the courtroom." Daniel scowled and shuffled uncomfortably on the desk.

"Are you sure it was her?" he asked. Lucy looked at him clearly annoyed.

"Yes Daniel, I'm sure. You don't forget a woman that cruel." Daniel grimaced then put his hand on her shoulder.

"Oh Lucy, I'm sorry," he offered sympathetically, "I don't know what to say." Lucy nodded sadly.

"There is nothing you can say," she replied, "and I don't even know why I'm upset about it." Daniel got off the desk and sat next to her on the edge of the armchair, then he placed a hand on her shoulder.

"You're upset because despite her horrible demeanour she's your mother." Lucy grabbed a tissue to stem the tears that were flowing down her face.

"I thought I was over her rejection," she said emotionally, "So I don't know why seeing her again would affect me so much." Daniel awkwardly rubbed her shoulder doing his best to give the little comfort he was able to offer her.

"I don't think it was seeing her again that affected you," he suggested. Lucy did not reply but waited for him to elaborate. "I think it was the fact that when you saw her you thought she had finally decided to be there for you," continued Daniel, "but then she left just as quickly. I don't understand it though, why would she turn up in court only to walk out just as fast?" Lucy felt more tears roll down her cheeks as she re-lived the moment all over again in her mind.

"Neither do I and that's what hurts the most. It's the not knowing." She stood up and began to move around the room finding herself unable to sit still. Daniel also stood up watching her, as if he was trying to figure out the best course of action. "It's almost like she was toying with me," continued Lucy bitterly, "I mean I was nervous for my first day as it is and then she showed up…it was just too much." Lucy put her hands around her arms as if cold and then began to sob once more because it didn't matter how much she told herself that the woman meant nothing to her. The truth was all she had ever wanted was someone who believed in her and who loved her unconditionally. Daniel looked pained as if struggling with some internal battle, eventually he sighed, crossed the room, and embraced Lucy in a hug. To his surprise, Lucy returned the hug and leaned into it as if she needed this form of comfort.

"We all get overwhelmed sometimes," he said kindly, "the important thing is there are people there for us who pull us back from the edge." Lucy pulled back and looked straight into his eyes wondering why it was this man wanted to pull her back from the edge? Without thinking about it or without warning Lucy leaned her face towards Daniel's and kissed him. Daniel gasped in shock, and it took a moment for him to recover before he quickly pulled away from her.

"Lucy you are my patient!" he said firmly, while moving away from her. Lucy flushed red in embarrassment; she wasn't sure what she had been thinking and now she was mortified.

"I know," she said exasperated. Did he really think she was that stupid? She thought there was something between them, but now it was quickly becoming clear that she had imagined the whole thing.

"No, I don't think you do," said Daniel seriously. He shoved his hands in his pockets and shifted on his feet awkwardly.

“All I know is that you’re the one person who makes me feel as if everything is going to be ok,” said Lucy in barely more than a whisper. It was the most honest she had ever been with him because she needed him to know how much he meant to her. Even if they could never be anything more than friends or just doctor and patient. Daniel looked like he was struggling to find any words in response and Lucy lowered her gaze to the floor feeling foolish.

“I’m glad about that,” offered Daniel honestly, “but Lucy I’m your doctor; there can’t be anything more between us.” Lucy scoffed in annoyance; she thought there already was something more between them; certainly more than doctor and patient at any rate. She wasn’t even sure why she had made the stupid decision to kiss him, except perhaps she had wanted some comfort.

“Just shut up. It’s fine. Just forget it,” said Lucy firmly, “In Fact if you want me to get a new psychiatrist I understand.” Daniel’s eyebrows shot up.

“That’s not what I want,” he replied, but offered nothing further. This only served to make Lucy even more angry; she was sick of having to second guess everything.

“THEN WHAT DO YOU WANT?” she yelled “I’m sick of trying to figure it out!! You say you care, and I talked to other patients about what you’re like with them and they say you’re nice and professional. They know you care, but you’re different with them than you are with me.” Daniel put a hand to his head and nervously ran it through his hair.

“Lucy,” he began awkwardly, “I’m sorry if I gave you the wrong impression.” Lucy suddenly forgot her anger and stared at him wondering what impression he thought he had given and whether it had even been real.

“What impression? The impression that you care?” she said emotionally, “That you tell me how lovely I am despite how shit I feel about myself? The impression that you hug me when I need comfort. Or was it all just a shitty act? Did you just be nice to me so I would tell you more about everything because you know I hate authority? Tell me the truth and stop lying to me!! I can take it!!!" Daniel looked pained as he opened and closed his mouth.

"We should probably leave it there today." He looked towards the door as if he himself wanted to run through it. Lucy knew she shouldn't push him, but regardless of the mistake she had made, he needed to know his behaviour was not acceptable either.

"Oh here we go again," said Lucy sarcastically, "Daniel clams up just as things are about to get serious. And you accuse me of keeping my defences up." Daniel lowered his gaze from hers.

"I don't know what you want me to say?" replied Daniel quietly. Lucy crossed her arms and moved towards him. He involuntarily took to take a step backwards, but Lucy moved another step towards him undeterred.

"Anything as long as it's the truth," said Lucy. Daniel suddenly looked terrified, so much so that Lucy's mouth dropped open as she wondered why anybody would be so scared of the truth? Then she remembered that it was her very fear of the truth that got her here in the first place. It was so hard to try and hold others to a higher standard given all of her own self-loathing.

"The truth is complicated," said Daniel finally. He was still avoiding her gaze, as if he thought the truth would come spilling out if they looked at each other properly.

"Then let me make it nice and simple for you," said Lucy angrily "Fuck off until you start being honest with me. I can take you just seeing me as another random person you want to help, that you feel sorry for, but I can't take you constantly hiding and lying by omission, while expecting me to reveal everything." Daniel remained silent, but his face suggested he was deeply conflicted. Before he could regain his composure, Lucy took one last look at him before she fled the office wondering what she had actually expected him to say.

Chapter 14: What am I supposed to do now?

I'm without a doubt well and truly fucked! What am I supposed to do now? I had no idea that she has feelings for me too; I still don't! Maybe it was just a spur of the moment thing because she needed comfort. Anyway, it's completely wrong and messed up; I'm her psychiatrist! I should know better! Elijah was right, I'm in way over my head. I couldn't help being intrigued by her when we first met, because we are actually quite alike. From what I had read in her file I was expecting to meet someone who was rebellious and had a bad attitude, but that's not the woman I met. Instead, I met someone beautifully captivating; intelligent and compassionate. She doesn't think a lot of herself, she thinks one mistake makes her unlovable, but only if she could see herself the way I see her.

Elijah teases me that I'll be alone for life now. He's one to talk; he's never been married! He doesn't know what it's like to love someone completely, to trust someone so much then to be torn apart as they completely destroy your confidence in not only them, but yourself. You start to question; was it me? Was I just that stupid to not be able to see it?

That's why I can't go there with Lucy, I can't do that to myself again!! I'd be lying to say that I don't feel there is a connection between us. I keep telling myself she's out of my league, I'm 16 years older than her after all, but the truth is, she's more than out of my league, she's out of bounds. I'm her doctor, that's what I keep reminding myself anyway.

None of it matters though because she still doesn't know the truth and not just about my feelings for her, but about everything else too. If she did, I don't think she'd have kissed me today; she'd probably slap me again. Despite knowing she'd probably slap me; I still want to tell her. I want to tell her everything about me, about how I came to be here and why, but I am terrified in case it makes things worse between us.

I know I need to keep my distance and stay back for now. I also know I should report what happened, but it would mean I can't be her psychiatrist anymore and I still want to help her; I have an obsessive need to help her. Deep down I know it's more than that though. I was hoping to be able to bury what I'm feeling towards her, but how can I do that now? I can't stop thinking about her lips on mine; it was only for a split second, but it honestly felt like I had been struck by lightning. I've never felt like that before, not even with my ex-wife. I know it makes me completely crazy and unethical, but I can't help but wanting to be struck by that lightning again, no matter how much it may hurt us both.

Chapter 15: Musings of the Past

The next morning found Lucy sitting half asleep in the meeting room talking to Elijah. It was 7am in the morning and Lucy had hardly got any sleep the night before because she was so worried about what had happened between her and Daniel. She wondered if they would ever get past it or if he would just leave and assign her a new psychiatrist. The thought made her desperately unhappy and frustrated, but perhaps it was for the best. Despite being half asleep, Lucy noticed that Elijah also seemed somewhat lost in his own thoughts. Stifling a yawn, she decided to see what was on his mind, because it was easier than discussing what was on hers.

"Something is bothering you." Elijah suddenly blinked as if he had only just realised she was there.

"Yes, it seems insignificant, but I can't put it down," acknowledged Elijah thoughtfully. Lucy suddenly forgot about her own troubles as her curiosity peaked.

"What?" asked Lucy, waiting for him to elaborate.

"We must have been over that night a thousand times," began Elijah, "each time you've told me exactly what happened step by step." Lucy rolled her eyes; talk about stating the obvious.

"Yeah and…" she said wearily. Elijah shrugged his shoulders.

"At no point did you ever mention the victim touched the knife?" stated Elijah. Lucy sighed feeling disappointed, wondering why something so small and irrelevant had got Elijah thinking.

"It was dark," she offered, "he might have done." Elijah nodded although he still did not seem satisfied.

"If you were as terrified as you say," began Elijah "then you were holding to it for dear life. Did he grab it once you'd stabbed him with it?" Lucy crossed her arms becoming slightly frustrated with

Elijah; what did it matter if Alex Pembrokeshire had grabbed the knife or not?

“I don’t think so cause he went straight down,” she affirmed sadly, “Like the medical examiner said I hit a vital artery, he was probably dead within seconds.” She shivered as she recognised the harsh reality of her words. “It hardly seems important; I mean what does it matter?” she insisted, “Are you going to make out he committed suicide?” Elijah shook his head.

“No, I don’t know,” he said, clearly frustrated, “It probably doesn’t matter, but I can’t shake it.” Lucy nodded and then frowned. She knew that feeling very well because her thoughts, over the last 12 hours or so, had continually consisted of Daniel. Thinking about what she had done and how she could have got it so wrong.

“Believe me I know that feeling of not being able to shake something off,” she mumbled. For the first time, Elijah studied Lucy properly for the first time since she had entered the room.

“What do you mean?” he asked. Lucy sank back into her chair and shrugged her shoulders feeling embarrassed.

“He’s told you, hasn’t he?” she replied pointedly. Elijah raised his eyebrows in surprise.

“I’m not sure what you’re talking about,” he said honestly. Lucy looked at him cautiously; judging from the conversation she had overheard yesterday, Daniel and Elijah held each other in high confidence.

“You two tell each other everything.” Elijah suddenly sat up a little straighter as if he realised that what she was about to say was important.

“Ok now I’m really curious,” offered Elijah seriously “what is it that you did?” Lucy didn’t reply at first, she really had expected Daniel to tell Elijah about her mistake and what he should do about it, she hadn’t expected to be wrong.

“You really don’t know,” she said nervously. Elijah sighed.

“You and Daniel have quite a bit in common. He’s not exactly an open book either. You really think we get together after work, and he pours out all his secrets to me?” Lucy blinked in surprise; that is exactly what she thought. Ok maybe it was an exaggeration to think Daniel might put his heart out every night, but she assumed he would want to talk about something so serious to someone. Then her heart dropped into her stomach as she realised that perhaps it might be because it was something unimportant to him.

“Oh. I thought he was just being like that with me,” she suggested, “because well professional boundaries.” Elijah shrugged his shoulders sadly.

“Sadly, Daniel’s professional boundaries extend to close friends and family as well.” This time Lucy felt a little more reassured that perhaps Daniel was not keeping her at arm’s length after all. Perhaps he had in some small ways lowered his guard a little more with her, then her thoughts returned to his reaction yesterday and she groaned. Elijah studied her carefully, waiting for her to divulge what was on her mind. Being a man who always spoke his mind albeit politely, he found it frustrating when people just couldn’t just say what they intended.

“Wow that’s…” began Lucy, “I suppose we are similar in a way.” She knew she was guarded around most people, but it still frustrated her that she had lowered her guard substantially with Daniel and was yet to receive the same in return.

“So I ask again,” stated Elijah wearily, “what did you do?” He held her gaze, calmly waiting for an answer that Lucy really didn’t want to give, but she had no one else to talk to about what had happened.

“You’re not going to like it,” she admitted nervously. Elijah tensed up as if he was expecting the worst, but his expression still remained calm.

“I’m sitting down already.” Lucy lowered her gaze to the table between them as she spoke.

“I may have tried to kiss him,” she confessed. Elijah groaned and put a hand to his face, which made Lucy feel rather defensive. “I know, it was stupid and totally inappropriate. I was really emotional over something, and Daniel tried to comfort me, then I wanted to be comforted a little bit too much…in the wrong way." Elijah folded his arms waiting for more, but when she did not offer it, he sat up and leaned forward.

"Then what happened?" he said forcefully. Lucy felt it was an odd question because there was nothing more to tell.

"Well what do you think happened?" she stated sheepishly. "Daniel put me in my place, and I was mortified. I still am and usually when I am feeling something I talk to Daniel but obviously I can't so I'm talking to you instead." She watched Elijah curiously waiting for his response when suddenly he smiled slightly and snickered.

"I have no words." Lucy sank further down into her chair. She could feel her cheeks burning red and wished the ground would swallow her up.

"I can probably think of all of them anyway," she said humiliated, "You're not going to report him, are you? I mean he did nothing wrong; it was all me." Elijah looked surprised at her question.

"Lucy, Daniel is one of my best friends. Why would I report him?" he asked seriously, "Besides if he is doing his job correctly, he'll have to report it anyway." Lucy's face fell as she realised how utterly stupid she had been. Of course there would be consequences to what she had done. Daniel was her doctor, not her friend.

"Oh crap!" she whispered quietly, "I really screwed up." Elijah nodded and Lucy wanted to run from the room. Perhaps she should have said nothing to Elijah.

"Well to put in bluntly yes you did," warned Elijah honestly, "There is a good chance that Daniel will probably not be able to be your psychiatrist once he reports it." Lucy's stomach suddenly felt like she was going to be sick. Daniel was the one person she could talk to, but now she would be back right where she had started: alone.

"Why?" she asked frustrated, "I made a stupid bloody mistake! I've had enough of all of this. Can I not just enter a late guilty verdict and go to jail?" She looked up at Elijah with desperation etched on her face and despite being annoyed over her actions, he suddenly felt concerned and surprised at her statement.

"You want to plead guilty just because you might get a new psychiatrist?" queried Elijah. Lucy shrugged her shoulders in response.

"I just want this whole thing to be over," she explained, "to stop hurting people, to stop making mistakes and to stop feeling so crap." For once Elijah's calm demeanour slipped and his mouth fell open as he looked blankly at his client. For a few moments they descended into an uncomfortable silence and Lucy could tell that Elijah was deep in thought. Exactly what he was thinking she couldn't tell, but she found sitting here waiting for him to say something deeply unnerving. Eventually Elijah sat up and narrowed his gaze towards Lucy.

"Feeling crap is not going to go away just because you go to jail." Lucy scowled at him, sick of feeling shame. Who did he think he was?

"How do you know?" she asked bitterly, "I bet you've never had to deal with anything like this personally. Probably always at the other end of the spectrum, looking at your clients' problems but never really experiencing any of them." Elijah blinked and then sighed.

"You think I always had it so easy, do you?" he asked, trying to keep his voice level. Lucy shrugged her shoulders but did not argue with him. She liked Elijah and that made it harder for her to project her feelings of loathing on to him, but it was easier than feeling worse about herself. "I was a black man growing up in a busy suburban town," explained Elijah, "I have a funny accent, so everybody knew I wasn't from there. Many people didn't want me to succeed." Lucy looked at him curiously.

"Yeah, but you still did," she noted sourly.

"And I suppose you think I just did a somersault and became a lawyer?" asked Elijah pointedly, "One day I just fell out of bed, put on a suit and walked into a courtroom?" Lucy opened and closed her mouth in response, not quite knowing what to say. She knew that Elijah had probably faced hardship, but she had been so caught up in her own drama that she never once thought of what it might have taken for him to become a lawyer. "When your best friend gets accepted for a scholarship," said Elijah passionately, "but you don't, and you realise that it might just because you are black…because you were not born where somebody wanted you to be born, you start to want to change the world you live in. I decided to stop moaning about the problem and fix it." Lucy stared at Elijah in awe; she had never really thought about him being black, that it might have put him at a disadvantage. It was inspiring that he had risen above his circumstances, but she also knew there was no such hope for her.

"I can't fix the fact that I killed somebody," stated Lucy sadly, but she wished more than anything that she could.

"No, you can't, but what can you fix? There are millions of people like you, you know, who end up battered and bruised by the system, living on the streets…are you prepared to be just another lost cause? Or will you fight to get in a position where you can help them? So that no other person will ever find themselves in your position." Lucy wasn't sure what she could say to that? He almost made her sound selfish for not standing up for herself and it was something that made her head hurt.

"You should be a preacher," she offered seriously.

"My dad was a preacher," replied Elijah, grinning slightly. Lucy's face took on a more pained expression.

"Poor you." Elijah did not look offended.

"He was a great man." Lucy nodded and then suddenly her thoughts turned to Bella; she had been a great friend; would she tell Lucy to use her plight to help others?

"I never told you why I pleaded not guilty in that hearing," said Lucy. "It was because of my dead best friend Bella. I don't know if I dreamed it; at first, I thought I had, she told me that I shouldn't give up on myself. Maybe it was my own conscience speaking to me, but then I thought I saw her in the courtroom that day." She expected

Elijah to look at her like she was crazy, but instead he nodded as if he understood.

“She must have been quite a friend.” Lucy nodded.

“She was the bestest friend I ever had,” Acknowledged Lucy honestly. “There was just something I could never… I always think if she was here now…what would she say? I can’t imagine her being unkind even now.” Elijah tilted his head and smiled at her sadly.

“It sounds like she believed in you more than you believe in yourself.” Lucy dropped her gaze from his and nodded because it was true; Bella had always been the best part of her.

“I think maybe she did,” explained Lucy. “I remember the first time we met. It was in church. I went in so I could rage at God, to tell him exactly what I thought of him. Only when I got in there, I just couldn’t do it…I mean there was nobody around, but it still didn’t feel right. Then Bella found me, the first words she ever said to me were ‘Are you speaking to God?’ I told her I didn’t think he would have much to say to me.” Lucy wrapped her arms around herself, feeling a barrel of mixed emotions wash over her as she recalled the memory.

“What made you think that?” asked Elijah curiously. Lucy shrugged her shoulders, she liked Elijah, but she needed him to know where her hate for God came from. That it wasn’t just based on some random impulse or illogical, but it came from knowing that God had used a man to defile her.

“I was sexually abused by a catholic priest when I was seven,” confessed Lucy sadly. “How could any God allow that to happen?” Elijah reached out and put a hand on her shoulder.

“Sometimes God’s plans are not black and white,” said Elijah, “particularly if we are at the centre of them.” Lucy scowled; how could anyone’s plan be what she had been through.

“You can’t imagine the emotions I went through. Blaming myself, blaming Father Graham and then blaming God who allowed Father

Graham into the church." Elijah nodded and Lucy appreciated that like Daniel, he was not quick to make rash judgements.

"It's understandable of course," said Elijah "We as humans are always looking for the source of our suffering, but we never seem to look for the source of our happiness. Why is it do you suppose that we blame God for our suffering, but not for our happiness?" Lucy was so thrown by the question that she forgot to be angry with him. Instead, she took a moment to consider it, when had she last been truly happy? It was probably when she was with Michael, and she hadn't taken the time to consider that God could have orchestrated that as well.

"I suppose it's easier," answered Lucy finally, "It gives us something to focus on. When we're happy, we are just in the moment, when we're suffering, we're trying to hold on to something that is no longer happening, with no way of changing it." Elijah's mouth dropped open slightly at the depth of her answer.

"Wow, that's quite insightful. I can understand why you and Daniel get on. Have you ever heard of a disciple called Paul?" Lucy sighed; she hadn't expected to get into a religious debate with him and did not really care for fictional figures who spent time with an imaginary god. However, she didn't want to offend him either.

"Not really," she replied honestly, "I scanned the bible once, but I didn't get any answers, so I didn't see the point in re-reading." Elijah smiled as if he was enjoying some kind of secret joke.

"Paul was a stubborn old battle axe who hated God for many many years." Lucy grinned at him, appreciating the comparison he was trying to make.

"Sounds like a decent bloke to me," said Lucy slyly. Elijah chuckled slightly but seemed undeterred.

"Then one day he saw God and he became a changed man." Lucy sniggered at this; she was way past being able to rejoice in fairy tales.

“Let me guess,” proposed Lucy sarcastically “He lived happily ever after telling lots of people the great news of his good old pal Jesus.” Elijah shook his head and Lucy found herself feeling intrigued.

“You’re only partly right,” explained Elijah in amusement. “Paul suffered a great deal because he told people about the good news of Jesus.” Lucy shrugged her shoulders, feeling unsympathetic.

“Maybe he should have kept his trap shut then.” She chanced a quick glance at Elijah to see if he was offended, but as always, Elijah maintained his calm exterior.

“Paul didn’t see it like that.” said Elijah coolly. “It only made him more determined about why people needed to hear the good news.” Lucy rolled her eyes; it just meant the guy was stubborn and didn’t know when to quit.

“Well hopefully God will show his face to me at some point,” she began, “so I can give him an earful.” Elijah raised his eyebrows and looked at her pointedly.

“You may live to regret saying that you know.” Lucy shrugged her shoulders thinking that the chances of God actually revealing himself to her were very slim. “How are you feeling about today?” asked Elijah suddenly. Lucy sighed, because she had been avoiding thinking about the fact that she would have to take the stand.

“Like I’m going to be sick in front of a courtroom full of people,” she said honestly. Elijah nodded, but then suddenly grinned.

“Well if you are sick,” he began, “please promise me you will try your best to aim for Jacobson.” Lucy sniggered; she hadn’t realised that Elijah had such a sinister sense of humour. She stood up to leave the room feeling their meeting was over. Looking at the clock she realised she still had some time to compose herself before they had to leave.

“Remember,” said Elijah cautiously, “Try not to scowl at the witnesses, the jury really don’t like it.” Lucy sarcastically gave Elijah the thumbs up before she headed for the door. She knew she ought to go to the cafeteria and try to eat some breakfast, but she wasn't even sure she could stand the sight of food right now so instead she headed back to her bedroom. She wanted a few last moments of calm before the pain of today would begin to rear its ugly head.

Back in her bedroom, Lucy lay down on her bed trying to calm the dark thoughts that were invading her mind. She did not mean to fall asleep, but the next thing she knew she was walking down a long corridor. At first, she did not recognise it, but then she caught sight of a famous painting and she realised that she was back in Michael's house. Though she knew she was dreaming, she suddenly felt anticipation building inside of her at the thought that she might see Michael again. What would she say to him? She slowly and cautiously made her way down the corridor and into where she knew was the garage. She had no idea how she knew he would be there, but she did. Lucy was terrified of seeing Michael again, which was odd considering she knew it was a dream. She opened the door of the garage and began to make her way down the large concrete steps. She looked around nervously, but Michael was nowhere to be seen.

Slowly, she made her way passed the rows of expensive cars looking for any sign of Michael. She was just beginning to think that maybe her dream was really a nightmare tormenting her with hints of Michael without actually revealing him. Then she gasped as she caught sight of him. He was standing in the shadows like a dark brooding stranger, leaning against the wall behind an expensive red Audi. His messy black hair and boyish good looks, despite being what many would call middle aged, remained the same as the day she had met him all those year ago. Time hadn't changed him in the slightest, but then why would it? He was dead and therefore couldn't age. When she approached, his expression was a mixture of sadness and anger.

"How could you think so little of me?" he stated. Lucy's mouth dropped open in shock, surely, she was the one who had a right to be angry with him.

"What?" she stuttered. "I..." Michael held up his hand and she fell silent. It amazed her that even after all this time, he still had such a powerful effect on her.

"You really thought I didn't love you," accused Michael sadly, "that I was just using you." Lucy shrugged her shoulders and lowered her gaze to the floor.

"Other people have used me. What was I supposed to think?" Michael narrowed his eyes at her, feeling deeply offended.

"Oh come on Lucy," he scowled pointedly, "don't link me in with those arseholes." Lucy sighed; he was right, he had never given her any reason to doubt him when he was alive, but that didn't make it ok that he had not told her about his family.

"You kept something from me," she said quietly. Michael raised his eyebrows.

"Yeah, you were an open book," he replied sarcastically. "Come on Lucy, even our first meeting you lied." Lucy's mouth fell open and she glared at him.

"Wow," she said shocked, "you're really going to throw that in my face?" Michael held his hands up in surrender.

"I don't want to fight." Lucy nodded her head agreeing with him, she hadn't seen him in so long and all she wanted to do was step into his familiar embrace. She knew that would be strange though after he had been gone so long, so she settled for shuffling slightly closer.

"I don't want to fight either," she admitted, "I couldn't grieve for you, you know. Finding out that you had a wife and child, that you had kept a big part of your life from me, it made me feel like I was just a dirty secret! That I hadn't meant anything to you. If I hadn't meant anything to you what right did I have to grieve for you?" Michael appeared as though he had been kicked in the stomach. He reached out and took Lucy's hands in his.

"I don't know what more I could have done to show you how much I love you." said Michael emotionally, "I even told you." Lucy shivered as Michael's touch felt very real.

"But you didn't tell me about a huge part of your life." Michael sighed and let go of her hands.

"I know," confirmed Michael, "but my wife and I had been separated for a long time by that point, and I was going to tell you, but I didn't expect to die that night before I could." Lucy nodded, realising that what it all really came down to was shit timing. Yes, he should have told her about his family sooner, but then the had been going to and what mattered the most; is that he had genuinely loved her and hadn't just been using her to pass the time.

"Where do you think we'd be right now if you hadn't died?" she asked curiously. "Do you think we'd still be together?" She held her breath while waiting for an answer, she wasn't sure she wanted to hear. If he said that he did think they'd still be together then she might be able to begin to mourn for what they might have had. However, if he didn't think they'd still be together she would have to cope with the pain of knowing that they hadn't be good enough; that she hadn't been good enough. Michael shoved his hands in his pockets and looked at her somewhat sheepishly.

"It's hard to think like that when you're actually dead," he offered seriously, "but I'd like to think so. We'd possibly be sunning ourselves on that Caribbean Island." Lucy grinned, then suddenly her smile faded as she realised that it would never happen and that the time had finally come to mourn.

"Why did you have to get involved with all that bad stuff?" asked Lucy quietly. Michael lowered his gaze from hers feeling ashamed.

"I managed a PR firm that looked after famous celebs, it was hard not to. All I did was pay some people off to make a few problems go away. I didn't think it would all get me killed." Lucy suddenly felt she no longer had any words left to say about it; his choice not to tell her about his wife, his death because no words would change anything. Instead, she blurted out something she felt she needed to tell him.

"I'm on trial for murder." Suddenly she felt foolish; she knew this was a dream so what did it matter if Michael knew or not, but somehow it seemed important.

“I know,” acknowledged Michael. “You’re not the evil person you think you are you know. We all do things we regret when we’re scared, angry or even sad.” Lucy reached out and took Michael’s hand in hers.

“I can live with the regret,” admitted Lucy, in little more than a whisper. “It’s something that I might eventually be able to come to terms with,” she continued, “but someone is dead because of me. I can’t make that right.” Michael shook his head disagreeing with her.

“Maybe,” he replied, “Maybe not.” Lucy opened her mouth to ask him what he meant by that, but suddenly Michael disappeared, she felt nothing in her hand, and everything went black.

A few moments later, Lucy opened her eyes to find herself back in her bedroom. She knew he hadn’t really left, but the dream and everything in it had felt so real. She hadn’t thought about Michael much since his ex-wife had revealed to her that he had really loved her all along because she didn't feel lovable; not anymore, not after what she had done. As she began to comb her hair and make herself look presentable for the trial, she wondered whether knowing Michael had loved her at the time would have changed things. If he’d be honest with her before he died, would it have made any difference?

Chapter 16: What if he had told the Truth…

Michael leans forward, I think he is going to kiss me, and I smile in anticipation, but instead he does something better, he leans into my ear and whispers, "I love you; you know," and I think I am going to faint. All this time, I've been worried that he was just using me to pre-occupy his time, but he genuinely loves me. My heart feels like it could soar, and I am grinning from ear to ear. When I come back to reality, I realise that Michael is looking at me in part curiosity and part amusement. That's when I realise, I love you is usually followed by something else, but wait, do I love him? Then I sigh, of course I bloody love the man, I don't just fool around with every man that comes along.

"I love you too," I say, and I try to put as much feeling into it as possible so that he knows I mean it. "Is that the important thing you wanted to tell me?" I ask smiling. Michael suddenly looks worried and shakes his head.

"Actually no," answers Michael. "There's something else, only I don't know how you'll feel about it." Shit, he's going to propose!! Is three months long enough to get engaged? Especially if one of you is an employee of the other one? Oh what the hell I figure, he's hot, I love him and he's a successful rich man, this is what every girl dreams of marrying into. I am just about to ask him what he wants to tell me, when suddenly the waiter approaches our table, I look at his hands in eager anticipation only to release he is not carrying our food. He smiles at me and then looks at Michael.

"Sir, you have an urgent message from your chauffeur outside," he states, and Michael looks puzzled.

"Why doesn't he just ring me?" he enquires, and the waiter shrugs his shoulders, looking embarrassed.

"I'm afraid I don't know, sir. He did say it was quite urgent." Michael nods and looks over at me apologetically as the waiter walks away. Then suddenly he shakes his head.

"Waiter!" he calls. The waiter turns back around and looks at Michael expectantly. "Tell my chauffeur that if it's urgent, he can ring me or come inside." I look at Michael in surprise; he is not one to delay something when it's seemingly important.

"Are you sure you don't want to find out what that's all about?" I ask. Michael shakes his head once more and takes my hand in his.

"No," insists Michael, "Like I said, I have something really important to tell you." I lean forward in anticipation. Does he want to marry me that much? Maybe he really does love me! "I hope you remain calm when I tell you this," he continues nervously, and I blink, because it seems such an odd thing to say if you are about to propose to someone. If he is not going to propose, then what is he about to tell me? "This is something I probably should have told you right at the start of all this. The only reason I didn't is because it didn't seem that important at first, but now…well things are different between us." I look at him in curiosity. Ok, so he's definitely not going to propose. What has he been keeping from me? Maybe it's that he can't have children or maybe it's that he's not ever looking to get married? I can probably cope with not getting married, but not having children? That's a big thing to accept right now, especially because I am so young. Then I mentally scold myself, there is no point overthinking it; not until I actually know what he's about to tell me.

"The thing is…" he begins looking nervous. I take a deep breath, whatever it is, it can't be a good thing, not if he is this nervous. "I'm actually married," he states finally, and my mouth drops open. Out of all the things I expected him to say, that was not what I was expecting; he already has a wife? Is he just using me? "Married but separated," he quickly adds. Oh, I guess being separated isn't that bad, I mean he should have told me, but at least he's not having an affair. I try to remain calm and compose myself as I look back at him, he squeezes my hand looking for reassurance.

"How long have you been separated?" I ask anxiously. I glance around the fancy restaurant to see if anybody is paying any attention to us, but they are engaged in their own conversations. Hopefully theirs are going better than this one.

"A long time. A year; probably more really." I nod, but I'm really surprised. I did my research about him on the internet, and it never mentioned he had a wife, but then it didn't really mention anything about his personal life at all. Suddenly, something occurs to me, maybe it's because I have trust issues, but I can't help asking him my next question.

"Does she know you're separated?" I question cautiously, but then I instantly regret it because Michael narrows his eyes at me in anger.

"Do you really think I'm that kind of guy?" he asks pointedly. I shake my head, deep down I know he wouldn't do that, but my mind is still trying to process everything.

"No, I don't think you are," I reply, "but I am struggling to understand why it's taken you this long to tell me." Michael exhales loudly and I can tell it's not something he likes to talk about.

"The only reason we're not divorced is to keep up appearances," he explains. "She accompanied me on lots of business trips and made nice talk with my business colleagues, but then we even started arguing over that stuff and decided to keep our distance." I nod, but deep down I am also concerned; is that what he now wants me to do? Schmooze up to his business colleagues? Accompany him on business trips? I'm not sure I'm suited to all that stuff. "Another reason we haven't really got divorced is…" he begins, but he trails off very quickly. I glance at him expectantly waiting for him to continue. What possible other reason would a couple have for not getting divorced when they were basically separated? Then the truth suddenly dawns on me, and my throat goes dry. I have to swallow before I attempt to confirm my suspicions.

"You have children, don't you?" Michael slowly nods and I release his hand; how could he not tell me about any of it? I can understand maybe not mentioning the wife, but I genuinely love this man and now I find he's kept a big secret from me for months, a big part of his life.

“I have two,” he says, “They mean a lot to me.” I frown; if his children meant that much to him then why did he feel the need to keep them a secret?

“Why didn’t you tell me about them then?” I accuse him, trying to keep my voice calm and controlled.

“Well, I never really planned on being a father,” he answers. “I suppose you could say it happened by accident.” I roll my eyes, thinking that everybody knows how babies are made so unless he accidentally had sex then I have no idea what he is talking about.

“Didn’t your mother have the whole birds and the bees conversation?” I enquire. Michael suddenly grins.

“You can tell me about it later if you’d like,” he says suggestively and I grin, then I remember that I’m annoyed with him so it’s probably not a good idea to be flirting. “My wife had kids when we met,” he continues, “I consider them mine.”

“If you consider them yours, why didn’t you care to mention them?” I shoot back, but Michael throws up his hands in frustration.

“Because I wasn’t looking to meet someone like you,” Michael protests. “I was separated with an impending divorce, I wasn’t really looking for anything, but now things are becoming more serious between us and less business like. I don’t want to keep secrets.” I open my mouth to tell him that it still doesn’t make it right but then I realise I don’t care. Yes, it’s bizarre that he kept his wife and children a secret from me, but I guess I can understand it given how we met, and I suppose the important thing is he’s telling me now, because he actually loves me.

“I’d love to meet them one day,” I suggest, as I take his hand in mine. I smile, thinking nothing can come between us now.

Predicated Verdict: Guilty

Chapter 17: The Real Question

Lucy met Elijah at the main exit by the reception. Elijah opened his mouth to speak when she arrived but then closed it again as he seemed to be looking at somewhere behind her. She turned and to her dismay, saw Daniel approaching cautiously; it was the last thing she needed before her trial.

"Lucy I…" began Daniel, he looked at her beseechingly as if he did not know what to say and hoped she might have some words for him instead. Finally, he seemed to realise that she didn't, so he put his hands in his pockets and looked sheepish. "I hope today goes well." Lucy did not respond; instead, she strolled to the button by the security door and pushed it. Ten seconds later there was a buzzing sound, Lucy opened the door and walked through it without glancing back. Elijah gave Daniel a pained expression before he turned and followed Lucy out the door.

Once they had arrived at the court and made their way past the swarm of relentless photographers, Lucy and Elijah took their places in the courtroom. Elijah turned towards Lucy, and she could sense that he was going to give her another warning or lecture. Knowing that she was not in the mood to deal with it, she quickly spoke up first.

"I know, I know," said Lucy impatiently, "Speak only when spoken to and remain calm." Elijah sniggered slightly.

"Actually," he stated, "I was just going to ask you if you have noticed the tie that Jacobson is wearing today?" Lucy looking somewhat puzzled, glanced across the courtroom and as her eyes fell upon Jacobson, she grinned. He was wearing a bright yellow tie with blue diamonds on it.

"Do you think his wife made him wear it?" asked Lucy amused. Elijah shook his head.

"I don't think he has a wife. He's made that fashion blunder all on his own." Lucy's grin widened but faded quickly as she saw the bailiff head to the front of the courtroom. Silence fell as people quickly took their seat waiting for the proceedings to start.

“All rise for the honourable Judge Redford,” said the bailiff. Everyone stood up as the judge entered and took her seat.

“You may be seated.” The judge banged her gavel, and everyone sat down. “Prosecutor, would you like to call your next witness.” Jacobson stood up eagerly and Lucy tried hard not to glare at him, after all it wasn’t his fault that she was on trial; it was entirely her own.

“The prosecution would like to call former Police Officer Mark Myers to the stand.” Lucy looked around as a middle-aged man wearing glasses made his way towards the front of the courtroom. She instantly recognised him as one of the officers who had arrested her on that night. Once Mark Myers was in the witness stand and had sworn the oath, Jacobson wasted no time in getting right down to business.

“For the court can you please describe what you found when you arrived on the crime scene?” he stated confidently. Mark took a quick glance in Lucy’s direction before answering the question.

“I saw a frightened woman; Miss Boragas,” he began, “clearly alarmed, surrounded by a group of young people and a dead body on the floor surrounded by blood.” Lucy tensed up as she felt herself remembering that night all over again.

“Did Miss Boragas say anything?” asked Jacobson. Mark shook his head.

“She screamed ‘I didn’t mean to, I was scared.’ as we led her away.” he replied. Jacobson looked towards the jury with a thoughtful expression on his face. Growing tired of his throwing gestures at the jury, Lucy wondered why he would need to do that if he were a good lawyer. Then she reminded herself that despite having a criminal justice degree that she wasn’t actually a lawyer and therefore it wasn’t up to her to decide what defined one.

"In your professional opinion, do you think she was scared?" asked Jacobson. Mark nodded his head and frowned.

"Yeah, I mean she looked pretty roughed up and terrified," he stated seriously, "I obviously can't say what her intentions were at the time though." Lucy sighed feeling like this whole situation was pointless because what it ultimately came down to was her words and perception versus everyone else's.

"but in the aftermath," continued Jacobson, "once she was taken to the police station, did she express remorse?" Lucy had to admit to herself that the part where she had been taken to the police station and put in a cell was still a complete blur. She couldn't recall it no matter how hard she tried.

"Not as such," replied Mark, "She acted like she wasn't bothered in the slightest." Lucy scowled, but it was hard to be annoyed with the witness when she could barely recall much about that time herself. Jacobson once again looked pointedly towards the jury.

"That's odd," he said thoughtfully, "considering she claims to have acted in self-defence. No further questions."

Jacobson walked calmly back over to his chair with a smug smile plastered on his face. A face that Lucy had a growing desire to slap. Elijah stood up and walked over to the witness stand.

"So, Mr Myers," began Elijah politely, "you said Lucy seemed frightened and alarmed when you arrived on the scene, but once she was taken back to the police station that she showed no remorse is that correct?" Mr Myers slowly nodded.

"It was almost as if someone had flipped a switch," he replied. "One minute she was screaming that she hadn't meant to do it and the next she was adamant she hadn't done it, but it's not unusual as some people do that once they realise, they want to appear more innocent." Lucy scowled at Mr Myers and then sighed; she had genuinely thought she was innocent! Suddenly, she had a longing for the days when she remembered nothing, before she knew she was a cold-blooded killer. She finally realised that an old saying really was true; ignorance is bliss.

“Liked a switch had been flipped?” repeated Elijah coolly, “Tell me would someone who was suffering from Dissociative Amnesia express remorse?” Mark blinked, appearing confused by the question.

“I’m not even sure what that is to be honest.”

“Let me tell you,” stated Elijah kindly. “Dissociative Amnesia happens because your brain cannot process an experience. To preserve a safe mental state, it blocks out something entirely.” Mark put a hand to his chin thoughtfully, as he considered this new information.

“Well, I guess if she didn’t actually remember committing the crime,” he began, “it would explain why she was so disorientated afterwards. She didn’t seem to know where she was or how she got there.” Mitch Jacobson rose out of his seat with a face like thunder.

“Speculation!” he exclaimed. “He has just put an idea in this man’s head, and he ran with it.” The judge sighed softly as if she found the whole business rather tedious.

“What do you say to this Mr James?” she asked. Elijah looked coolly at Jacobson before he straightened his tie. Lucy was amazed how calm he could remain under fire.

“My client has been diagnosed with Dissociative Amnesia by a qualified professional, namely a doctor,” replied Elijah. “I was merely asking if the witness had known that at the time, would he have expected her to show remorse? I understand you’re a good lawyer Mr Jacobson, but I did not realise you were a doctor too?” There was a small laugh heard around the courtroom and Lucy was sure that she saw the judge smile slightly but, in an instance, it was gone as she turned towards the prosecutor.

“Overruled,” noted the Judge with a slight air of smugness. Lucy felt a huge surge of pride and respect for Elijah as she saw Jacobson turn red in anger before begrudgingly throwing himself back down into his seat with force.

"No further questions," said Elijah calmly. He nodded at the witness before making his way back to his seat. Lucy would not have blamed him for sending a smug smile in Jacobson's direction, but instead he made his way back to his seat demonstrating a level of humility that Lucy was sure she could not have managed in similar circumstances. Jacobson was soon on his feet again eager to level the playing field.

"The prosecution would like to call Miss Lucy Maria Boragas to the stand," said Jacobson. Lucy's heart fell through her stomach and her legs wobbled as she tried to stand up. She knew this had been coming, but now the moment was here, it felt like she was not prepared in the slightest. Elijah put a hand on her arm reassuringly and nodded before she walked over to the stand. Once she was seated in the witness box, the bailiff stepped up beside her and held out the bible. Lucy looked down on it in disdain.

"Do you solemnly swear to tell the truth, the whole truth and nothing but the truth so help you God?" asked the bailiff. Lucy did not place her hand on the bible instead she held it up as if making some kind of salute.

"I solemnly affirm to tell the truth, the whole truth and nothing but the truth," she responded. Swearing on the bible or asking for God's help was certainly not something she wanted to do right now. She knew what she had said was a legally acceptable alternative, but still felt a little disheartened when she saw that Elijah looked slightly disappointed with her decision. Jacobson walked confidently towards the witness stand with a determined expression and Lucy steeled herself for the impending attack.

"How did you end up living on the streets Miss Boragas?" asked Jacobson curiously. Lucy shrugged nervously.

"My life fell apart for various reasons," she admitted, "mainly due to drug use brought on by a traumatic event." She lowered her head in shame, wondering how an earth the downward spiral into drugs had begun, given how she had first felt about others using them.

"For the sake of the jury, would you mind sharing the traumatic event that led to your drug use?" questioned Jacobson. He observed her carefully waiting for her reaction. Lucy took a deep breath and tried to remain calm; she had no intention of sharing something so personal with a room full of strangers.

“How is that even relevant?” she asked. “It has no bearing on the crime whatsoever.” Then she saw Elijah looking at her pointedly and sighed, remembering what he had said about keeping her cool and answering the questions put to her honestly. “I sought out my birth mother who I had never met,” she stated, through gritted teeth, “she was working in the states. I went and surprised her, and she outright rejected me saying that she didn’t care about and never wanted me.” Elijah’s mouth dropped open in shock and even Jacobson seemed to be at a loss for words. Lucy looked around the room angrily daring anyone to think of her any differently because of what she had shared. She was more than just a girl who had been rejected by her mum.

“Erm right,” stuttered Jacobson, “Well that’s er...so you were doing drugs on the streets?” Lucy rolled her eyes and snickered, wondering where Jacobson had actually received his education.

“I could barely afford food and you think I could afford to buy drugs,” suggested Lucy firmly, “I was clean for at least two months before that night of the crime. I did miss taking them though; they helped to manage the feelings of everything I’d been through.” Lucy saw Jacobson’s expression soften slightly and she felt rage flare within her. The only thing worse than being provoked with questions was having Jacobson feel sorry for her and she was determined not to allow it. She crossed her arms and stared at him defiantly waiting for him to continue.

“So why did you take the knife in the first place?” said Jacobson. He looked a little less sure of himself and Lucy was at least glad for that.

“To protect myself,” replied Lucy. “A night earlier some big mean homeless man came and dragged me out of my sleeping place for the night and there wasn’t a thing I could do to stop him. It made me feel vulnerable.” She flushed red, feeling embarrassed at having to admit she had been unable to defend herself.

"Why did you stab him?" persisted Jacobson. He did not look remotely interested in the fact that Lucy was feeling embarrassed. Lucy took a deep breathe realizing this was her chance to make everyone understand why she had done it; the frame of mind that she had been in that night.

"I had just been attacked by a man down an alley way and was running away. The man...Alex, tried to grab me and I just wanted to be left alone. To not be terrified that someone might hurt me." Jacobson observed her sceptically, but for the first time she did not feel remotely challenged by him because she knew that regardless of what he believed, she was telling the truth.

"Can you describe this man you ran away from?" enquired Jacobson. It sounded like a challenged, but Lucy undeterred, answered the question without any delay.

"Big duffle coat, curly hair?" she began. "It was dark, but I still remember the dead pan cold stare he gave me...he looked me up and down like I was nothing more than a piece of meat." Jacobson nodded and glanced towards the jury. Lucy could tell from the way he observed them shrewdly that he was trying to weigh up what they were thinking.

"Did he just come forward and attack you?" asked Jacobson. His voice sounded sympathetic, but Lucy wasn't fooled by his showman act. Nevertheless, she answered the question choosing to address the court instead of the pitiful excuse of a man before her.

"No," said Lucy honestly. "I asked him if he had any change and he asked me what I would do to earn it?" She scowled as she remembered feeling intimidated and angry that he had thought there was a chance she might degrade herself like that.

"What was your response?" replied Jacobson. Lucy glared at him but tried to keep her voice even and calm as she answered.

"Despite what you think of me Mr Jacobson, I have never actually been a prostitute," she stated brazenly. "I told him I wasn't interested so he tried to attack me instead and then I ran." Jacobson observed her curiously. Lucy wasn't sure this time if he was genuinely interested in what she'd had to say or whether he was just trying to work out his next move in his line of questioning.

"Why didn't you just run away from Alex?" he asked. Lucy knew that this question might be asked because Elijah had warned her. She supposed it was a fairly logical question given that she had ran away from one man and stabbed another.

"Why didn't he?" replied Lucy adamantly, "I only got the knife out to threaten him, to let him know that I would protect myself if he tried to hurt me. Yet he chose to try to lunge at me instead of backing away." She wasn't particularly happy with the answer, but it was one that Elijah had given to her to memorise. If she were using her own words, she would simply say she ran away from one man because she was scared and stabbed another because she was tired of being scared. Yet Elijah's answer seemed less likely to send her to jail.

"Your attitude would imply that you don't have regret for what you did?" said Jacobson. He smiled at her slyly as if goading her and this time Lucy felt her blood begin to boil. How dare he try to tell her how she was feeling when he didn't have the first idea. Lucy saw Elijah stand up ready to protest, but before he could utter a word, Lucy had already jumped up from her chair on the witness stand.

"Of course I regret it!" shouted Lucy angrily. "I am filled with regret! Do you honestly think I'm ok with the fact that I took the life of another human being? It makes me sick! It haunts me and I can't do anything to change it...ever! but that doesn't change the fact of why I did it. I didn't do it to kill him, I just wanted him to stay away, to not hurt me...He was trying to take my knife…my only form of protection...do you know what it's like to live on the streets? Especially when everyone else is so much stronger than you are. If I could go back, I'd change it, but stop trying to put words in my mouth Jacobson...it makes you a pathetic excuse for a lawyer!!" A silence descended over the courtroom as everyone seemed to be shocked with Lucy's outburst, everyone that is except Elijah, who despite looking shellshocked, had the slight twitch of a smile playing at his lips, as he sat back down. Finally, the judge seemed to regain some sort of composure and banged her gavel down.

“Miss Boragas, you will refrain from shouting and having outbursts of anger otherwise you will be removed from this courtroom,” she instructed. Lucy scowled and crossed her arms as she sat down.

“Yes, your honour,” she said through gritted teeth. Lucy’s blood boiled as she saw that Jacobson seemed to be quietly pleased with her being scolded.

“As for you Mr Jacobson,” began the judge, “I’m inclined to agree with the accused here. You should not be implying anything, stick to the facts; as a lawyer you ought to know this.” Lucy could not help but smirk slightly in Jacobson’s direction because he suddenly did not look as smug.

“I apologise, Miss Boragas,” said Jacobson, but Lucy was pretty sure that he didn’t mean it. However, to go along with formalities and prove to him that she could play the showboat game too, she decided to respond politely.

“Apology accepted, Mr Jacobson,” she stated. He nodded at her curtly, but Lucy knew that inside he must be raging, and this gave her a small sense of satisfaction.

“So do you recall the moment that you decided to stab Mr Pembrokeshire?” asked Jacobson and Lucy almost smirked in response. However, realising that this might give the wrong impression she refrained from doing so. She knew that he was trying to slip her up with this question, but also knew he wasn’t going to, because the truth was the truth no matter how it was painted.

“I didn’t decide to stab Mr Pembrokeshire,” replied Lucy. “He tried to grab me, so I got out my knife to intimidate him, but then he tried to grab my knife, so I slashed at his arm. He got really angry with this and called me a stupid fucking bitch and lunged at me. He seemed to take great offence to the fact that I didn’t want his help.”

“Why didn’t you want his help?” replied Jacobson, “Surely after months of living on the streets without any means of surviving, someone offers you a lifeline you take it.”

"I hardly call grabbing someone or lunging at them offering a lifeline," stated Lucy calmly.

"If he did indeed grab you or lunge at you. No further questions." Then he walked coolly back to his seat with a small smile on his face. Lucy scowled at him angrily; she knew he was only doing his job, but it was frustrating to know she was telling the truth and still having people treat her like a liar. Before Elijah could stand up to cross-examine his client, the judge cleared her throat indicating that she wanted to speak.

"I think perhaps we should have a recess for lunch," she proposed calmly. "Give time for the tension in here to cool down." Lucy was not sure whether this was aimed at her or Jacobson, but she didn't care because the truth was after that dramatic showdown, she needed some fresh air and a drink.

Over lunch, Elijah talked to Lucy about the kind of questions he would ask her next in the cross examination. Once again Lucy didn't eat and this time Elijah did not insist, she did because he could tell how emotionally exhausted she was.

Once they were back in the courtroom and the judge had called the trial back in session, Lucy once again entered the witness stand. This time feeling slightly better that it was Elijah doing the questioning. Elijah came and stood before her giving her a small smile before he began.

"Lucy, can you tell the court why you were so averse to receiving help from Alex Pembrokeshire that night?" he asked. Lucy sighed; she knew what she should say, the textbook answer that Elijah had given her, but she felt that above all else; the truth was more important. Giving a nervous glance at Elijah, she took a deep breath and began to improvise based on her own experience.

"In my experience people rarely offer their help unless there is something in it for them," explained Lucy sadly. "I was...am sick of being used by people who always want something in return. That's why I didn't accept his help; I was afraid of what he wanted from me. Why would he help someone like me? Someone who couldn't even help themself! Someone who has ruined their own life through a series of bad choices. I guess what it comes down to is this…I didn't feel like I was worth saving and the possibility that someone thought I was, terrified me; it still does."

Elijah blinked at her in shock, but Lucy wasn't sure if he was disappointed or not. A silence descended amongst the courtroom once more and even Jacobson seemed to be lost for words, as he did not know where to put his face. However, Lucy did not notice as the reality of the situation began to take hold causing tears to cascade down her face as she realised that it was not about whether she had killed someone or not? She had known ever since she had finally remembered that night that she had killed someone. The real question, the one that she had been avoiding for months now was a question which would ultimately decide what happened next for her; was she worth saving now?

"Why do you think that Alex approached you that night?" asked Elijah. His question drew Lucy out of her overwhelming thoughts. She curiously studied Elijah's expression to see if he had been disappointed with her previous answer and when he smiled at her reassuringly, she shrugged her shoulders in answer to the question.

"I don't know," she replied, "maybe he genuinely wanted to help. I can't say for certain, but I don't know why he had to be so forceful about it." She took a quick glance at the jury to see if any of them were wearing expressions that may give away what they thought of her, but they all wore the same neutral expression.

"Have you ever attempted to commit a crime in the past?" asked Elijah. Lucy quickly shook her head.

"No, never," she replied honestly.

"Did you have any intention of killing Alex?" asked Elijah. If it had been Jacobson asking the question Lucy knew she would have felt attacked. The fact it was Elijah made it different somehow, because she knew he was a good man.

"Of course not. I didn't know him. I just wanted to be left alone." Elijah nodded and Lucy took a look over at Jacobson. He was whispering something in the ear of his assistant next to him. Lucy was so busy trying to work out what he might be whispering that she almost completely missed Elijah's next question.

"You developed Dissociative Amnesia after that night," said Elijah, "so you couldn't remember having done anything, so what was that like?" Lucy paused to give his question some serious thought. How could she make people understand, she had thought she had known herself; been sure of her innocence and then to have that all ripped away in the instance she had remembered. It was like someone had removed a piece of her soul and replaced it with something much darker, something which she didn't recognise, but was now a part of her.

"I remembered living on the streets," began Lucy earnestly, "I remember being arrested and being taken to the police station, but up until a few months ago I thought I hadn't done anything at all. Then to remember…" Lucy trailed off thinking that it was somewhat pointless to go on. The fact was, she could never make someone understand what it felt like to suddenly realise you were a killer when you had never seen yourself that way. Elijah sensing her hopelessness gave her a small gesture of encouragement with his hand.

"It must have been quite a shock," he offered. Lucy sighed; she knew Elijah had mentioned the importance of her telling the court about her having Dissociative Amnesia; but it was difficult when she wasn't even sure she understood it herself.

"I had a mental breakdown when I remembered," she admitted sadly, "Imagine thinking that you were never capable of ever hurting anybody, then suddenly you remembered you had done worse than hurt them. It's like hearing someone else tell your life story and you don't recognise it." She paused for a moment as Elijah gave her a slight warning look as if she was about to implicate herself so she decided to choose her words more carefully, "I know what I did, I did it in self-defence," continued Lucy, "because I genuinely thought he was going to hurt me, but the fact that I killed another human being, that will stay with me for life regardless of what the jury decide." Elijah gave her a small smile then nodded.

"No further questions." Lucy sighed in relief as she stood up, she had to hold on to the witness stand for a moment because her legs felt like they had a mind of her own. Wishing she could run from the courtroom and catch her breath before the trial continued, she resigned herself to the fact that it wouldn't happen and focused on regulating her breathing.

After a few moments, Lucy felt stable enough to walk to her seat, but as she got down from the witness box, she became aware that her feet were getting wet. Looking down at the floor, she realised that she had been treading through a steady pool of water, which seemed to be spreading around the courtroom floor at an alarming rate. It was already a few inches deep, and Lucy tried to isolate the source of where it was coming from. She looked around to see several other people on their feet seemingly confused and the court bailiff was also moving quickly around the courtroom trying to figure out what was happening. Jacobson who was on his feet inspecting the bottom of his rather wet trousers. Looking thoroughly annoyed he held up his hands and looked at the judge. Lucy had to stop herself from laughing. "Your honour, I think we're going to have to leave it there for today," stated Jacobson. Judge Redford's mouth opened in surprise as she observed him sternly. She was clearly not used to being told what to do in her own courtroom. "I apologise, your honour," said Jacobson, under her strict gaze. "It's just that the bottom of my pants are doing a good impression of the last scene from Singing in the Rain down here." The judge blinked not having the slightest clue what Jacobson was talking about. Jacobson sighed looking exasperated. "There's a leak!" he stated loudly. Judge Redford stood up and gazed down at the courtroom floor finally understanding what Jacobson had been trying to tell her. Then she spotted the court bailiff making his way towards and he leaned up to quietly whisper something to her. Then she banged her gavel to refocus the court's attention.

"I have no choice, but to put this court into recess for the rest of the day. I am awaiting further news from the court bailiff, but I very much doubt judging by how quickly this started, that this courtroom will be in a usable condition by tomorrow morning. Therefore, I suggest we reconvene the day after tomorrow if everyone is agreed."

She looked from Jacobson to Elijah, who looked at each other solemnly before nodding at the judge.

Lucy almost sobbed in relief; she could not believe her luck if it even was luck. Not only did she get to leave this wretched place early today, but she would not have to come back tomorrow either.

Once Elijah had gathered his things and the court had near emptied, Lucy almost skipped down the court aisle feeling such an overwhelming sense of relief. Then she was brought back to reality again upon leaving the courthouse, by the waiting photographers, all crying out for blood.

She was silent on the way back to the car. Elijah knew it had been a taxing day for her and he wanted to offer some words of comfort. However, based on everything she had said in court today, she already knew how she felt about everything and nothing he could say would change that. When they were finally back at the institute, Elijah walked Lucy back to the reception in silence, when the security door was open Lucy ran through it without a single word or glance back, because she simply wanted to be alone. Elijah sighed debating whether he should tell Daniel about what had happened. He knew Lucy would not be happy with him if he did, but the fact of the matter was Lucy needed the comfort of a friend. Making up his mind, he headed for Daniel's office closing the security door behind him.

Chapter 18: Tell me I'm a Monster

Lucy was sat on the bench outside in the garden deep in thought with tears free falling from her eyes. She had been sat there for around fifteen minutes when she heard footsteps approaching. Quickly trying her best to wipe all traces of tears from her eyes, she turned to see who it was, but when she saw it was Daniel wearing a concerned expression on his face, the tears started falling all over again. Daniel said nothing at first, instead he sat down on the bench next to her and placed his hand on hers giving it a squeeze. This made Lucy feel worse because she didn't want to be treated with kindness right now.

"I'm sorry," she blurted suddenly. Daniel looked at her in confusion, but she could not bring herself to make eye contact with him.

"What?" he enquired.

"For the other day," Lucy admitted, "I don't know what I was thinking." Lucy could feel her cheeks flushing red in embarrassment. How had she ever had the audacity to think it had been a good idea to kiss him? Daniel shrugged his shoulders and waved his hands into the air as if not bothered in the slightest.

"Oh it hardly matters now." This time Lucy turned to face him, wondering how he could be so flippant about the situation. Daniel said nothing, only looked at Lucy expectantly waiting for her to speak.

"It does matter," insisted Lucy emotionally, "because now I have to get a new psychiatrist." Daniel raised his eyebrows in surprise.

"What?" he replied, in confusion.

"Elijah said you have to report me or something." Daniel's mouth dropped open in shock.

"You told Elijah?" he groaned, "Why?" Daniel put his hand to his face clearly annoyed and this irritated Lucy.

"Cause I needed to talk to someone," she said adamantly, "and obviously it couldn't be you, could it?" Daniel suddenly stood up, moved away from the bench, and faced away from her.

"Oh for Fucks sake, Lucy!" he retorted, "do you know the lectures I'm going to get off Elijah now?" Lucy jumped off the bench; her embarrassment soon giving way to anger because Daniel had never once treated her like this.

"Yeah, that's right; make me feel worse!" snapped Lucy. "I've already had the day from hell, but why not stick the knife in some more? I get it ok; I'm a horrible person, you've every right to be angry with me and I deserve to go to jail…happy now?" She crossed her arms and waited for him to respond or even look at her. When Daniel turned around his expression had softened, and he took a step towards her.

"I'm angry at you, but that doesn't mean I don't care," he stated honestly. "You're a good person!" He shoved his hands in his pockets looking nervous, as if such honesty was not something he was comfortable with. Lucy for her part, scoffed at him, not believing what he had said in the slightest; good people don't kill.

"Tell me what you really think," Lucy challenged, taking a step towards him. Daniel looked rather intimidated by this and took a step backwards nearly falling into a flower bed, filled with red and yellow roses.

"That is what I really think," admitted Daniel hesitantly. He looked around cautiously as if to see if anyone else was witnessing this dramatic episode. Fortunately, the rather large willow tree partially shaded them from and there was nobody else to be seen due to it being dinner time.

"LIAR!" shouted Lucy, placing her hands on her hips. Daniel sighed in exasperation and raised his.

"For goodness sake Lucy!" he retorted "Do you want me to hate you? Tell you that you're worth nothing because of one mistake you made?" To his utter disbelief, Lucy nodded, and Daniel's face fell.

"Yes!! That's exactly what I want!!" snapped Lucy earnestly, "I want to not have to look at you and feel a glimmer of hope. I want to not feel better about myself when I'm around you just because you make me laugh and challenge me at the same time. I want you to put me in my place and tell me that I should hate myself for what I did." Daniel appeared genuinely terrified and desperately sad at Lucy's admission.

"You're not going to get that from me," he said quietly, looking at the floor.

"Why not? I killed someone…it would make everything so much easier, if you hated me…if you told me the truth." Daniel raised his eyes to hers.

"I've already told you the truth," he replied. He took another step towards her, but this time it was Lucy who backed away.

"Stop lying to me!!" shouted Lucy angrily. "Tell me I'm a monster, tell me I'm a horrible human being that doesn't deserve kindness or love or anything that is good because that's…" Lucy was cut off mid-sentence because suddenly Daniel took three strides towards her, pulled her face up to meet his and kissed her. Lucy was so shocked that she did not respond straight away, but then she sighed as a warmth spread through her; a feeling she had not felt for the longest time. It was a mixture of joy, hope, passion, and tenderness all combined into one electrifying moment, as his lips moved against hers. Then suddenly Daniel pulled away and looked her in the eyes. The expression in his eyes was so intense that it made Lucy want to run and stay at the same time. He stroked Lucy's cheek with his thumb affectionately as he spoke.

"You're not a monster," he said emotionally, "you're a good person. You deserve kindness and love because they are basic human rights, not bonuses for people who feel they deserve them." Lucy opened her mouth about to protest when Daniel kissed her again and she lost all sense of coherent thought. In that moment Lucy forgot about her guilt, she forgot about why she was always so sad and why her heart always felt heavy in her chest from carrying an un-liftable burden. All she could think about was Daniel's lips on hers and how right it felt, despite knowing that it was wrong. What it came down to was despite everything, this annoying stupid man not only made her feel like things would be ok, but that just maybe they could get better.

Chapter 19: Heart First; Head Second

I can barely believe that I did that. She was saying all this bad stuff about herself, and she wouldn't believe me when I told her she is a good person, somehow, I ended up kissing her. How the fuck did that even happen? One minute I am stood there trying to be the voice of reason and the next thing I know I am making out like a lovestruck teenager. I know it was stupid, anyone could have seen us, but I can't bring myself to regret it. How can I regret something that felt so right? There is no doubt it's wrong though and they'll fire me in a heartbeat if they find out. I should probably do the right thing and get her a new psychiatrist or report myself for misconduct, but I just know that I'm not going to do that. It would mean I wouldn't see her anymore and I'm pretty sure that would be so much worse for both of us. I know I'm a complete fool; of that I have no doubt either, as soon as I knew I was developing feelings for her I should have put a stop to it all, but instead I continued to charge ahead heart first head second. I've never done that before, even with my ex-wife I was always the logical one; the one who made smart decisions. Now I've been brought down by a woman who is on trial for manslaughter. Not that I could ever judge her for it; not after the things I've done. I need to end it before she finds out the truth because it will destroy her and destroy me along with it.

Chapter 20: Sabotage

The next morning, Lucy was in a meeting with Elijah. They were meant to be discussing the dramatic parts of the trial from yesterday including what was expected to happen next, but Lucy was only partly listening. In her head, she was replaying the kiss with Daniel and how it had made her feel. She had not felt happiness like that in such a long time, and even though the moment had been brief, she clung to it, because it offered her a small piece of hope. Not just for what might happen with Daniel, but the notion that someone might actually care; that she was worthy of something more than what had already been given to her.

"Are you ok?" said Elijah suddenly, "You seem a million miles away at the moment." Lucy flushed slightly red, relived that he could not read her thoughts.

"Yeah, I am," she said. Then she smiled at him, and Elijah blinked.

"You seem a lot happier than when we last spoke."

"Maybe I'm starting to believe that my life, me…" she began, "maybe I'm worth fighting for."

"That's excellent," replied Elijah. However, his expression was filled with concern and Lucy knew he was wondering what had brought about the change in her attitude. She certainly wasn't going to tell him it was the fact that Daniel had kissed her.

"I'm not saying what I did was ok," said Lucy quickly.

"You can want to fight for yourself while still having regret," he offered kindly, "it's not about trying to make out what you did was acceptable, it's about showing them it was unavoidable." Lucy nodded but still avoided his eye contact and drummed her fingers nervously on the table.

"I used to think it was more black and white. That you are either a killer or you're not, but life isn't like that? I mean of course there are people who choose to kill but then there are people like me who don't choose to kill, but somehow end up killing. Does that make it any different? Obviously not for the person killed, but it should mean something to me…to the jury." Lucy almost believed what she was saying, wanted to believe it, but there was still a small voice inside of her that rang out 'you are a killer; no excuses!'

"Everyone is worthy of redemption, Lucy."

"I know but accepting that also means that everyone who has ever hurt me is also capable of redemption to. If I can't offer redemption…and I really can't…I've tried to forgive, but…if I can't offer it…what right do I have to accept it?" She hugged herself as if trying to protect herself from the truth of all.

"Ahh but in my understanding it's only once you receive it you can offer it to others," explained Elijah, "After all, how can you offer somebody a gift that you didn't get first." Lucy groaned; she felt like her head was going to explode, it was just too much to think about. It was like a game of ping pong being played in her head with one side screaming for her to accept she was a killer and the other to accept that she had simply made a terrible mistake.

"If you're talking about God," began Lucy, "then I don't want any gifts from him. Taking a gift from him would mean I believe he exists, but if I did believe he exists then I'd also have to accept that everything I've been through, every amount of pain I've felt has also been part of some sick twisted plan…I don't want a gift from a God like that," Elijah gave a frustrated sigh.

"Right," he replied, "well I have some interesting news regarding the trial." This time Elijah had Lucy's full attention, as she tried to decide what he had meant by the use of the word interesting.

"It's been cancelled?" suggested Lucy hopefully, "They've decided I should just stay in here?" Elijah blinked and Lucy gasped slightly at the realisation of what she had just said. Did she really want to stay in here? That wasn't the plan, was it?

"No," said Elijah bluntly, "That water pipe that burst, it's going to take a few days to fix, the trial will not re-commence until Monday."

Lucy sighed in relief; she was not sure she could handle another day of trial tomorrow. She had expected the trial to be gruelling, but she had not expected it to be so emotionally exhausting.

"Well at least that is something." Elijah shook his head and looked at her pointedly.

"That's not the interesting part." Lucy raised her eyebrows.

"No?"

"Somebody sabotaged the water pipe on purpose." Lucy's mouth fell open, as she leaned back into her chair crossing her arms.

"Why would anyone sabotage a water pipe in a courthouse and how?" she asked. "That place is swarming with security." Elijah shrugged his shoulders looking equally puzzled at the strange turn of events.

"That's the worrying thing," he noted, "nobody can figure out who did it or why?" Elijah looked thoughtful as he considered this, but Lucy did not have the same curiosity. It did not matter to her who had done it or why, because it meant at least for now she could have a few days break from it all.

"Well, if you ever find out give them a thank you from me," said Lucy happily. "I could do with a recharge." Elijah didn't smile back at Lucy, instead he furrowed his eyebrows as though concerned.

"This could put us at a disadvantage. In my experience, the longer the jury has to think about things, the more difficult it could get." Lucy knew Elijah was trying to keep her informed, but she honestly didn't care.

"Let's be honest," began Lucy, "most of them have probably already made up their minds. The likelihood is I'll be found guilty." Elijah opened his mouth to protest, but Lucy held up her hand to stop him. "Don't get me wrong I'm going to fight. I did act in self-defence, but I also know the law. I wasn't supposed to be carrying a concealed weapon regardless of the circumstances. That's probably going to be the main argument for the manslaughter charge and it's a pretty good one." Elijah looked torn between acknowledging what she said to be true and offering some form of hopeful reassurance. "You forget that I know the law," continued Lucy earnestly, "As good as a lawyer as you are, and I do think you are very good, short of a miracle it's more than likely I'll be going to jail." Once again Elijah opened his mouth to protest, but Lucy quickly cut him off. "I don't blame you," insisted Lucy, "and I'm glad I didn't take any plea deal because I have a right to have my story heard, to let people know why I did it, but I'm not stupid, I've resigned myself to the fact that we'll probably lose." Elijah shook his head and crossed his arms, with a determined expression on his face.

"Well as your lawyer, it's a good job, I haven't resigned myself to the same conclusion," acknowledged Elijah. "I meant what I said, I still think we can get you off on self-defence and there are other leads I'm looking into." Lucy tilted her head and looked at him curiously.

"Care to share?" she asked. Elijah shook his head and Lucy felt slightly disappointed.

"Not yet," he stated, "It could be something or nothing. I don't want to get any hopes up."

"Or give any hope at all?"

"I tried to give you hope," insisted Elijah, "but you keep shooting me down." Lucy sighed; she had to come to appreciate Elijah's council and she knew he was a good man, but that didn't mean he was always right.

"You always bring hope back to god," said Lucy bitterly. Elijah shrugged his shoulder as if the answer was straight forward.

"To me the two are mutually exclusive," he explained. Lucy held up her hands with a grin.

"Guess I've got no hope then."

"Let's leave it there for today," sighed Elijah, "I'm sure we're not far off your appointment with Daniel." As he spoke, he studied her carefully to see what her reaction would be. Lucy noticed this and for a moment wondered if he was aware of what had happened between her and Daniel yesterday, but then brushed the thought off. Daniel wouldn't have told him because he was annoyed that she had mentioned it to Elijah. So, confident that hers and Daniel's secret was safe, she stood up to leave.

"So, when is our next meeting then?" asked Lucy, as she headed for the door.

"We'll probably meet again on Friday 9am," said Elijah, "More to touch base than anything and just review what will happen on Monday. See you then." As she left the room and walked down the corridor, Lucy realised that this time, he had not told her to pass on his greetings to Daniel, which meant even if he didn't know anything about what had transpired between then, he did at least have his suspicions. Trying not to worry too much about what that could mean, she headed to her room to retrieve her book thinking she would read until it was time for her meeting with Daniel.

Forty-five minutes later, Lucy was outside Daniel's door, and she couldn't understand why she was feeling so nervous. Her and Daniel had left things unsaid yesterday and she wasn't sure what was going to happen next between them. Whatever happened though, Lucy knew she would not find out by waiting outside the door, so she took a deep breath and knocked.

"Come in," shouted Daniel. Lucy turned the handle and opened the door. She shuffled into the room feeling awkward, she was about to speak when Daniel looked at her and she felt unable to find any words.

"Lucy," he said, standing up, "I must apologise. Yesterday I…" Lucy did not allow him to finish what she knew would be a grand speech about how he must remain a professional. Instead, she strolled towards him with a determined look on her face.

"Don't," she said simply and then she kissed him. Still in shock, he did not respond at first, but eventually he relented. It was a passionate kiss that consisted of what they could put into words, consisting of an outpouring of mixed emotions, which they had been denying for so long. When they finally broke apart, Daniel had a slight boyish grin on his face.

"Why do you have to be so damn stubborn?" he asked wearily. Lucy grinned.

"For the same reason you always try to be so damn professional." she sighed. "It's who I am and all I know." They both looked at each other for a moment, each trying to figure out what they should do or say. Daniel opened his mouth to speak but closed it again. Instead, he wrapped an arm around Lucy's waist, pulled her towards him and kissed her again. Lucy was more than ok with this because it was so much easier than trying to talk about everything. Yet, suddenly talking was no longer an option and Lucy wasn't even sure what was happening, but she was vaguely aware that Daniel was now sitting on the armchair and somehow, she had managed to sit on his lap. It was like her body had a mind of its own because her hands had already pushed aside Daniel's tie and was working on undoing the buttons of his shirt. Daniel gasped when Lucy put her hand on his bare chest and lurched forward so suddenly that Lucy fell to the floor in a heap.

"Hey," she yelled. Daniel quickly jumped up from the chair and held out his hand to help her off the floor then he took a few steps backwards to put some distance between them. Lucy still feeling rather breathless looked at him in confusion.

"Well for starters the doors, not even locked," warned Daniel firmly "and secondly; Lucy…I…we've got to be so careful."

"Ok I get it," Lucy teased. "I'll lock the door; you get the candles." Daniel blinked causing Lucy to grin mischievously and laugh. "I'm joking obviously." She went to move towards him, but Daniel held up his hand to stop her.

"Will you just do me a favour and stay there?" he pleaded. Lucy pulled a face, but followed his instruction, feeling a little deflated. Daniel began buttoning back up his shirt, much to her dismay.

"It's not that I don't…it's just…" began Daniel, "oh for fucks sake!" Daniel put his hand to his head and nervously drew it through his hair.

"I know," sighed Lucy. "You have to be professional."

"Oh, Fuck professionals," stated Daniel bluntly, "I think we both know that went out the window a long time ago." Lucy looked at him curiously waiting for him to elaborate, but when he didn't, she raised her hands in frustration.

"Are you worried about your job?" asked Lucy, "Of course I'm not going to say anything ever; you know I wouldn't that." Daniel shook his head slowly.

"No, it's not that," he said quietly.

"What is it then?" said Lucy in exasperation.

"You…" said Daniel, "you're worth more than just some cheap screw on an office desk." Lucy blinked then suddenly started to laugh, and Daniel rolled his eyes at her.

"What's so funny?" he demanded, looking rather offended.

"I don't know," admitted Lucy, "I just…I'm on trial for manslaughter and I have no idea how that's going to go…a cheap screw on an office desk might be the best offer you are going to get." Daniel chuckled and shoved his hands in his pockets.

"It might be the best offer I'm going to get," said Daniel, "but I doubt it's the best offer you'll ever get." Lucy smiled at him, feeling touched that he cared about her so much that he didn't want anything to happen to feel meaningless. She wasn't sure it could ever feel meaningless where Daniel was concerned though. Lucy really couldn't even begin to understand what it was that Daniel saw in her, she had killed someone and was on trial. What could he see in her that so many others had just dismissed without so much as a second glance? Aside from that, he was definitely a good-looking man with a great career, yet he was trying to suggest that he wasn't good enough for her.

"Don't sell yourself short."

"Same to you." For a moment, they just looked at each other carefully and Lucy felt her heart pounding in her chest.

"Have you heard anything about the trial from Elijah?" asked Daniel suddenly. Lucy groaned and rolled her eyes.

"You really know how to kill the mood, don't you!" she stated. Daniel grinned sheepishly.

"I am still your psychiatrist," he said, "although gosh it sounds really wrong to say that now." Lucy chose to ignore his comments as she didn't want to open that kettle of fish. She knew it would only serve to make Daniel more unsure of them and she didn't want that.

"Elijah told me the water pipe was sabotaged on purpose. They're investigating it I guess, but no leads." Daniel went and sat on the chair behind his desk. Lucy took it to be a sign that he was trying to put his professional head back on so she sat in her usual place on the armchair.

"Do you think it was to delay your trial?" asked Daniel.

"I dunno," answered Lucy honestly, "I'd say I'd have done cause it's a smart idea, but I had armed guards watching my every move and another courtroom was flooded too. Though that one was apparently somebody who had dodged far too many speeding tickets, so I very much doubt that was worth delaying, unless the person knew somebody in higher places and I…" Daniel looked at her pointedly and held up his hand to cut her off, looking rather amused.

"Lucy you're rambling." Lucy leaned back in the armchair and nodded.

"I know; to be honest I'm relieved," she acknowledged. "Yesterday it was…it was a lot. I just need some time to process everything." Daniel took his glasses off the desk and placed them back on his face.

“That’s understandable,” he paused, “Your mom is coming to the trial, right?” Lucy did not need to ask him which mum he was referring to and she quickly tried to push thoughts of her birth mother from her mind.

“She’s flying in on Friday; it was the first flight she could get. To be honest I thought she might not come at all.” Daniel’s eyes bore into hers.

“Don’t say that. I’m sure she cares about you.” Lucy sighed but nodded.

“I know, but the way I treated her in the past…it was awful…I wish I could take it back,” she explained. “It’s got be a balance hasn’t it…between taking responsibility for your own choices…your own experiences and letting people take responsibility for theirs, but how do you decide which is which?” Daniel looked rather amused with her statement.

“When you figure out that balance you let me know. I’ve got a feeling I could make a lot of money with the answer to that question.”

Chapter 21: I've Spent so Long Hurting

The next day, Lucy had just finished her breakfast and was heading from the cafeteria to the recreation room when she walked straight into Max. Lucy looked at him curiously, wondering whether she ought to say hi or carry on walking. She fiddled with the water bottle she was holding nervously, while debating what to do.

For the last few months, Lucy had made a point of ignoring Max because she was worried about how he would react if she spoke to him. In response, Max had seemed perfectly happy to do the same, only this time he didn't just walk away. He shuffled his feet uncomfortably and opened his mouth, but then closed it again.

"Hi Max, are you ok?" Max nodded, then he started to walk past Lucy who turned to walk away. However, Max then seemed to think better and quickly followed Lucy and touched her on the shoulder.

"I'm sorry I haven't really spoken to you," admitted Max nervously "it's just everything went nuts after that attempted breakout. It really took a toll on my mental health." Lucy nodded and then shrugged her shoulders. It was then that she took the time to really study Max's appearance properly. She noticed the dark circles under his eyes that suggested he wasn't sleeping and his chiselled cheekbones, sharper than usually indicating that he had lost weight. Lucy was suddenly confronted by a pang of sharp guilt, only this time it had nothing to do with what she'd done. This time it was because of something she hadn't done. She had been so wrapped up in her own issues, her own situation, that it hadn't occurred to her that Max had been battling his own demons too. Perhaps she should have been doing more to help him.

"I get it!" she replied, "no judgements for me."

"I came and saw you, you know," explained Max, "when you were in the hospital, you weren't awake yet. Nurse Elaine told me you'd been sedated. I heard Remy attacked you, is that true?" Lucy nodded slowly looking around to see if anyone had overheard, then she gestured for Max to follow her into the recreation room, so she didn't have to worry about being overheard.

"It's true!" confirmed Lucy quietly, as she sank into the armchair. She placed her bottle of water that she had brought from the cafeteria on the table. Max sat down on the arm of the chair watching her carefully. "She wasn't who she said she was," admitted Lucy. Max looked around the room before he asked his next question.

"Who was she?" he enquired. Lucy took a deep breath, knowing that she owed Max the truth, especially considering how horrible she had been when he respectfully asked her questions about her actions the first time.

"She was…" began Lucy, "is the sister of the person who I killed." Max's mouth dropped open and his eyebrows shot up in surprise.

"So, you did kill someone?" enquired Max. Lucy broke eye contact with him and hung her head in shame.

"Yes, but I didn't mean to. I thought they were trying to hurt me. I wish I could change it." She looked back up at Max to see that he was suddenly looking rather uncomfortable. Lucy couldn't blame him; it wasn't every day that somebody told you they had killed someone.

"Well at least you know what you did was wrong and it's not like you planned to murder someone so I suppose there is that…I mean I can't talk…" murmured Max apprehensively, "I've done some bad stuff…some questionable stuff…true nothing like killing but still…I suppose that some people might consider some stuff to be…erm..." Lucy held up a hand to cut him off.

"Max, it's fine," she said, "You don't have to pretend you're ok with it…I'm not." Max let out a shaky breath and smiled sheepishly.

"Oh thank god for that! Cause to be honest…it really does make me very uncomfortable. Don't get me wrong I know you had your reasons, but I can't begin to understand them. Just do me a favour?" Lucy tilted her head as she looked at him, wondering what he was about to ask.

“What?”

“Just promise me you won’t try to kill me, and we can still be friends.” Lucy’s mouth dropped open, her face flushed red in anger and her hands clenched into fists. Max upon realising this quickly started to flap his hands wildly. “It was a joke!” he said exasperated, “I do actually have a sense of humour you know. I don’t actually think you’re going to kill me or anyone else here. You said you regret what you did; I believe you.” Lucy blinked, then playfully punched him in the arm.

“Dickhead!”

“Is that the best you can do?” challenged Max, teasingly.

“Probably.” Max moved further back on the arm of the chair and put his feet up on it.

“How come you’re not at your trial today?” he asked, “I saw you on the TV outside the courthouse.” Lucy smiled as she remembered the good news, she had got yesterday. Though she wasn’t happy to hear she had made the headlines.

“It got postponed. Somebody purposefully flooded two court rooms.” Max gasped loudly.

“Why?”

“Dunno, perhaps to delay my trial?” she explained, “They’ve done me a favour to be honest as it’s all been so emotionally exhausting.” Max nodded and shivered slightly.

“I can imagine. I don’t know how you put up with the intense scrutiny, with all of it to be honest. I’d be a nervous wreck.”

“Dan…” began Lucy, but then she caught herself realising that she couldn’t go around calling Daniel by his first name with anybody else in the institute, especially now. “Doctor Robertson has been a big help,” she said firmly. Max smiled slightly.

“Yeah, I quite like him,” he said earnestly, “he tells it how it is…he doesn’t sugar coat things like a lot of people do.” Lucy was about to agree with him but decided better of it. The more she spoke about Daniel out in the open, the more chance there was of her allowing something to slip out and that was the last thing she wanted. Trying to think of something to change the subject she caught sight of the news on the TV. The headline along the bottom of the screen read 'Man's lies are exposed.' and instantly she thought of Jacobson. It wasn't like he was a liar; he was worse than that, he was somebody who twisted the truth, distorted it so much that he could still call it the truth while also implying a lie.

"The prosecutor in my trial is a nasty piece of work," said Lucy suddenly. "Every time I see him, I have a sudden urge to punch him in the face." Max sniggered.

"I've met many people like that in my life." Lucy laughed and suddenly felt a small burst of affection for Max. It felt good to laugh with Max, because as much as she loved Daniel's company, things were different between them. She was always trying to impress him or challenge him in some way, with Max, he felt more like her equal.

"I never noticed before," began Lucy, "you do have a good sense of humour." Max held up his hands as if was blindingly obvious.

"If only I had the stunning good looks to go with it," he said sadly. Once again Lucy laughed.

"What, to impress all the ladies?" she enquired. Max shook his head grinning slyly.

"It's not the ladies I'd be wanting to impress," he stated pointedly, with raised eyebrows. Lucy stared him, then realised what he was trying to say and smiled.

"Ahh you're looking for a nice handsome man eh?" she teased. "Shame it's slim pickings in here!" She picked up her bottle of water from the table and took a sip.

"Yeah. The only handsome looking man in here is Dr Robertson." Lucy spat out her water at this and Max looked surprised, as he dodged out the way.

"Really?" replied Lucy, "You think he's handsome?" Max titled his head and narrowed his eyes at her.

"Are you gay as well?" he asked. "He's a really good-looking bloke and he's clever; a lot of people go for that." Lucy flushed slightly red as she thought; *well, I definitely do.*

"Yeah, I suppose," she offered quietly. Max not noticing Lucy's nervous disposition, shrugged his shoulders.

"But people like him; they're always married to their work," he stated sadly, "makes it impossible for them to have a decent relationship with." The conversation was heading in a direction that Lucy was extremely hesitant to travel.

"Maybe he's gay?" she suddenly blurted out. Max looked surprised, but then shook his head.

"No I don't get that vibe," he said, "I could be wrong…oh God I hope I'm wrong, but I think he might be straight." Lucy pretended not to be remotely interested and took another sip of her water.

"I've never really thought about it," Lucy lied. Max then jumped up from his position on the arm of the chair.

"Anyway, I've got group therapy. How come you stopped coming?" Lucy sighed as she remembered the friendly warning that Elaine had given her about attending group therapy in future. The orders had come from higher up, but she could guess why it had been recommended. The only reason Lucy had not pursued it further was because it suited her interest; she had always hated group therapy.

"They said it was probably best not to attend for the time being. I think they are worried about me blurting something out about Remy…there is an investigation, did you know?" Max nodded and seemed uncomfortable as he shuffled his feet.

"Yeah, they made me sit in front of all these scary people and answer some questions about her," he stated. "I thought it was to do with our escape attempt, but I guess not." He paused for a moment and then grinned slightly. "I nearly threw up on some guy's suit," he explained. Lucy laughed hoping that it had been the lead investigator, the one which she had taken an instance disliking to, Simon Banks.

“Really?”

“Yeah, but it was ok, it was a horrible suit anyway. To be honest I think it might have been the real reason I thew up. See you later.” Max then gave her a wave as he headed out of the recreation room leaving Lucy feeling torn. She liked Max, he was a good person, but then she remembered she didn’t have the past instincts when it came to patients in this facility. Looking down at her watch, she realised that if she didn’t hurry up, she would be late for her meeting with Daniel, so she too left the recreation room and headed down the corridor.

When she arrived, she knocked on the door to Daniel’s office and was about to reach for the handle when the door opened. She smiled expecting to see Daniel, but she took a step back when she realised that was not who had opened the door. Instead, she saw to her dismay, that Simon Banks was standing on the other side.

“Erm maybe I got my appointment wrong,” suggested Lucy hopefully, but when she saw Simon smile, she knew that was not the case.

“Lucy, please come in.” Lucy did not budge; under no circumstances would she be entering a room alone with him, because she knew he would probably goad her into saying or doing something she regretted. She leaned forward to glance into the room without stepping forward and Simon seemed to understand what she must be thinking. “Doctor Robertson is expecting you for an appointment,” he noted, as he stood aside to let Lucy through the door. Lucy tried to ignore the knots forming in her stomach as she entered the room. Once inside she saw Daniel seated behind the desk, he gave her a pained smile and indicated she should take a seat. Lucy looked at Simon as she cautiously sat down in the armchair.

“Simon is here to supervise today’s meeting between us,” explained Daniel politely. Lucy wanted to ask why, but she was afraid of the answer. Surely, it couldn't be about their relationship because the last thing they would do if they suspected her and Daniel of being romantically involved would be to allow them to continue meeting, even supervised. Then Lucy remembered that Simon Banks was the lead investigator on Remy's Case so it must have something to do with that. Feeling a little more at ease, Lucy decided to just ask the question.

"Why is he here?" she asked calmly. She looked over at Simon sourly and he looked slightly put out.

"He does have a name," stated Simon pointedly.

"I know," retorted Lucy, "but I can't exactly call you what I've been calling you in my head, can I?" Daniel started to laugh slightly, but then quickly turned into a loud cough, as Lucy tried not to smile.

"Hilarious," stated Simon sourly. "I'm here to supervise this meeting between you and Dr Robertson, relating to the investigation into Remy."

"And what if I'm not comfortable with you being here?" asked Lucy "What I talk about is personal and it doesn't have anything to do with Remy."

"You can of course decline," proposed Simon. Lucy opened her mouth to speak, but he held up his hand wearing a rather contrite smile on his face. "But it would really help us to assess Dr Robertson's skills as part of the investigation." Lucy had to stop herself from groaning out loud, the idea of having to sit here talking with Daniel while in the presence of Simon Banks was enough to make her run from the room. While Simon was making a note on the clipboard on his lap, Lucy chanced a glance at Daniel. He looked at her cautiously, but nodded slightly, which Lucy took to mean that they had to do this. Once Simon was finished writing on his clipboard, he looked at Lucy enquiringly, waiting to see if she would protest.

"Fine," sighed Lucy, "you can stay." She scowled at him, but then sat up straighter and looked at Daniel expectantly.

“So, Lucy we were talking in our last session about your trial,” said Daniel politely. “You said you were relieved that it’s been postponed, has it given you time to process things.”

“Erm…” blurted Lucy, then she paused. This was not usually how their conversations worked and she was unsure what to say, not wanting to put her foot in it or make things worse for Daniel. “Yes,” she stated, “I mean I was shocked to hear that somebody sabotaged the water pipe on purpose, but I can’t say that it’s not been…”

“Sorry to interrupt there,” interjected Simon, “but what sabotage are you referring to?” Lucy rolled her eyes, wondering if she would have to spend the whole session explaining to Simon things he didn’t know or understand.

“Oh, I’m sorry I forgot you were here,” said Lucy condescendingly. “Somebody sabotaged a water pipe at the courthouse and my trial got delayed. Now that you’re all caught up can I continue to explain to the Doctor how I’m feeling about it.” Simon did not respond instead he waved his hand dismissively and started writing on his clipboard.

“So where was I before Simon, it is Simon isn’t it, interrupted?” she stated. “Oh yes, so I was shocked when I found out my trial had been postponed, but also relieved because it’s been such an emotional journey…it’s changed me so much.” Daniel straightened his tie slightly giving the distinct impression he was trying to be professional, but there was an amused twinkling in his eyes that Lucy had come to recognise quite well.

“In what way do you feel it’s all changed you?” he asked. Lucy looked at Simon, who seemed rather curious to hear her answer and knew she had better come up with something good. She didn’t exactly want Simon to hear her thoughts or feelings, but she knew that allowing him to do so might make Daniel look like he was very good at his job. So, she took a deep breath before she began to speak.

“Well as you know, for a long time after the event I felt like I hadn’t done anything,” she stated earnestly, “like I was being punished for something I hadn't done. That I could never do something so vile. Then when I realised, I had done it. Well, I had that breakdown and felt like I was this evil person. Now I'm slowly coming to the realisation that I had a reason for doing what I did. It doesn't excuse me from what I did, but it makes it's so it's not so black and white, that I'm not just this evil person…not completely." Daniel blinked and studied her carefully for a few moments, before he seemed to remember that Simon was also there with them.

"That's huge progress Lucy."

"Thank you." She wrapped her arms around herself suddenly feeling exposed, but she had started pouring out her soul, so she might as well finish. "It's like this eternal battle is going on my head," she continued. "One side is saying I'm a good person who did a horrible thing, and the other side is saying I'm a horrible person who did a horrible thing. If the side which says I'm a good person wins it means that I've also got to accept that people who hurt me in the past must have had their reasons too. If the side of me that says I'm horrible person wins then what else is there? There's no hope at all. So, you see Doctor, I'm screwed either way." Daniel's mouth fell open in shock. Lucy could not blame him; she had never shared this much in any of their sessions before.

"And you feel like you need to choose a side?" he Enquired. "Why?" Lucy sighed and shivered. She had never revealed as much of herself, and it irritated her that Simon was sitting just a few feet away.

"Because if I don't, then I feel like the anger, regret and rage will consume me," she admitted. "If I pick a side then I feel like I might be able to contain it." She looked at Daniel carefully to see if she could measure how he was responding to her dark confessions, but his expression was unreadable.

"Is it enough to contain it?" Daniel questioned. "Don't you want to get rid of that anger and hurt completely?" Lucy maintained eye contact with him as she slowly shook her head.

“No,” she replied quietly. Lucy spotted Daniel looking over at Simon who seemed to be completely hanging on to Lucy’s every word. She wasn’t sure whether she should feel relieved or concerned about it.

“Why not?” asked Daniel curiously. Lucy lowered her head, unable to make eye contact with anybody while she admitted something that she had scarcely admitted to herself before.

“Because I have no idea who I am without it,” she said emotionally “I’ve spent so long hurting. Fighting to overcome the injustices I’ve experienced. What if all I am, all I’ve ever been, all that I’ve ever fought for, ceases to be important the moment I accept that I no longer have any control over it.” A long silence passed followed Lucy’s admission. Daniel seemed to be frozen and unsure what to do next. Lucy knew if they were alone, he would probably try to comfort her by offering her a hug or holding her in his arms. At the thought her mouth suddenly felt dry and she found she could not break eye contact with Daniel. Then Simon Banks coughed, and the spell was broken.

“So, if we go along the line of, you’re a good person who did a horrible thing,” said Daniel politely, “and you are starting to realise that good people can do bad things, which person do you think it might be the hardest to forgive? Who has upset you the most?” Lucy blinked; she had never even asked herself that question before so it took her a few moments before she could answer it.

“Can god be a contender?” she asked suddenly. Daniel nodded slowly, not taking his eyes of Lucy.

“He can be if you want him to.” Then Lucy sighed and put her head back, so she was looking at the ceiling.

“It’s easier to blame something like god for all my suffering because then it would seem like there is some journey, some purpose to it,” she confessed, “but the truth is my suffering is nothing but an endless scattering of bad choices and difficult experiences. No purpose, no final destination, just life.” She looked over at Simon who appeared to be thoughtfully writing something on his clipboard.

Trying not to concern herself too much with what he was writing, she continued to think about which person she would say had hurt her the most. “If I had to answer your question about who hurt me the most?” she Continued. “I think it goes back to the very first person who hurt me…the person who betrayed my trust…Father Graham.” Daniel nodded and took a deep breath as if to calm himself.

“Sexual abuse is a terrible to go through,” he stated, “but to go through it at such a young age it’s just awful.” Simon Banks cleared his throat loudly, causing both Daniel and Lucy to look at him in surprise.

“Sorry, Doctor Robertson,” Noted Simon sincerely. “I’m just wondering if it’s appropriate to make a personal opinion on that.” Lucy scowled at Simon as her hands clenched into fists, while Daniel blinked at the question, but managed to remain calm.

“Are you saying that there is any other opinion valid than sexual abuse is wrong?” he enquired, looking at Simon, “because if you are then I’d have to report that I have no confidence in your ability to do your job.” Lucy tried to cover up her smirk with brushing a strand of hair from her face. She looked at Daniel with admiration wondering how she had been so lucky to have a man like him actually notice her at all. Then she remembered they were not alone and quickly turned her gaze to the floor instead.

“N…No of course not.” said Simon, looking outraged. Daniel nodded politely, but Lucy guessed how annoyed he must be.

“Then I’ll continue.” Daniel turned his attention back to Lucy. “What would closure look like for you, over what happened with Father Graham?” he asked. Lucy shrugged her shoulders.

“I don’t know. He wrote me a letter. I never told you because I don’t even want to think about it. That monster not only did what he did, but he had the nerve to write to me about it, back when I was seven years old. My mother kept the letter for twenty-nine years until she showed it to me about five months ago.” Lucy raised her eyes back up to meet Daniel’s and found that he looked deeply hurt. She guessed it must be because she hadn't already confided the information to him.

"Was this before or after your breakdown?"

"Just before." Daniel raised his eyebrows at her, and she knew he was trying to convey his hurt without speaking. She also knew that next time they were alone together, they were probably heading for an argument.

"What did it say?" he asked curiously, "Did you read it?" Lucy nodded her head. She turned to look at Simon's expression to see if it would portray outrage or disgust but was annoyed to see that he was just scribbling away on his clipboard.

"He said he regretted what he did. It sounded like maybe his father did the same to him. He said that the devil had tempted him, and he'd been weak. That his hope for me was not to allow what had happened to corrupt me or my future…like it had corrupted him. I guess I failed in that because I still carry so much hurt over what he did." Daniel took a deep breath as if he were trying to control his anger.

"Are you trying to say you're weak because you never got over being sexual abused?" asked Daniel in disbelief, "In our first meeting you told me no one ever gets over it." Lucy noticed Daniel was trying very hard to keep his voice calm as he spoke. She also knew he was right; that is what she had said. She lowered her head sadly trying to figure out what she could say in response.

"Lucy," he said kindly, "He had no right to write you that letter."

"Wouldn't you say that's a leading opinion?" interrupted Simon. Daniel opened his mouth to respond, but Lucy, angry at his question spoke up first.

"So, you think I'm stupid then?" queried Lucy. Simon blinked looking rather confused.

"Sorry?" he replied. It took all of Lucy's restraint to remain seated in her chair.

"You think if someone states an opinion, and to me it sounded like a professional opinion you might offer to someone whose been sexually abused," said Lucy, "then I'm just going to accept it without question because I can't think for myself?" Lucy chanced a look at Daniel who shot her a warning look, but this only served to irritate her even more. Simon didn't reply to Lucy's comment instead, he scowled, gathered his pen from his lap and began writing things on his clipboard furiously. Lucy jumped up and picked up a clipboard and pen from Daniel's desk. Daniel looked at her questioningly but seemed hesitant to ask what she was planning with Simon there. Lucy sat back down in her chair, then she looked over at Simon and began writing too. Daniel's eyes flicked from one to the other.

When Simon had finished scribbling his notes, he looked at Lucy then his expression changed to one of confusion and curiosity. He leaned forward to see if he could make out what she was writing, but Lucy moved the clipboard out of his eyesight. She chewed on the end of the pen for a moment, before looking at Daniel who seemed to be waiting with bated breath.

"Doctor, I've hit a blank," she explained, "how do you spell obnoxious?" Simon jumped up out of his seat in outrage and snatched the piece of paper from Lucy. He looked down at it for a moment before he scowled.

"You are an extremely challenging individual," shot Simon through gritted teeth. He threw the paper down on Daniel's desk. Daniel still rather perplexed picked up the piece of paper and then laughed when he saw what Lucy had written; '*I bet he really wants to know what I'm writing*'. Simon glared at Daniel for laughing and Daniel held up his hands in protest of his innocence.

"Oh come on," insisted Daniel politely, "it's a little funny." Simon sank back down in his chair in defeat.

"If kindergarten jokes are your style I suppose." Lucy was about to snap back at him when she realised that Daniel was still under supervision by this guy. She didn't want to just storm out because it would make Daniel look bad. At the same time, Lucy knew that if this continued then she would end up saying something she would regret, but what could she do? She thought for a moment about faking being ill but knew that would probably be too obvious. Then an idea came to her and without a moment's hesitation she decided to put it into action.

Suddenly, Lucy started crying hysterically, she put her hands over her face to cover up the lack of tears and sobbed earnestly. Daniel blinked looking at her with a pained expression and then at Simon. Once she had managed to muster a few tears, Lucy looked up making sure that Simon could see her tear-stained face. Simon looked like he wanted to run a mile, as he it was fairly obvious that he was not used to being around emotional woman. Daniel leaned forward and offered Lucy the tissue box off his desk from which she took a few tissues.

"I'm sorry…I just…it's that…what I did," sobbed Lucy, "and the investigation with Remy…and then it's just all…I need…I just need…everything is too much and…I…do you know what I really need?" She looked at Simon who almost looked terrified of finding out what it was she wanted and then she looked to Daniel who held up his hand to encourage her to continue.

"I need a cup of tea," she said emotionally. "Do you mind if we leave it there for today? I know it's early, but I just think everything is getting on top of me." Daniel blinked as he studied Lucy for a moment, she stared back at him urging him to get what she was trying to do and suddenly he seemed to understand.

"Well, that's ok with me, as long as Simon doesn't have anything to add?" Simon for his part, continued to look extremely uncomfortable at the sight of Lucy crying, but shook his head slowly.

"Erm no," muttered Simon nervously. "I think I have what I need."
"Well then," said Lucy, as she stood up, "I think I'll go and get a drink and sit in the garden for a while." She looked at Daniel hoping he would get the message.

"Goodbye Doctor," she said kindly, "Goodbye Steven." The last thing she saw as she closed the door to Daniel's office was Simon scowling at her and it gave her a deep sense of satisfaction. Smiling slightly, she headed for the cafeteria; to grab a bottle of juice before hopefully meeting Daniel in the garden.

Ten minutes later, Lucy was sat on the garden bench with a bottle of orange juice, and her brain was beginning to work overtime. She was thinking about how awful that meeting had just been and what might come of it. Lucy really hoped that she hadn't done or said anything that would get Daniel in trouble, because she wasn't sure what she would do if one day he just suddenly wasn't there. Then Lucy's stomach did a little lurch as she realised that for her and Daniel; this was all there was! There would probably never be any normal, they'd never be able to go out on a date or spend a cosy evening in front of a TV with a takeout. She started to think about the last serious relationship she'd had before it had all gone wrong. The one that had happened almost ten years ago with a man she once thought she might marry, before his demons had overwhelmed them both.

Chapter 22: What if I'd had a family…

"Mummy Mummy," I hear, and I sigh. "Bella hurt me," continues the voice. I roll my eyes and try not to laugh, as I walk out into the big garden and survey the 'crime scene'. Bella, my oldest, is stood with her hands in her pockets of an expensive fashionable Gucci dress, looking like butter wouldn't melt. While Zackery, my youngest, looks on the verge of tears. The garden is picturesque, with a large area of green grass surrounded by colourful flower beds. I wish I could take the credit, but the truth is we owe it all to an expensive, highly qualified gardener.

"Bella, did you hurt your brother?" I tower over her observing her carefully for any signs of undeniable guilt. She looks up at me and despite her nervous expression, I cannot help but feel a burst of affection. She is such a beautiful little girl with long brown hair and sparkling blue eyes. I know I might be a little bit bias, but I still can't believe I helped to make something so perfect. Bella suddenly breaks eye contact and lowers her head to the floor.

"No mum," she argues, "I didn't hurt him." I look over at Zack who looks at me in outrage waiting for me to do something. Then I gently brush a hand through Bella's hair.

"You forget darling that I'm a lawyer," I state, "and a tell-tale sign you are lying is when you cannot look me in the eye when giving me an answer." Bella looks up at me again and I wonder if she is about to argue with me, but suddenly she puts her hands on her hips and sighs loudly.

"He was annoying me!!!" she protests.

"You wouldn't share the tree house with me," retorts Zack. I put a hand to my head in frustration, debating whether to continue to be involved or just bow out quietly and let them argue it out. The large treehouse we got them last Christmas has caused more trouble than it was worth. At least, I had insisted on a small lift being installed, as I had a fear of one of them breaking their neck, falling out of the large oak tree, which held it.

"Do I really want to intrude on this?" says a voice, and I turn to see Jake has arrived home from work. Bella and Zack rush towards him shouting, "Dad!" I smile as Jake picks up Zack and spins him round. Then he puts an arm around Bella and gives her a hug, before placing Zack back on the ground. Jake walks over and kisses me gently on the lips; I still feel goosebumps every time he does that which is quite remarkable after two children.

"How was work?" I ask.

"Stressful. The Brontes' are determined to fight this thing all the way, despite the company's desire to settle things out of court, which reminds me, isn't your firm representing them?" He raises his eyebrows at me, and I fake a look of innocence.

"I couldn't possibly say," I reply sweetly. I only work three days a week now. Jake and I had that big discussion when Bella was one years old, and we decided we wanted another child. I wanted to be around for the children, and I feel blessed that we have the money coming in that I can do it.

"I bet I can get it out of you later," says Jake flirtatiously. I shiver slightly in anticipation and then remember that the children are playing only yards away.

"You'll have to wait and see," I reply playfully, "It's nearly time for dinner." I'm excited for him to try this recipe I've experimented with today. I'm not much of a cook, usually we order from a gourmet service where everything is cooked for us, but I'm trying to learn a new skill. As much as I love being home with the children, it's not exactly intellectually challenging and I must admit the other night when I came home, and the nanny had cooked the children this wonderful authentic meal, I had a pang of jealousy. Instead of continuing to wallow in my jealousy I've been on a mission ever since to prove that I too can make a nice meal for my family.

A little while later, I am just cleaning around the kitchen and starting to load the dishwasher, when I hear Bella shout for me from the front room. I walk into the living room to see Zack has fallen asleep on the sofa again, for the second day in a row. I gesture for Bella to be quiet and leave him that for a moment. Five minutes later, Jake comes down after having a shower. He is wearing jeans and a white shirt and it's my favourite look on him.

"Honey, can you put Zack to bed please?" I sigh. "He's fallen asleep in front of the TV again." Jake blinks and then puts a hand to his face.

"Damn that kid has got to stop doing that," he says exasperated. "He'll be up at like 4am again." I look at him sympathetically then he turns and goes into the living room to deal with Zack while I start loading the dishwasher. A few minutes later, Bella walks into the kitchen and I can tell by the look upon her face that she is going to ask me for something.

"Mom," she moans, "Sissy Prescott says she's better than me cause she has a pony!" I stand up straight and put my hands on my hips, trying not to roll my eyes.

"Does she really?!" I reply, "Why does she think that makes her better?" Bella looks at me pleadingly and I can tell that she wants me to understand what she is trying to say without actually saying it. I'm not going to make it easy for her; I want my daughter to be well spoken and articulate, so she needs to at least argue her case.

"I don't know," she protests, "She just says it does!" I sigh thinking she really needs to work on her rationale.

"Knock it off, Bella. We're not getting you a pony. We took you to pony riding lessons and you said they were boring." Bella stamps her foot in frustration, and I shoot her my 'really?' expression.

"Cause I didn't own those ponies," she protests. Then she crosses her arms and scowls at me.

"Unfortunately counsellor, you do not present a valid argument so I'm going to have to say no on this occasion," I say seriously. Bella scowls even more and stomps her foot again.

"Stop trying to bamboozle me with big words." Then she turns around to walk away. I don't bother pointing out to her that bamboozle is actually quite a big word too.

"Make sure you do your homework!" I shout after her. I don't like saying no to her, but I don't want my children to be spoilt. They know we are well off financially compared to some of their friends, but that doesn't mean they get to have everything. I am only who I am today because I have had to work so hard to get here.

A few hours later, I am getting ready for bed when Jake comes in. "All clear?" he asks looking around. I laugh and give him two thumbs up.

"All clear," I confirm. Then Jake sighs as he sits on the bed and begins to remove his shoes. He looks towards me with a pained expression.

"I sometimes think the kids don't like us," he admits, and I raise my eyebrows at him in surprise.

"Really?" I reply, "What gives you that idea?" Jake stands up and removes his shirt and I feel myself losing focus.

"The mess they make, the fights they get into," he states, and then I catch the teasing tone in his voice.

"Are you saying they are a handful?" I tease. He walks towards me just wearing his jeans and suddenly my throat has gone dry; I can barely think straight.

"I'm saying they would probably be less of a handful if they didn't take after their mother so much."

"Hey!" I snap. "Are you saying I'm a bad mother?" I try to keep the tone light, because I know he is teasing, but I can't help being a little offended; I take being a mother very seriously. Jake wraps one arm around my waist and puts his hand under my chin, lifting my face to meet his.

“I’m saying I love our messy chaotic life,” he replies and my heart melts; he always knows just the right thing to say. I’m so glad we preserved through the rough patches in our relationship, like the jealously issues and the drug abuse; this was worth fighting for.

“Oh good. I was hoping you’d say that.” I take a step back from him and smile mischievously. I hope Jake is ready for what I’m about to say next.

“Why?” he asks flirtatiously as he tries to grab me. I resist and step back out of his reach, “Do you wanna create some more chaos right now?” he adds. Jake looks at me suggestively and I have to laugh slightly.

“I’m afraid we already have,” I reply quietly. Then I point down to my midriff and look at his face, waiting for him to understand what I’m trying to tell him. Suddenly his mouth drops open in shock and I can tell he’s finally realised.

“You’ve got to be kidding me?” he enquires seriously. For a moment, I panic slightly, we’ve never really talked about having more than two children; this just kind of happened. Then a wave of relief washes over me as I see Jake burst into a smile. He grabs hold of my hands and pulls me towards him.

“It’s a good job we’re experts at managing chaos by now.” He kisses me; a deep and long kiss that leaves me breathless and shaking to my core.

“I wouldn’t have it any other way,” I reply seriously, and I mean it. Then he scoops me up in his arms and begins to kiss me passionately while leading me towards the bed behind us, and I know without a shadow of a doubt that life doesn’t get any better than this.

Predicted Verdict: Guilty

Chapter 23: One Day at a Time

Feeling rather sad thinking about the simple happy life she might have led; Lucy sighed. Deep down she had always longed to be a mother, but it had just never worked out and was probably never going to considering she was likely going to jail for the foreseeable future. Lucy had just taken a sip of her water when she heard a small cough and looked up to see Daniel take a seat next to her on the bench.

"That was…" he began.

"Painful…frustrating…" interrupted Lucy.

"Yes," replied Daniel, "but not because of Simon being there." Lucy's eyebrows shot up as she turned to look at him in surprise. "Some of the stuff you said in there," continued Daniel, "really surprised me and made me feel like I'm not very good at my job." Lucy shuffled closer to him on the bench; that was the very opposite of what she had been thinking.

"What are you talking about?" she asked.

"You never mentioned any of that stuff before," Daniel said. "You've never been so open in a session before." The accusing tone in his voice stung Lucy, so she jumped up off the bench and rounded on him.

"Yeah exactly!" she said. "Do you think that was easy for me in there? I did it so Simon 'punch-me' Banks didn't suspect anything and would think you are an amazing psychiatrist." Daniel looked around carefully as if were making sure that they were not being overhead.

"So, he couldn't figure it out on his own huh?" asked Daniel, accusingly.

"Are you kidding me?" Lucy crossed her arms. "The guy's got as much brain power as a lump of concrete and was looking for excuses to trip you up. GOD!! I can't believe you are actually annoyed when I poured out my heart out to make you look good." Daniel jumped up feeling concerned that Lucy was raising her voice and would attract them the kind of attention he really didn't want. "I thought I was doing you a favour," said Lucy, "but next time I won't bother." She charged towards him and started whacking him gently on the chest in frustration. Daniel had a twinkle in his eye but was frowning as he grabbed her hands and for a moment, they just looked at each other trying to work out what it is they were each feeling. Daniel then suddenly broke eye contact, removed his hands from Lucy's and stepped back, as he looked around nervously.

"You should have told me about the letter," he sighed. His voice finally portrayed the hurt he was feeling. Lucy lowered her head because he was right. After all they had been through, all the support he had shown her; she should have told him.

"I know," she replied honestly, "but it was literally right before I had the confrontation with Remy, and besides, I've been pretending it doesn't exist." Daniel's eyes never left Lucy's, as he took a step towards her.

"I can't believe that bastard thought it would be ok to not only write it, but to send it to you at just seven years old," he said through gritted teeth. Lucy slowly nodded, feeling relieved that Daniel shared her anger and hurt over it.

"Well clearly he was fucked up," she stated, "otherwise he wouldn't have done what he did in the first place." Daniel visibly shivered as he studied Lucy carefully. She didn't appear to notice as she was lost in her own thoughts.

"Did you see Simon's face when you called him Steven?" He laughed. "I think I might have seen steam coming out of his ears." Lucy laughed, she knew he was trying to interject some much-needed humour into the conversation, and she really appreciated it.

"Or his face when you told him you might report him about his inability to do his job?" she replied.

"I'm going to get fired for sure," said Daniel jokingly. Lucy suddenly stopped laughing.

"Don't say that," she said seriously. Then she turned away so he couldn't see her face. Daniel seemed to realise he had said the wrong thing because he took a step towards her.

"Lucy…I…" began Daniel. Lucy quickly turned back around and shrugged her shoulders.

"It's ok," she said casually. "We both know we're on borrowed time; by the end of next week, I'll probably be in Jail." Daniel's face fell.

"Don't say that," he replied.

"It's true. Elijah must have told you," she said, trying to keep her voice calm. "The fact that I was carrying a concealed knife makes it really hard to prove self-defence." Daniel's expression changed to one of determination.

"You don't know Elijah like I do," said Daniel passionately, "he always finds a way."

"Is that you knowing or hoping?" she asked quietly.

"Both!" said Daniel earnestly. Lucy put her hands around her arms feeling a slight chill.

"I recon I'll get about ten years." Daniel flinched and Lucy mistook his reaction for what lay ahead. "I hope you know I don't expect you to visit me in Jail anything," she said kindly. "I'm sure they have TV and things." Daniel put his hands on her face tenderly and looked into her eyes as if searching for something.

"Let's just take it one day at a time. We'll deal with what happens next together." Lucy smiled as she looked into Daniel's eyes and placed her hands over his. She had always tried to be strong; to not depend on anyone else, but this man gave her hope that she hadn't felt in a long time, and the thought terrified her. Daniel then looked around anxiously and Lucy removed his hands from her face. He was right to be anxious; if anyone caught them then that was it; they'd probably never see each other again.

"I feel like I got blindsided in that meeting. I could barely concentrate. Then you came up with all those confessions and I think that's the biggest breakthrough I've ever achieved in any session I've had with a patient." He grinned slightly, but Lucy knew deep down he was still questioning his ability do his job.

"I've told you before I think you're a good psychiatrist. Why do you think I've kept you around so long?"

"I may have an idea," said Daniel flirtatiously. He took a step towards her, keeping his eyes locked on hers and Lucy knew if he continued then they could land themselves in a whole lot of trouble. She stopped him in his tracks by holding up her hand to ensure space between them.

"Do you really think flirting out in the open is the best idea?" she asked teasing. Daniel blinked and Lucy grinned.

"Not that I'm not enjoying it," she continued, "but I'm kind of hoping it continues and I can't see that happening if you get fired if people catch us flirting."

"You give a compelling argument." Then he took hold of her arm and steered her gently the towards main entrance of the garden.

"Where are we going?" asked Lucy curiously.

"Back to my office. So we can continue flirting." Lucy followed him, grinning all the way.

An hour later, Lucy was sat in the cafeteria eating lunch, she knew where she would rather be, but unfortunately Daniel had appointments with other patients. She almost felt sorry for him having to listen to everyone drone on and on about their problems.

They hadn't exactly done anymore talking when they got back to Daniel's office, although truth be told she was already beginning to get frustrated with his gentleman chivalry and his determination to respect her. Knowing that in all likeliness she was going to jail made it a more pressing problem than it should, but like Daniel had said 'one day at a time'.

"Penny for your thoughts?" said a voice. Lucy looked up to see Max stood in front of her and she looked at him in confusion. "Isn't that what you English say? I saw it once in a movie." Lucy blinked and then smiled.

"Oh yeah!" she replied, "I was just thinking that my mum is coming tomorrow." Lucy knew she was lying, but she couldn't exactly tell him the truth about what she had been thinking about. Besides, it wasn't exactly a lie, because in the back of her mind, she was anxious about seeing her mother again.

"Oh yeah, for your trial?" He sat down on the seat in front of her and Lucy noticed he had a bottle of juice.

"Yeah, I've not seen her in ages," admitted Lucy. "Last time I saw her, I yelled at her for thinking I was a killer." Max cringed slightly, and Lucy knew he probably still found her being a killer difficult to talk about.

"She'll forgive you," he said quietly. Then he took a sip of his juice.

"How do you know?" asked Lucy curiously.

"She's your mum, she has to; it's like a rule or something." Lucy sighed, she knew Max's heart was in the right place, but she still didn't believe that everyone was worthy of redemption.

"Surely there is only so many times someone can ask for forgiveness though?" questioned Lucy. Max shook his head.

"No, I think you can ask as many times as you want. It's more about whether someone is willing to forgive as opposed to whether you think you should ask." Lucy's mouth dropped open in surprise; since when had Max been so insightful, because he was right; a question was merely a question; it was the answer that was the most important.

“Fair point,” she said quietly. “Oh, by the way, Simon Prat Banks supervised my session with Doctor Robertson today. You know the one who is leading the Remy investigation.” Max raised his eyebrows in surprise.

“Really; why?” he asked. Lucy shrugged her shoulders.

“I don’t know really,” she said, “I mean it obviously has something to do with the investigation, but I can’t figure out why they are trying to pin it all on Da…the doctor.” Max stared at her and Lucy for a brief second wondered if he had noticed her little slip, but then he sighed.

“They’re probably just looking for a scapegoat,” he stated. “you know, someone to take all the blame.” Lucy nodded and scowled; knowing this place, it was probably about right. They’d replaced the director about five months ago thanks to Daniel’s complaint; they were probably looking for an excuse to get rid of him based on that alone. This made Lucy feel somewhat guilty as it was on her behalf that Daniel had made the complaint.

“Well, it better not be the doc, he’s one of the few decent people in this place.” Max nodded then looked at her sheepishly.

“I hope I’m on that list,” he stated. Lucy grinned at him then stood up.

“Don’t worry,” she reassured him. “You’re right near the top.” Then she grabbed her tray and began to walk away before looking back at him, “But that’s probably because it’s a very short list,” she added. Max laughed as Lucy ditched her tray and walked out of the cafeteria.

Chapter 24: You are Both Completely Crazy

The next morning, Lucy had her scheduled meeting with Elijah. Trying not to allow herself to be plagued with thoughts of seeing her mum in only a few hours, she tried to concentrate on what Elijah was saying.

"So, the repairs are almost finished," stated Elijah, "so we'll definitely be back in court on Monday." Lucy lifted her hands in the air in triumph, but her facial expression portrayed someone who was far less than happy.

"Woo-hoo!" she said, with no note of enthusiasm. She knew that the nearer they were to her trial, the nearer they were to this all being over, and her and Daniel would be over too. The very thought made Lucy feel like there was a rather large hole in her stomach.

"I can tell your enthusiasm is as strong as when we last spoke," Elijah replied amused.

"Yes," sighed Lucy, leaning back in her chair. It wasn't like she didn't want to be more enthusiastic. She wanted to be heard and to fight for her right to claim self-defence, but it would be foolish to think that would change the outcome.

"So, Daniel told me about an interesting session, you guys had yesterday." For a moment Lucy looked at him in shock. Surely Daniel hadn't told Elijah about their relationship and there was no way that he would be so calm about it. Then she remembered about Simon Banks, and she almost breathed a sigh of relief.

"Yep, I just don't understand why they are investigating Daniel so much," said Lucy sourly, "Is he the one who made the decision to allow Charlotte to come work here?" Elijah looked momentarily stunned.

"Charlotte?" he repeated. Lucy nodded slowly.

"Remy's real name?"

"I see," he said quietly. Lucy wasn't sure about how Elijah was processing this new information, because his expression was unreadable.

"I think perhaps they are trying to blame Daniel," continued Lucy, "because he put in that complaint about the director, and she got fired." Elijah raised his eyebrows slightly and then shook his head.

"No, she would have got fired either way. I think it was her decision to allow Charlotte to…" He trailed off and suddenly Lucy began to wonder how much he really knew about it all. After all, it was clear Daniel must have told him about the complaint to the director, otherwise Elijah would have asked what she meant. Then it dawned on Lucy that Elijah was not aware that she knew the truth about Charlotte.

"You don't need to be like that," she reassured him, "Daniel told me; I know he's not supposed to, but I basically screamed at him until he did. I was so confused about how she could have fooled everybody, faked being a patient. It never occurred to me they knew she was faking, and we were all part of some weird experiment." Elijah leaned closer to Lucy over the table with a serious expression etched on his face.

"Lucy," said Elijah wearily, "if anybody finds out that Daniel told you that then…" Lucy rolled her eyes; did he really think she was that stupid?

"I know," interrupted Lucy. "I wouldn't tell just anybody." Elijah leaned back in his chair and studied her carefully.

"Are things less awkward between you two now?" asked Elijah. Lucy did not need to ask who he was talking about.

"Absolutely. We had a serious talk; Daniel told me we should move passed it." Elijah's mouth dropped open slightly and for a moment Lucy wondered if she had said the wrong thing.

"He's not going to report you," stated Elijah. Lucy knew he was making a statement instead of asking a question. She didn't really know how she could respond to it, so she decided to just stay silent.

"I had an interesting dream last night." Lucy knew he had changed the subject on purpose, but she was glad he had.

"What?" she asked bemused.

"It was about you," stated Elijah, frankly. Lucy grinned sheepishly and leaned back in her chair, crossing her arms.

"Sounds like a nightmare. What happened? No wait let me guess…I was trying to stab you, or something wasn't I?" Elijah scoffed and raised his eyebrows.

"Fortunately, my imagination does not stretch that far," explained Elijah. "I dreamt that you were thanking me outside the courtroom." Lucy's mouth fell open in surprise, she wished she could have dreams like that. All hers were nightmares consisting of her committing the same crime over and over again without any reprieve.

"Wow…I…" began Lucy. She was unsure how to respond, without telling him that it was just wishful thinking on his part.

"I think it was a sign from God," interrupted Elijah. Lucy slammed her hands down on the table in frustration. Then she sighed and sank further down her chair, deciding that she might as well humour Elijah, since he was trying his best to help her avoid jail.

"Has God ever given you a sign before?" she asked curiously. Elijah nodded slowly.

"Yes," he replied, "sometimes." Lucy suddenly found herself wanting to know more. It wasn't like she didn't want to have hope or the comfort of knowing that God was on her side. However, with that comfort would also come some difficult questions about the pain and suffering she had endured.

"Have the signs usually been right?"

"Mostly."

"Interesting. So, they actually found me not guilty?" Elijah shrugged his shoulders.

“I’m assuming so,” answered Elijah. Lucy blinked at him in confusion.

“Eh?” she said. “You just said I was thanking you outside the courtroom. I wouldn’t be doing that if I was found guilty would I?” Elijah looked slightly amused at her statement.

“Knowing you and God, I wouldn’t rule anything out.” Lucy sniggered at him.

“I was probably thanking you for sabotaging a waterpipe on my behalf.” she retorted. This caused Elijah to chuckle.

“If Jacobson asks the exact same questions to this other witness from that night,” he began, “I might just do exactly that.” Lucy laughed and gazed at him in surprise.

“I knew you had a darker side,” she teased. She expected Elijah to be offended, but he looked far from it.

“I’d be sparing a lot of people a lot of boring,” he replied, “I think I could just about live with that.” Lucy laughed, deciding that she liked this side of Elijah a lot. Suddenly she looked down at her watch subconsciously.

“You are on countdown for seeing your mother.” Lucy scowled and then rolled her eyes.

“Daniel told you,” she guessed. Elijah sat up and straightened his tie.

“Actually, it was that lovely nurse, Elaine. She warned me that our meeting should not run over.” Lucy studied him carefully and then smirked.

“Lovely nurse Elaine, eh?” she repeated in amusement. Elijah blinked and flushed slightly.

“Don’t start,” he warned. Lucy shrugged her shoulders, but her eyes still danced with amusement.

“I’m not saying anything.” Elijah sighed and started putting the document in front of him into the briefcase he had brought.

"Good," he stated, "You should get going." Lucy nodded, stood up and headed for the door. Once she had opened the door, she turned back to look at Elijah.

"Ok. See you Monday. I'll tell Elaine you said Heeeeey!!" Then she quickly ran out of the door, slamming it shut behind her, before she could hear Elijah's reaction.

Half an hour later, Lucy had several knots in her stomach as she headed for the visitor's room to see her mum. She wondered whether her mum would be upset or angry with her. She hadn't cared before if her mum saw her as a monster because she was convinced that she wasn't one, but now that she knew she was exactly that, she didn't want her mum to believe it too.

Walking into the visitor's room, she nervously scanned the room for any sign of her mum. She had always hated this room; it never particularly seemed a happy place to her, despite its purpose. Perhaps it had something to do with the way it was set up, it reminded Lucy of a high school classroom, with tables all set neatly in a row and chairs dotted around them tidily. The small rectangular window at the far end of the room, was one of the only few in the institute which offered a view of the outside world. Not that there was much to see except tall grey walls ten yards away, but it was still nice to be able to see that life went on for other people, even if it didn't for Lucy stuck in here.

Finally, Lucy saw her mum sat at a table right at the end of the room. Her mum did not see her at first and Lucy was able to watch her for a few moments, trying to figure out how she was feeling about their impending meeting. She had cut her hair into a short bob since they had last seen each other, and she was wearing a bright red coat. Lucy couldn't be sure, but she seemed to have lost a bit of weight too.

Then suddenly, her mum's eyes met hers and Lucy froze unsure what to do. Hesitantly, she took a step forward, but then seemed to think better of it. Lucy's mum stood up and walk towards her.

"Hi," said her mum nervously.

"Hi," replied Lucy quietly. Then Lucy burst into tears and ran into her mum's arms. Lucy's mum started to cry too and everyone in the visitor's room turned to look at two grown women holding each other whilst sobbing. When Lucy had finally calmed down, she let go and slowly followed her mum back to the table. As they sat down, Lucy knew that she owed her mum an explanation.

"I didn't mean to; I was trying to protect myself," explained Lucy, "I honestly didn't just decide to kill him." Her mum nodded at her as if she completely understood.

"It's my fault," said her mum, tearfully, "It never occurred to me that you genuinely couldn't remember it. I thought you just wouldn't admit it. I knew there must be a reason though and I was hurt you wouldn't share it with me." Lucy sighed, talking had never been a thing in their family, but she wondered how many painful feelings could have been spared if that wasn't the case. Suddenly, she saw Daniel enter the visitor's room and was momentarily distracted, he never usually came in here and she watched him as he walked over to sit with one of the patients and their visitors.

"Who's that man?" asked her mum suddenly, drawing Lucy back to focus on her. Lucy tried not to blush at being caught out staring at her…boyfriend? She didn't even know if that's what Daniel was, their relationship was difficult to define. Lucy certainly wasn't going to share all of that with her mother though.

"That's my psychiatrist," said Lucy, trying to sound casual. Lucy's mum studied Daniel curiously and then turned back to Lucy.

"Oh really?!" said Lucy's mum, "I wonder if he wouldn't mind chatting for a minute." Lucy's mouth fell open; she couldn't imagine anything worse.

"Please don't do that," said Lucy quickly. She looked towards Daniel hoping to catch his eye contact and encourage him to leave as quickly as possible, but he was deep in conversation with the male patient and his visitors. 'At least he's currently occupied' she thought.

"I just wanted to know a little bit more about this condition you had," said Lucy's mum, "to help me understand it. I've never heard of it before." Lucy folded her arms, she was beginning to feel a bit irritated, what did it matter what condition she'd had? She could remember everything now and was worse of for it.

"Look it up online," retorted Lucy, but she noticed her mum was not listening. Instead, her mum's attention was focused on Daniel, as he stood up from the table he'd be sitting at and started to walk towards the door. Lucy watched in horror as her mum stood up and made a beeline for him as he was passing their table.

"Excuse me Doctor; sorry I'm sure you're very busy," she said apologetically. "I just wanted to ask you a few questions. I'm sure you know my daughter, Lucy?" Lucy's mum gestured to Lucy, and she literally wanted the ground to swallow her up. Daniel's eyes caught Lucy's and she cringed slightly, shooting him a pained expression. He then looked at Lucy's mum and nodded, holding out his hand for her to shake.

"Yes, of course. My name is Doctor Robertson. What questions do you have?" Lucy was amazed at how calm he was being; she felt like her stomach was going to fall through her chair.

"Well Lucy's obviously made excellent progress under your care," began Lucy's mum, "more so than with the other doctors. Lucy's told me that she suddenly remembered, and I wondered what would cause her to remember?" Daniel looked momentarily confused, he looked over at Lucy who shook her head slightly. It was then that Daniel realised that Lucy had not told her mum about the confrontation with Remy, so he chose his next words very carefully.

"Erm…a shock," he began nervously, "or something they come across reminds them of something from the event they've blocked out…it can be anything really. Lucy and I have been talking about events from her past. Things that may have influenced her decision to react in the way she did that night." Lucy's mum flushed slightly red and lowered her gaze to the floor.

“I’m guessing you have had quite a lot to talk about then,” said Lucy’s mum sadly, “I’ve not exactly won any awards for mother of the year; she’s very damaged.” Daniel suddenly looked rather uncomfortable as he shuffled feet and wouldn’t quite meet Lucy’s mum’s gaze.

“Erm well if you’ll excuse me,” he said politely, “I must be going…it’s nice to meet you. See you in our session Lucy.” Lucy could do nothing, but nod in response and then she watched as Daniel turned and walked away. Lucy’s mum sat back down in her seat.

“He seems like a very nice man,” she said warmly. Lucy had to try her very best not to roll her eyes; it seemed bizarre to her that her mum liked the guy she was…dating? seeing? She didn’t even know what it was.

“Yeah well…” began Lucy.

“He’s obviously a good doctor.” She studied Lucy carefully as she said it and Lucy had an uncomfortable feeling that somehow her mum could read her thoughts.

“Yes, he is.”

“He’s a little younger and better looking than I would have expected.” Lucy’s mouth dropped open, she must have misheard, because there is no way that her mum had just called Daniel good looking. I mean of course, he was, she knew that, but her mum wasn’t supposed to think it too.

“MUM!” she said loudly. “Can we talk about something else?” Lucy’s mum looked slightly surprised by her reaction but nodded regardless. “I’m guessing Ricky didn’t want to come?” asked Lucy sadly. Her mum fidgeted uncomfortably in her chair and avoided Lucy’s eye contact.

“It’s not that he doesn’t want to. It’s just so much has happened. He feels…” She trailed and Lucy already knew what she was going to say.

“He feels I abandoned you both after dad died,” said Lucy through gritted teeth. It was the truth, but she wished her brother would be more understanding. She had stopped taking Ricky’s calls as often when she had moved to America. It wasn’t because she didn’t love her brother, it was because he reminded her of the past that she had longed to forget. A past she wanted to leave in England but was still haunted by.

“I did try to explain,” protested Lucy’s mum, “I tried to tell him, that you’ve changed now.” Lucy blinked because she wasn’t sure it was the truth, had she changed? She supposed in a way it was true, she had begun to come to terms with the things she had done, but she still felt anger for everything she had been through.

“What does your lawyer say?”

“He’s hopeful, more hopeful than me.”

“Well, I suppose he knows what he’s doing…” Lucy quickly interrupted her. The last thing she wanted was for her mum to get her hopes up.

“Mum, I have a degree in law. Elijah, my lawyer, he’s an optimistic person. He’s not exactly going to tell his client that it’s looking bleak. I was carrying a concealed weapon, whether I intended to use it or not is irrelevant. Frankly, I’m lucky I’m not being prosecuted for third degree murder.” Lucy cringed as she watched her mum’s face fall and tears began to fall from her eyes.

“On the TV they are trying to make you out to be this horrible person. This feral person who was off their head on drugs, who just stabbed a poor defenceless man in the streets. They don’t know you; I get so angry with them. That’s my daughter they’re talking about, I think.” Lucy felt a sudden burst of affection for her mum, even knowing her daughter had taken someone’s life wouldn’t stop her from defending her.

“The press don’t exist to tell the truth mum. They exist to sell a good story.” She covered one of her mum’s hands with her own and gave it a squeeze.

“I know,” sighed her mum, “I’m glad your trial got delayed. Work wouldn’t let me come any earlier and I wouldn’t have forgiven myself if they had delivered the verdict while I was back in England.” Lucy shrugged her shoulders, as much as she appreciated her mum wanting to be there for her, it was one more thing that she had to feel worried about; seeing her mum’s face when the final verdict was delivered.

“Don’t thank me,” said Lucy. “Thank the person who sabotaged the water pipe.” Lucy’s mum opened her mouth to respond when suddenly a loud beep was heard and Lucy sighed, knowing that the noise meant visiting time was over. She looked at her mum sympathetically, there was still so much more to say, but it would have to wait. Her mum stood up and came around the table to give Lucy a hug.

“I’ll come by on Sunday. I’d come tomorrow, but…” She trailed off unable to give a convincing excuse. Lucy knew what she was thinking, but she didn’t want her mum to apologise for having a life outside of visiting her daughter in a mental facility.

“Don’t worry mum. I’ll see you on Sunday.” The guards came up to them and Lucy waved at her mum. She headed through the main door without looking back, because she knew if she looked back then she would probably cry.

An hour later, Lucy was heading to Daniel’s office, she knew she was a little early, but somehow, she didn’t think he’d mind too much. She wanted to apologise for her mum’s behaviour because she didn’t want Daniel to feel like he had been boxed into a corner. Lucy was walking past the meeting room when she heard voices; one of which she recognised as Daniel’s.

“You’ve got to do something!” he said. Lucy continued to listen because Daniel sounded much emotional that she had heard him before and she was curious to whom he was conveying his feelings.

“I’m doing the best I can,” said a voice, which Lucy quickly recognised belonged to Elijah. She debated walking away; she knew she should walk away. After all she had overheard their conversation before, and it had only served to make her more confused. Lucy moved back from the door and looked down the empty corridor, before beginning to slowly take a few steps down it.

“She can’t go to jail,” said Daniel passionately. Lucy stopped in her tracks and held her breath, there was no denying who he was talking about.

“I know we’ve had this conversation before,” said Elijah in a warning tone, “but I’m going to ask you again…is there anything going on between you two?” Lucy froze, wondering what Daniel would say, she had been right that Elijah suspected something, but surely Daniel would lie about it.

“Look I don’t want to lie to you,” stated Daniel hesitantly, “so just don’t ask me.” Lucy put a hand to her head in frustration. Elijah would surely know now as Daniel had not issued a complete denial; he should have told Elijah that the very idea was insulting.

“You are a complete idiot!” said Elijah loudly. Lucy found herself agreeing with Elijah, but for a different reason. How an earth could she and Daniel keep their secret if it wasn’t willing to lie about it?

“I am in love with her!!” said Daniel. Lucy gasped and fell against the door in shock, realising too late that it would give away her whereabouts. She heard Daniel groan and debated whether she should just turn and run. She could flat out deny that she was nowhere near later if he asked her.

“Lucy, I know you’re out there!” said Daniel loudly. Lucy froze in horror thinking how awkward this was. Before she could decide to run, the door opened and there stood Daniel looking at her. She knew she should apologise, but she couldn’t bring herself to say anything at all. Instead, she steeled herself for the lecture she knew that was coming about earwigging.

“I love you!” said Daniel. Lucy’s mouth dropped open in shock, of all the things she had expected him to say that was not one of them. Her brain was whirling at an incredibly fast speed as she looked passed Daniel to Elijah, who seemed to be watching both of them with a look of horror and disgust etched on his face. Lucy knew

Elijah was finding it difficult to understand, but the simple truth of the matter is that from the moment she had met Daniel, they'd had a connection and denying it had only worked for a set period of time.

"You… I…" began Lucy, feeling incredibly flustered, but then her eyes locked on to Daniel's and the answer seemed like the easy thing in the world "I...love you too," she replied quietly. For a moment they smiled at each other happily, until the momentary bubble of happiness was burst by Elijah groaning loudly.

"You are both completely crazy," he snapped. Lucy could not help, but grin at the irony of his comment, as Daniel pulled her inside the room and closed the door to ensure they were not overheard.

"I am in a mental institution," said Lucy apologetically, shrugging her shoulders.

"And this is where you will stay if they find out about you two," said Elijah angrily, "Daniel's testimony will mean nothing." He looked over at Daniel, who had the decency to lower his gaze to the floor feeling guilty.

"We'll just have to make sure that doesn't happen," said Daniel. He looked at Elijah pleadingly and Elijah scowled seemingly anticipating what Daniel was thinking.

"You are asking me to compromise my professionalism for your unprofessionalism," scowled Elijah. The anger in his voice scared Lucy a little, because she had never seen Elijah so cross; he was usually such a calm man.

"I'm asking you to be my friend!!!" said Daniel wearily. Elijah looked outraged and opened his mouth to respond, but Lucy quickly stood in between them. She knew it was only going to lead to a full-blown argument if they continued.

"Oi!" she said in a warning tone. Then she looked at Elijah curiously. "Elijah what are you going to do?" she asked. Elijah looked at her carefully before looking at Daniel with distain and Lucy realised who he held more responsible for the relationship.

“I’ll pray on it,” said Elijah finally.

“I…” began Daniel, taking a step towards Elijah.

“I’LL PRAY ON IT!” shouted Elijah. Then without a single word to either of them, he walked out of the room slamming the door behind him, leaving Lucy and Daniel to exchange worrying glances.

Chapter 25: I can't; I won't!

Well Elijah knows and boy is he mad! I can't say I blame him! I'm annoyed with myself for how I've handled this whole thing and yet I don't think I'd do anything differently. I'm not even sure if I could have done anything differently. I have no idea what Elijah is going to do, but I wouldn't blame him for reporting me. I can't say I'd be happy about it, but the bottom line is I'm a doctor and she's, my patient. I'm supposed to be in a position of authority, but when it comes to her, I feel like I have no authority at all. I should do the right thing and turn myself in, but I can't; I won't! She needs me and I need her because she's the only person who really gets it; gets me. It's only a matter of time though until it all goes to shit when she learns the truth about how I came to be here.

Chapter 26: I'm not going to Lie

Lucy was nervously pacing around Daniel's office replaying the awkward confrontation they had just had with Elijah. Daniel sat wearily on the chair behind his desk, watching her in amusement.

"What do you think he's going to do?" she asked finally. Daniel held up his hands in response.

"Honestly, I've no idea," confessed Daniel, "Elijah lives by a very strict code of honour. I think I've rather disgraced myself in his eyes." Lucy perched herself on the desk in front of Daniel taking his hand.

"He wouldn't report you though, would he?" asked Lucy in concern. Lucy looked into Daniel's eyes searching for some form of reassurance. Lowering her head to the floor when she could not find it, she felt Daniel give her hand a squeeze.

"I'd like to think not, but…" began Daniel. Lucy suddenly let go of Daniel's hand and jumped up off the desk feeling restless.

"We can just deny it; both of us," said Lucy fiercely. "I'll swear that nothings ever happened, that I think you're really ugly!" Daniel raised his eyebrows at her slightly amused.

"Gee thanks," he said sarcastically, "that's really considerate." Lucy laughed as she placed her hands on her hips.

"You know what I mean. They'd have no proof except Elijah's word." Daniel sighed as he reached for Lucy's hands, holding both in his. "We'd just have to…" began Lucy, but Daniel shook his head.

"Lucy, I'm not going to lie," he stated seriously "if this comes out, it comes out." Lucy's mouth fell open in shock; that was the worst idea she had ever heard of.

"But you'll lose your job," she retorted, "You might even go to jail" Daniel shook his head slowly and Lucy's heart sank, as she wondered why he was being so calm about the whole thing.

"They won't send me to jail," explained Daniel, "it's unethical, but not illegal per say. I'll just lose my job and get my licence revoked in all likelihood." Lucy's mouth dropped open, thinking she should really know that considering that she had studied Criminal Justice, but then there was really nothing in the textbook about doctors having relationships with their patients. Sadly, she suspected it was probably something she may have learnt more about in law school, not that it would have benefited her now.

"Losing your career because of me is not right," confessed Lucy sadly.

"It's not because of you," said Daniel. "I'm the doctor here." Lucy withdrew her hands from his grasp and glared at him angrily.

"It's not your fault," she snapped. "We're in this together." Daniel grinned in response to her fiery temper. Lucy felt like slapping him, why was he suddenly being so difficult? There had to be a way to convince Elijah not to report them; to save Daniel's job.

"You may be ok with this, but I'm not," continued Lucy stubbornly. Daniel took a hold of Lucy, pulled her towards him and pulled her down on to his lap.

"Lucy I am completely in the wrong here," he stated sternly, "you're my patient, this shouldn't have happened, but I can't help that I fell in love with you. Even now I should be a better man, I should get you a new psychiatrist and then this could work out better for both of us." Lucy shivered at the thought, as she leaned her head on Daniel's shoulder.

"It won't work out better for the both of us though," said Lucy bitterly, "because I wouldn't be able to see you anymore." Daniel sighed as he drew a hand through Lucy's hair.

"And that, selfishly, is why I haven't done it," admitted Daniel. Suddenly, he began to fidget twiddling his fingers nervously and looking around the room. Lucy looked at him questioningly. "There is something you need to know though," he began. Lucy put a hand to his mouth to silence him.

"Do me a favour," She said, "save another problem for another day. Right now, I just want to sit here with you and pretend that everything is ok." Daniel appeared conflicted but seeing the expression on Lucy's face, nodded his head.

Later that afternoon, Lucy was sat in the recreation room reading a book when she saw Max approaching. She knew from the look upon his face that he had something he wanted to say to her. So, she folded her page over and put the book down next to her.

"We need to talk," said Max sternly.

"So talk..." replied Lucy. Max looked around to ensure they were alone and then crossed his arms looking rather serious. Lucy raised her eyebrows in surprise, she had never seen Max so sure of himself and it was unnerving.

"You and Doctor Robertson," spat Max, "really?" Lucy's mouth dropped opened in shock and a feeling of nausea suddenly swept over her.

"You know?" She asked, hesitantly. Max nodded slowly then sat down on the sofa next to her.

"I saw you two together yesterday," admitted Max. "He's your psychiatrist!" Lucy did a quick glance around the room to ensure no one was listening in on the conversation.

"You haven't told anyone have you?" she queried. Max sighed and shook his head.

"No, I'm a decent person. I decided to speak to you first." Lucy suddenly felt she could breathe a little more easily. That was now two people that knew about her and Daniel, how many more would there be until the secret came out?

“Good,” replied Lucy. “It’s not as it seems you know.” Max did not look convinced.

“How do you know he’s not done it with other patients?” asked Max curiously. He leaned back into the sofa and crossed his arms looking at her sceptically.

“I trust him.” Max scoffed at her.

“You’re very trusting of a man who’s abused his position,” observed Max. Lucy shook her head in protest.

“It’s not like that,” she argued. “I kissed him first.” Max blinked and then put hand to his head as if exasperated by the whole situation.

“Why?” he asked.

“Because I love him,” replied Lucy earnestly. Max raised his eyebrows at her.

“Well good for you, but it won’t go anywhere,” stated Max bluntly, “It can’t! What’s he going to do, visit you in jail?” Lucy shrugged her shoulders sadly.

“I don’t know,” she replied honestly. Max sighed and appeared lost in thought, while Lucy felt her stress levels beginning to rise. If Max chose to tell anyone at the institute about her relationship with Daniel, she knew there would be dire consequences.

“Look I know that life in here is not easy,” began Max finally, “It offers very little hope of a better life or finding true love. In some ways it’s like living half a fucking life, but his position, the fact you’re in here…it’s so wrong.”

“I don’t know how I can make you understand,” pleaded Lucy, “Daniel and I, we’ve had this connection since we met.”

“Daniel??” queried Max, with his eyebrows raised. Lucy couldn’t avoid rolling her eyes at him.

“We’ve kissed Max,” she stated pointedly, “I don’t call him Doctor Robertson, I don’t have some kinky doctor fetish you know.” The corners of Max's mouth twitched, and his expression softened slightly, but he still wore a look of determination, which suggested he was resolute in his opinion.

"Face it Lucy," said Max seriously, "nothing good can come from this." Lucy lowered her head to the floor, refusing to acknowledge he was right.

"It's the only good thing that's come from this," she protested quietly.

"The man's your doctor," insisted Max appalled. Lucy turned towards him and put her hand on his shoulder.

"I know it's not ideal," she confessed. Max's mouth dropped open and Lucy suddenly got the distinct impression that this was how Daniel must feel when talking to Elijah about their relationship. It was so hard trying to make other people see that they were so good for each other, when how they had begun, was so wrong.

"Not ideal?" retorted Max, "are you taking the absolute liberty? He could lose his whole career for what he's done." Lucy put her head in her hands, unable to deal with the fact that her happiness was now in someone else's hands.

"I know," said Lucy emotionally, "that's why you've got to promise you won't tell anyone." She gazed at him beseechingly, but Max looked uncertain.

"I don't know Lucy. I mean that thing with Remy was messed up enough. Did he know about it?" Lucy stared at Max but said nothing, eventually he got the message. "Fucking hell! You must have a brain injury," he snapped. Lucy threw her hands in the air.

"She blackmailed him," she protested. Max's eyebrows shot up.

"She what?" began Max, "over you and Robertson? That's fucked up!!" Lucy nodded, relieved that she and Max could at least agree on that.

"I know. I still don't think they should have let her in, in the first place," acknowledged Lucy, "but we can't change that now." Max brushed a hand through his wavy black hair as he took a few moments to think. Lucy didn't rush him; she knew she was asking a lot of him to keep her secret.

"Are you going to carry on with him?" asked Max finally. Lucy knew that this was the moment that she should lie. She knew she should tell Max that she would end it with Daniel immediately if he promised not to report them, but then Daniel's words came back to her; 'I'm not going to lie'. She sighed because Daniel was right; more lies would just cause more problems.

"He makes me happy," answered Lucy, "I've been so sad for so long. Please don't make me give up the one thing that makes me happy." Lucy took a deep breath, as she looked at Max fearfully knowing that his response could change everything. Max studied Lucy's face carefully for a few moments before he sighed in frustration.

"Oh, for fucks sake!" stated Max, "I don't approve but you're a fucking adult! You can make your own daft choices. I just hope it doesn't end up in a complete shit show." Lucy felt so relieved that she wanted to hug Max, but she wasn't sure how he would feel about that, so instead she squeezed his arm.

"You're the best max," she said earnestly, "honestly you're such a good guy and I still feel bad about that night we planned to escape." Max rolled his eyes.

"So it's just a coincidence that you couldn't tell me that before I'm keeping your secret?" questioned Max. For a moment Lucy thought that he was serious before he broke out into a goofy grin. "Are you hungry?" he asked, "I'm starving…let's get food."

After dinner, Lucy was heading back to her bedroom, when suddenly the new patient Jill blocked her path. Lucy wasn't in the mood for idle chit chat, so she folded her arms and glared at Jill, waiting for her to move out of the way.

"Do you want any stuff?" asked Jill. Lucy blinked, wondering what an earth Jill was talking about.

"Sorry?" she replied. Lucy had gone out of her way to purposefully avoid Jill, ever since she had moved into the institute. She was now weary of new people in a way that she hadn't been before meeting Remy. Jill looked around cautiously, moved closer to Lucy and then pulled a small little bag containing white powder from her pocket.

"Stuff? Stuff?" replied Jill, "good stuff, isn't it?" Lucy's mouth dropped open in shock as she looked up and down the corridor unable to take in the strange situation.

"Are you offering me drugs?" asked Lucy loudly. Jill scowled at her, then looked towards the security camera behind them before putting the little bag back in her pocket.

"Keep your bloody voice down!" said Jill menacingly. Lucy realised as she looked towards the security camera that Jill must have done this before. She knew exactly where to stand so her back was to the camera blocking the view of the illegal substance she was offering.

"I'm not interested," said Lucy firmly. She shook her head fiercely and began to walk away. Jill quickly followed her, grabbing her by the shoulder.

"You should be," warned Jill, "it ain't gonna get any better, you know. I seen you on the TV, you're going to jail. Might as well get your kicks where you can." Lucy scowled; who did this Jill think she was?

"I said I'm not interested!" snapped Lucy, "ask me again and I'll smash your face in or report you, depending on my mood." Then she quickly walked away in the other direction.

It would have been so easy to say yes to the drugs that Jill had offered her, to feel the sweet release that she knew they would bring, but she wasn't that person anymore; couldn't be that person anymore. Lucy knew how stupid it was, but she wanted to be a better person. Someone who acknowledges their mistakes and deals with the consequences of them. Now that she had Daniel; she wanted to the be that better person, not just for him, but for herself.

Once she arrived back at her bedroom and threw herself down on the bed, her mind began to wander. She was suddenly plagued by the thought that she could have said yes to the drugs, she remembered how hard it had been to come off them. It wasn't like she'd had a choice; she hadn't been able to afford them once being made homeless. She had barely remembered those first few days sober; it had been pure hell and she was convinced that she might die, as she slipped in and out of consciousness.

The drugs hadn't been an issue at first. She had only done them recreationally, but it had been a slippery slope with no one to pull her back from the brink. She hadn't asked anyway to pull her back because she had jumped off headfirst, enjoying the rush and release they had given her. Would she have accepted help if it had been offered to her? Who would have helped her and where would she have ended up? These questions swirled in her mind as she fell into a deep sleep.

Chapter 27: What if I'd got help…

I take a deep breath and stand up to address the many people gathered around the circle. I have been dreading this moment for a while, but I know that I need it. I've come so far; this is just another hurdle. "My name is Lucy," I say anxiously, "I was living in the states, a lot of things happened to me over there. I ended up with the wrong type of men and one of them got me involved in drugs, mainly cocaine. I thought he loved me. I managed to get myself clean, but then I tried to track down my birth mum and she outright rejected me. I couldn't handle the pain and got hooked on the drugs again. I came close to living on the streets. I could have died or worse. Instead, I plucked up the courage to come back to England, back to my mum. She helped me and now I am here, I'm determined to get better and be at a better place in my life." I pause and look around the circle, everyone is watching me; are they judging me? Or is there silent admiration there? I take another deep breath. "I guess what I should say is my name is Lucy," I continue, "and I'm a drug addict." Suddenly everyone around the circle bursts into applause. My first instinct is to roll my eyes, but I stop myself. Instead, I enjoy the moment, it wasn't easy taking this path, admitting I needed help, but I did it and I deserve this.

Each person takes their turn to tell the circle why they are here; actually, nobody did that except me. Everyone else just went with the standard 'My names blah blah and I'm a drug addict' which is all well and good, but I want to share my journey too. A drug addict is not all I am, not any more anyway. Once, we've gone around the circle, we take a break to get refreshments before listening to the group therapists. I'm not a big fan of all this, but I know it will do me well in the long run. Just as I am helping myself to a sandwich, I turn to my right and see a gorgeous looking guy with dark hair looking at me curiously.

"My name's Luke," he offers. "That took a look of courage." I can't help but swoon a little at his thick gorgeous Irish accent. I also flush red feeling slightly embarrassed that this amazing looking guy already knows one of my darkest secrets.

"Yeah well..." I begin hesitantly, "everyone has been really supportive." Luke grins, but then slowly shakes his head.

"I don't mean the speech you gave," replies Luke, "I mean as impressive as it was, I meant the courage to come back from America and ask your mum for help. I don't know you at all, but you come across as quite a proud person. That must have taken a lot of guts." My mouth drops open because it's like he already knows me. It was the most difficult thing I'd ever done, asking my mother help, especially after the way I'd treated her, but I knew if I didn't do it then things would only get worse. How does he know all that? Why don't I know anything about him?

"How did you become addicted?" I ask. Luke grins and holds his hands up sheepishly.

"Me? No, I'm too much of a goody-goody to ever even drop rubbish on the floor," he says earnestly, "let alone become a drug addict, no offence?" I shrug my shoulders, I used to think I was too good of a person to ever do drugs, that feels like a lifetime ago.

"None taken," I reply, and I mean it. I can't be mad at him for not wanting to have anything to do with drugs. Frankly, I'm surprised he wants anything to do with me.

"I'm actually here supporting my sister," he states, "she got addicted while at university over here." I nod at him sadly.

"Lots of drugs on the party scene," I admit.

"Well, the main thing is getting better," acknowledges Luke and I smile at him. He's right; it's not about what I used to do; it's what I do now that matters. "Anyway," he continues, "I was wondering, in a few weeks when you are feeling a bit better, and you are more up to it. Do you want to grab a drink sometime? Coffee or something." I blink, it's been years since anyone has asked me out, I'm not sure I'm ready for it, but then I look into his eyes: they are kind and caring. I could do with kind and caring, in fact it might just be exactly what I need right now.

“That would be nice,” I reply, then I look around the room. “So...” I begin, “are you going to introduce me to your sister then?” He smiles and nods, before leading me to where his sister is sitting in the circle.

Predicted Verdict: Guilty

Chapter 28: The Secret he Keeps

Lucy felt rather curious as she headed for the small meeting room. It was a Saturday morning and she had been eating her breakfast when Elaine had approached her and explained that Elijah had wanted to see her. It seemed to her rather strange, as they had only met to talk about the trial yesterday, but she was now worried that he might want to talk about her relationship with Daniel. As she stepped into the meeting room, she saw Elijah stood by the desk leaning against the wall. Her heart sank as she observed him carefully. He looked like a man who had been defeated by some unknown force; had she and Daniel done that to him?

"I requested this meeting Lucy," began Elijah, "because the truth of the matter is, I'm not sure I can represent you anymore. There is a conflict of interest now." Lucy's mouth dropped opened and her stomach fell through the floor; surely, he wouldn't just abandon her? What would she do without a lawyer? Would her trial be delayed again?

"Don't be like that Elijah," Lucy pleaded, "I'm really sorry about how you found out and I'm sorry you got put in this position, but my trial would be delayed again if I suddenly had to find a new lawyer. Don't do that to me!" Elijah sighed and kicked the chair in frustration, which caused Lucy to flinch slightly. She didn't like this side of him very much.

"You should have told me about you and Daniel," stated Elijah accusingly. Lucy lowered her head to the floor in shame; she hardly had a valid defence.

"I know," she replied, "but you and Daniel are good friends. I thought he might have told you and if not, there was a reason why." Elijah nodded slowly then put a hand to his forehead.

"That's why I'm so angry with him," said Elijah bitterly. "He's put us both into difficult positions. You with I, and I with you, especially with your trial happening."

“It’s not all his fault,” argued Lucy, “I know you think he took advantage of me, but that simply isn’t true.” Elijah walked a few steps towards her then smiled at her sadly: his eyes full of sympathy.

“Lucy, he is your doctor,” said Elijah seriously. “That by definition means he is taking advantage.” Lucy shook her head and stamped her foot in frustration. She knew it made her look childish, but she didn’t care.

“I’m not just some victim,” retorted Lucy, “I’m of sound mind, I know exactly what I’m doing. Do you know how many shitty doctors I had before Daniel? How lost and without hope I was? Meeting Daniel: it was like someone had flicked a switch; I finally had a little bit of hope. Without it, I probably would have killed myself, once I found out what I did.” Elijah blinked, and his mouth dropped open at Lucy’s frank confession.

“Wow,” said Elijah .“That’s...” he trailed off as he seemed lost for words.

“Intense I know. I’m not an idiot. I know how psychology works, but I can’t blame myself for falling in love with Daniel because he’s the first person that ever made me feel like anything at all; like I wasn’t some…murderer.” Elijah groaned as if he was having some kind of internal conflict.

“I can even understand it from Daniel’s perspective to be honest,” said Elijah, “there are things you probably still don’t know about him. Things I doubt he’s told you.” Lucy narrowed her eyes at him inquisitively.

“What are you talking about?” she exclaimed. Elijah shrugged and put his hands in his pocket. He looked away from Lucy as he spoke next.

“Daniel never used to be so closed off or secretive,” said Elijah quietly.

“He’s not secretive with me,” protested Lucy. Elijah turned towards her and observed her sceptically.

"Are you sure? Have you asked him everything about himself?" Lucy blinked, of course she hadn't asked Daniel every single question, but she assumed because he loved her, he would want to tell her everything.

"What are you saying?" enquired Lucy, "does Daniel have this big secret?" Elijah remained silent and looked away.

"Like I said I'm not sure me representing you is the best thing," said Elijah earnestly. Lucy crossed her arms and sighed.

"I can't make that decision for you," she said "but you told me you'd pray on it. Are you telling me that God told you to give up on me? Is that it?" Elijah groaned, putting both hands to his face. Lucy could tell that there was a fierce battle raging inside of him.

"Unfortunately, there is nothing in the bible about this sort of thing," said Elijah, through gritted teeth.

"No but there is plenty about God," explained Lucy, "is he the kind of God who would do something like this?" Elijah blinked and then his expression changed to one of anger.

"So all of a sudden you have faith in God now?" he asked angrily.

"Maybe I want to believe," snapped Lucy. She could feel her own temper rising now; did he think she enjoyed having nothing to cling to, like he had when things were difficult? Like Bella had when she was lay dying? "The idea of having that kind of hope is appealing," continued Lucy bitterly, "if not rather flawed." Elijah held her gaze as though searching for something there that he could not quite fathom.

"I can't tell if you're saying that just to appease me," said Elijah honestly. Lucy shook her head.

"I'm not, but even if I were, would it change what God would do?" enquired Lucy, "I've made some bad choices in my life, so maybe I deserved some of the pain and suffering I've been through, but I can't help, but wanting a chance to get things right…not just to survive…to rot away in some jail cell…I can't help wanting to live!"

Elijah picked up his briefcase that had been sat on the table and sighed.

“I’ll see you on Monday,” said Elijah, without looking at her. Then he started to walk towards the door before he turned back to look at her. “Don’t tell Daniel about anything I’ve said,” warned Elijah. Lucy sighed, as he closed the door behind him. She felt stuck in the middle of a raging war between two good friends.

Later on in Daniel’s office, Lucy was wondering what it was he could be keeping from her. She knew she couldn’t just ask him out right. That would betray the trust that Elijah had asked her not to break; Lucy didn’t want to do that again. She knew she had to be tactile in how she approached it, so she decided to be subtle.

“Ok I know I have no right to say this,” said Lucy, “but why are you acting so weird?” It wasn’t a lie; Daniel had been tetchy since she had arrived in his office, although she suspected it was more to do with her trial re-commencing on Monday.

“I’m not,” insisted Daniel, as he leaned back in his chair and studied her carefully. Lucy stood up and walked around the desk perching on the edge of his desk in front of him.

“Ok take your poker face off for a minute,” said Lucy firmly, “this is me you’re talking to, what’s going on?” Daniel sighed and put a hand to his head.

“I need to tell you something,” he said suddenly. Lucy nodded wondering what secret Daniel was about to share with her. He looked extremely nervous and restless.

“You know you can tell me anything. I want you to tell me everything.” She looked at him beseechingly, eager to hear his secret, wondering what it could be.

“There’s a reason why I felt drawn to you,” said Daniel, “why I see you.” Lucy’s mouth dropped open in surprise; surely his secret wasn’t about her?

“What do you mean?” she asked curiously.

“I mean the truth is, in the past…” began Daniel. Suddenly there was a knock on the door and Lucy almost groaned in frustration at the bad timing; their meetings were never usually interrupted. Daniel gestured to her to go and sit in the armchair which she found a bit insulting, but she could understand why. Then he went to open the door. Outside the door stood Elaine with a panicked expression on her face.

“Doctor Robertson, it’s Max,” she stated nervously, “he’s having an episode; they’ve tried to help him, but he’s asking for you. He’s in the library.” Lucy jumped up from her chair; poor Max, maybe she could help him.

“I’ll be right there,” he said, then closed the door. He looked at Lucy for a moment. “You’ll be alright here…” he began.

“I should come with you,” said Lucy, “It’s Max.” Daniel shook his head.

“No, I should deal with this. Stay here; I won’t be too long.” Lucy sighed; he was probably right as despite her and Max being friends, she had no idea how to help him. Not when she could barely help herself.

“Go!” she said wearily, “I hope Max is ok.” Daniel nodded then quickly opened the door and left. Lucy sighed sitting back down in the chair wondering how long he would be.

As she sat alone in Daniel’s office, Lucy looked around thinking how ridiculous it seemed that he had a big secret; what could it be? Suddenly Lucy had a sinking feeling in her stomach; Daniel wasn’t married, was he? Was that why Elijah was so angry about it all? After all, she didn’t get to see him outside of the institute.

Feeling like she desperately needed an answer, she stood up and began to look at the papers on Daniel’s desk, she knew it was snooping, but the overwhelming urge to know more, spurred her on as her insecurities, threatened to overwhelm her.

Lucy noticed the filing cabinet on the right-hand side, but she knew it would be locked and besides, she was pretty sure Daniel’s secret wouldn't be in there, she hoped not anyway. The filing cabinet was where all the patient's files were kept with their personal information. Instead, she focussed on Daniel's desk and opened the top drawer, staring cautiously at the door, hoping that Daniel would not return and catch her. Lucy saw nothing in there but a bunch of newspaper articles, she was about to close the drawer, when she gasped and withdrew the papers, the articles were all about her case. Lucy supposed, she shouldn't be surprised about the fact that Daniel had taken such an interest given their relationship. She sighed, going to put the articles back into the desk drawer wondering how much her trial must be playing on Daniel's mind. As she was putting the articles back, something fell out from between them and on to the floor. Lucy bent down to retrieve it, it appeared to be a photo that had landed face down.

She turned the photo over and smiled as she saw Daniel standing with a female friend, smiling at the camera. Then her mouth fell open as she caught sight of the friend. They looked slightly different with darker hair and the fact they were smiling, but there was no mistaking the piercing eyes; it was Remy!!

Suddenly, the door opened and in walked Daniel, he stopped, frozen to the spot as he caught sight of the open desk drawer and the photo in Lucy's hand. Their eyes locked, and they could do nothing for a few moments except look at each other in shock, as Lucy tightly gripped the photo in her hand.

Chapter 29: Please Lucy

Daniel took a step towards Lucy cautiously, but she took a step back suddenly unsure of everything she thought she knew.

"Why is there a photograph of you and Remy together," asked Lucy confused, "and a bunch of clippings from my case?" Daniel sighed and lowered his head, avoiding eye contact with her.

"I really didn't want you to find out like this," admitted Daniel honestly. Lucy scowled at him, realising that man she thought she knew might just be an illusion.

"You know Remy or Charlotte?" stated Lucy, "whatever her name was? You're investigating my case. Who are you?" Daniel looked at her beseechingly, as he took a few steps forward.

"Please Lucy…" he began. Lucy took a few more steps away from him; she didn't know this man; he was a stranger to her.

"No, stay away from me," she said, "tell me the truth." Daniel put his hands in his pockets and shuffled his feet nervously.

"You should sit down," he said seriously. Lucy shook her head fiercely; he had no right to tell her what to do.

"I'm not doing anything you tell me," she snapped, "not until I get some answers!" Daniel looked rather hurt but nodded.

"I wanted to tell you, but…" he began. Lucy crossed her arms.

"What?" retorted Lucy. Daniel suddenly looked tormented.

"I was worried what it would do to you." Daniel went to take a step forward, but then seemed to think better of it. Lucy tapped her foot on the floor impatiently.

"What have you been keeping from me?" asked Lucy quietly.

"Remy…Charlotte she's the reason I went for this job here," stated Daniel, "I swear I didn't know what her real intentions were. If I did, I would never have…"

"Why would she have got you a job here?" interrupted Lucy impatiently.

"She's my daughter," replied Daniel reluctantly. The truth of his words crashed over Lucy like a wave, one which she felt drowning her, as everything faded to black.

When Lucy came to, she felt something cool on her face and heard Daniel's voice full of concern saying her name. Then what had happened, started coming back to her and she sat bolt upright in shock.

"Woah! Take it easy," said Daniel. Tears began to quickly cascade down Lucy's cheeks, as she finally realised the reality of Daniel's secret.

"I don't understand," she cried, "if Remy…Charlotte is your daughter then that means that…" Daniel nodded slowly with a haunted expression on his face.

"Yes," he replied. Lucy sobbed even harder, now realising why Daniel had taken such a keen interest in her case. "I had no idea he existed until you told me what Remy/ Charlotte said," said Daniel emotionally. He looked on the verge of tears himself but was trying to maintain some composure.

"And where is she now?" asked Lucy. She suddenly wondered if Remy and Daniel had planned their twisted sick game on her together. Was that all she was? Just a pawn in somebody else's clever game?

"I've not seen her since that day I confronted her, the day she attacked you," said Daniel earnestly, "I've tried to call her and get in contact, but she's determined to avoid me." Lucy lowered her head in shame; she had never felt so guilty and worthless in her whole life. After a few moments of trying to compose herself; she reached out for the desk to pull herself up off the floor. Daniel reached out to help her, but she moved away from his touch. How could he stand to be in the same room as her? Despite him lying to her about Remy/ Charlotte, what she had done was so much worse!

"Do you hate me?" asked Lucy. She could not bear to look at him as she asked the question. Daniel did not respond straight away, and Lucy thought it might be because he was trying to spare her feelings. "I wouldn't blame you if you do," she added.

"It would certainly make all this easier to process," said Daniel, with a pained expression. Then he noticed the sheer look of hurt on Lucy's face at his comment. "Of course I don't hate you," he said emotionally, "how do you not know that by now?" Lucy angrily brushed the tears that still refused to be silenced away from her cheeks.

"Why didn't you tell me?" she stated angrily. Daniel put a hand through his hair looking deranged, then sunk on to the floor, as if he no longer had the energy to stand.

"She was here to do research as part of her PHD…at first it was because of the professional aspect, but after she did what she did I was shocked. I felt so guilty, and you already had so much to deal with I didn't want to add to it. Then you told me about what she had said about it being her brother and I was really confused. At first, I assumed it was her half-brother because my ex-wife went on to have other partners, but then I wondered why she had never mentioned him after we reconnected…not even once." Lucy's mouth fell open in shock; feeling dizzy she sat in the chair, looking over at Daniel on the floor a few feet away.

"So, you never even knew he existed?" asked Lucy. Daniel pulled up his knees and put his elbows on them, putting his head down as he spoke.

"No, my ex-wife never told me about him," said Daniel bitterly, "She must have been only two months pregnant when we split up and she never even thought to mention it." Lucy got up off the chair and went and sat beside Daniel on the floor. In a strange way, she could understand why he had kept it from her, but that did nothing to quell the messed-up implications of all of it.

“Now because of me you’ll never get to know him,” said Lucy sadly. Though his head was still down, Daniel reached out and put his hand on Lucy’s.

“That doesn’t change why you did it,” he said quietly. Lucy shook her head and withdrew her hand from Daniel’s.

“Your kindness is more than I can bear,” sobbed Lucy emotionally. Daniel finally looked up at Lucy; it was obvious that he had been crying too.

“It’s because you’re not used to kindness,” he stated quietly. Lucy scoffed, feeling that she of all people did not deserve any kindness right now; she could not reconcile the idea with the monster that she now saw that she was.

“Being kind to someone who is good is easy,” said Lucy, “but being kind to someone who is bad, who’s wronged you, it’s…it doesn’t make any sense.” Daniel suddenly sat up straight, reached out his hands and gently put them on Lucy’s face so that she had no choice but to look at him.

“He was a stranger to me,” said Daniel, “yes; biologically he was my son, but that doesn’t change the fact I knew nothing about him…his life, but I know you Lucy.” Lucy lowered her eyes to the floor feeling like that simple truth did not make her any more human.

“Does the director know?” asked Lucy quietly. Daniel let go of Lucy and sighed.

“That Charlotte is my daughter, yes,” said Daniel, “that’s why I am at the centre of the investigation.” Lucy gasped as she realised how stupid she had been.

“Of course,” she stated, “that makes a lot more fucking sense now.” Daniel once again put his hand on Lucy’s, she looked down at it curiously, but did not immediately pull away.

"They don't know that the victim in your trial is my son." Lucy stared at him in surprise.

"Why?" she asked cautiously, "Shouldn't you tell them." Daniel did not look at her as he spoke.

"I probably should," he said wearily, "but I'm not going to." Lucy could not fathom his mindset; he should want revenge. She knew she would if anybody had done the same to somebody she knew.

"Why?" she asked. Then Daniel turned his face towards her.

"For the same reason I never reported you when you kissed me," said Daniel hesitantly. Lucy suddenly jumped up off the floor, quick as if she had been struck by lightning.

"No," said Lucy forcefully, "you can't…you need to…" She waved her arms as if it would make him suddenly move away and see sense. Daniel stood up and walked towards her calmly. "Don't you dare," she pleaded.

"I still love you." Lucy scowled at him angrily knowing that he must be very confused over everything; this wasn't how he was supposed to feel, this couldn't be how he felt!

"You're deluded…You're confused," said Lucy passionately, "you don't know what you're saying…I killed your son." Daniel reached out his hands and drew Lucy's face up to his, so she had no choice but to look at him.

"It was a mistake," said Daniel. Lucy could not stop the tears that started to fall freely once more from her eyes. Full of shame, she lowered her gaze to the full. To find out she had killed someone was bad enough, but to find out now that it was Daniel's son, it just brought back the waves of guilt more intensely, she was a wicked person underserving of anything.

"You do realise that is completely fucked up, don't you?" she stated quietly. Daniel sighed and dropped his hands from Lucy's face.

“Yes! Do you not think I know that?” he stated annoyed, “do you think I’m that stupid? Out of all the people I could have fallen in love with, do you think I’m happy that it’s the person who killed my son? But I know why you did it…I know why you felt you didn’t have a choice. It’s fucked up, but I don’t care because I know how I feel…I know you and I love you.” Lucy lifted her gaze to meet his shaking her head fiercely. She knew she should tell him that their situation could not continue, that there was too much drama and emotion surrounding their relationship. She opened her mouth to speak, to tell him that this would change everything between them, but the words she meant to speak would not come out. Instead, filled with self-hatred, she uttered words of sheer madness.

“I love you too,” whispered Lucy, and she meant it. Moving forward, their relationship would be messy and difficult, there were so many demons, so many bad choices and too much mess, which she knew they would have to talk about, but the simple truth of the matter was that Lucy needed him. As Daniel held Lucy tightly in his arms; she felt perhaps that he probably needed her too. In spite of everything she had done, this monster she had turned into, somebody loved her and needed her. It was illogical and overwhelming, but it was the hope that she continued to cling to.

Chapter 30: I'm Good At My Job

On Monday morning, Lucy was pacing the corridor nervously when she spotted Daniel making his way towards her from the other end of the corridor.

"Has Elijah not arrived yet?" he asked. Lucy shook her head sadly in response. "Maybe he's planning on meeting you there?" suggested Daniel. She sighed; she knew he was trying to be supportive, but the fact of the matter was Elijah was AWOL. "I can come with you," continued Daniel, taking a few steps towards her. Lucy shook her head quickly.

"It's nice of you," said Lucy, "but it would look weird, and we don't want to draw attention to…us…not today!" Daniel sighed and Lucy looked at him nervously; things had been different between them since she had found out the awful truth; there had been a distance between them that wasn't there before. Lucy knew she had probably put that distance in place herself. The truth was as much as she knew that Daniel loved her, and she loved him, she was no longer sure that was enough. She wanted it to be so badly, but how could they overcome such sadness and trauma?

"You'd really be ok if they found me not guilty?" asked Lucy suddenly. They had talked a lot over the last two days, and though he had told her over and over again that he didn't blame her, she still couldn't understand how he was so ok with her killing his son. When she had pressed him on it, he had told her that he had his reasons, but Lucy was beginning to think he was merely blinded by infatuation. That there would come a time in the not-too-distant future where he would suddenly lose the rose-tinted glasses and see her for what she really was. Though she prayed that wouldn't be the case, it was the only way she could explain his behaviour.

"I've already told you I don't hold you responsible," stated Daniel adamantly.

"I know," she said, "but I still think there must be a small part of you that must want me to pay…to burn for what I did to him."

"Lucy even if you went to jail that won't bring him back. It's not like you're a danger to society." Lucy shrugged her shoulders in response and then looked at her watch before anxiously glancing down the corridor.

"I suppose I better go," she said wearily, "I'll just have to inform reception that it'll just be me and the guards." Daniel moved forward and lifted up her head gently so he could meet her eyes.

"I will see you there," he said.

"I won't hate you, you know," said Lucy seriously, "if you have a change of heart on the stand. If you want to tell them I'm crazy…I'll get it." Daniel did not reply, instead he quickly looked up and down the corridor then pulled her face towards his and kissed her. Lucy could tell he was trying to put all of his feelings into the kiss, because he could not make her understand, but when they broke apart, Lucy was more confused than ever. None the less, she tried to smile at Daniel reassuringly, wanting him to know that even if she didn't understand, she appreciated the effort he was trying to make.

"I'll see you later," she said. Then she made her way towards reception, still secretly hoping she might find Elijah waiting for her there.

Once she was in the courtroom, Lucy was dismayed to find that Elijah was still nowhere to be seen. Perhaps he had decided he could not represent her after all. She sat in her seat alone at the defendant's desk feeling awkward. She took a glance over at Jacobson, and found him deep in conversation with a young man who she was almost certain was one of the journalists who had been hassling her outside on her way in. Whatever he was telling Jacobson was making him look rather happy indeed and Lucy knew that wasn't a good thing. Suddenly she was distracted as a briefcase was dropped on the desk next to her and to her relief, she looked up to see Elijah straightening his tie looking rather forlorn.

"I thought you might not show up," said Lucy bluntly. Elijah looked down at her with a weary expression on his face.

"To be honest, I nearly didn't." Lucy grimaced slightly, thinking about what she could have done if he hadn't made the decision to turn up. She'd have just been sat here without a lawyer.

"What made you come?" she asked quietly. Elijah pulled out the chair from under the desk and sat down on it slowly.

"The sheer will of God," he replied, through gritted teeth.

"Hopefully, that means he's on my side," offered Lucy. Elijah opened his mouth to say something, but then seemed to think better of it and closed it again. Lucy knew what it must have taken for Elijah to have shown up here today, because she knew he was still angry with her and the whole situation. Lucy wished she could have that kind of self-control, but then Elijah had said it had not come from him anyway.

"Elijah," she said quietly. He turned towards her waiting for her to continue. "I know," she said. Elijah shrugged his shoulders.

"Know what?" he replied.

"About Charlotte/ Remy," she stated, "Daniel told me." Elijah suddenly looked really uncomfortable and shuffled his feet under the desk.

"Ahhh," he replied. Lucy couldn't blame him for having nothing else to say in response. She felt bad that he had been put in such an awkward position and it made her feel rather annoyed with Daniel too that he had recommended him. Then it dawned on her that he might have done it to ensure his secret had stayed with someone he could trust.

The bailiff stepped to the front of the courtroom and a hushed silence descended upon the crowd. The door at the front opened and the judge walked in. She surveyed the courtroom over her glasses carefully before she sat down and banged her gavel. "You may be seated," she said calmly. Not a pin drop could be heard as the court waited for the judge to start the trial.

"The case of Lucy Boragas vs the state is now in session, prosecutor, you may call your next witness." Jacobson stood up and smiled. Lucy could tell he relished being back in court.

"The prosecution calls Marcus Lightsonburge to the stand." Lucy turned to see a man in his mid-twenties heading down the aisle. He was smartly dressed in a crisp white shirt, a grey suit, and a green tie. His blonde hair was brushed back in place and his green eyes sparkled, with a hint of amusement. Lucy had never seen such a well-dressed handsome witness. Once Marcus was on the stand and had taken his oath, the questioning began.

"Mr Lightsonburge," he stated, "could you describe Alex's character for us?" Marcus nodded and cleared his throat to speak by coughing slightly.

"Alex was a good person," he said boldly, "He was always trying to help anybody who needed it." Jacobson turned pointedly towards the jury and Lucy rolled her eyes, wondering if they could see through his act.

"He did drugs, though didn't he?" asked Jacobson curiously. Marcus nodded but smiled in amusement.

"Yeah, but nothing too heavy," he said casually, "his mum made him go to rehab one time cause she thought he was addicted but he only ever did it recreationally."

"So, that night, what happened?" questioned Jacobson, "why did Alex approach Lucy? Talk us through it?" Marcus took a breath, and looked around the court, as if he were steading himself to tell an interesting story.

"Well, we'd just come out from a swanky little bar 'Limons' I think it was called, we were all just laughing and joking, then we clocked this girl running from down a side alley. She looked distressed and Alex being the person that he was, he wanted to help her." For a fleeting moment, Lucy's heart sank into her chest; had she really got it so wrong? She had thought in her heart of hearts that he was trying to hurt her, but maybe she had just been that terrified. Then suddenly Alex's words came back to her like cold water being poured all over her fickle human heart; "You stupid fucking bitch!"

"So then what did Alex do?" continued Jacobson.

"He approached her saying it was ok and he wanted to help her," said Marcus, "but she withdrew a knife from somewhere and nearly slashed his arm causing him to swear." Lucy scowled, knowing he wasn't being truthful. She wasn't stupid, there was a difference between swearing at someone in shock and insulting someone.

"Then what happened?" enquired Jacobson impatiently.

"Before he had a chance to do anything else, she took the knife and stabbed him through the chest," spat Marcus bitterly, "I could only look on in horror. I think I might have screamed his name. I could tell it was bad as soon as she pulled the knife out." Lucy shivered; she knew what she had done, but that didn't take away the raw pang of horror of it, even though she had re-lived that night a thousand times in her head.

"No further questions," said Jacobson, as he calmy walked back to his seat. The judge looked over at Elijah expectantly.

"Defendant, do you wish to cross examine the witness?" she asked. Elijah stood up and nodded.

"Yes, your honour." Elijah walked towards the stand. "So you said Alex approached Lucy to help," began Elijah, "did he say anything at all?" Marcus paused for a moment and put his hand to his chin, taking time to think. Lucy wondered whether he would be honest and admit that Alex had called her a stupid fucking bitch or perhaps he hadn't heard?

"Erm yeah I think he said, 'Calm down Lady, I'm trying to help you'." Answered Marcus, "Then when Lucy pulled the knife he said 'Woah, no need for that; give me that knife'." Lucy blinked, because the words did seem quite familiar to her, perhaps Marcus was trying to be truthful, but she waited with bated breath to see if he would reveal Alex's insult.

"I see," said Elijah, "and what was Lucy's response?"

"When he asked her to give him the knife she screamed 'Stay back or I'll use it.'"

"Ah, she warned him to stay away," After a pause Elijah continued "so did Alex at this point move away from her?" Marcus looked sheepish and straightened his tie, as he slowly shook his head. "No…look he probably should have backed off," admitted Marcus, "she was obviously distressed, but that didn't mean he deserved to die, did it?" Elijah looked thoughtful as he took a casual glance around the courtroom.

"No one here is asking whether Alex deserved to die Mr Lightsonburger," stated Elijah seriously, "I was asking why you think after being given fair warning, he decided to still try to intervene in Miss Boragas' situation?" Marcus looked rather annoyed with Elijah's question at first, but then he sighed, put his head down and shrugged his shoulders.

"I don't know," he answered honestly, "he just wanted to help, I guess. He got in over his head, he always did that…went too far out of his way to help others."

"But Lucy did in fact look destressed? Terrified even?"

"Yeah," admitted Marcus, "I mean she looked very unhinged." Lucy sighed quietly; she could just imagine what she must have looked like based on how she had felt at the time. That combined with the fact that she hadn't showered or brushed her hair in days, would have made her look terrifying.

"No further questions." Then he walked back to his seat and Marcus got down from the witness stand. Lucy looked around the courtroom anxiously, she knew Daniel was the next witness and she wondered if he was here already.

"I propose we take a small recess for Lunch before we continue" stated the judge, "I know it's slightly earlier than usual, but any objections?" She looked at Elijah and Jacobson who did not make any comment. "We'll reconvene in an hour at 12:30," she stated, then banged her hammer on the gavel. Lucy let out a breath that she hadn't even realised she was holding.

"Let's grab some lunch," suggested Elijah. Lucy raised her eyebrows at him. "Ok, I'll grab some lunch, you sit and drink your water." Lucy gave him a pained expression as they made their way out of the courtroom towards the upstairs café.

When they were walking down the corridor, Lucy spotted Daniel down the corridor in front of them. For a moment, time stood still as Elijah and Daniel just stared at each other; each unsure of what they should say or do. Lucy watched them both in concern, she hoped they wouldn't start arguing in the middle of the corridor. Then suddenly Elijah turned towards the stairs and continued to make his way to the café, gesturing for Lucy to follow him. Lucy feeling torn, gave Daniel an apologetic look before she quickly followed Elijah to the café.

An hour later, back in the courtroom, Lucy felt restless and nervous, she didn't think that Daniel would actually say anything bad about her, but she almost wished he would, because it would mean he actually had pent up anger. It made more sense to Lucy that Daniel would be hiding his anger from her rather than having none whatsoever, given all that he knew.

Once the judge had called the court back into session, she looked down at her papers in front of her before addressing Jacobson. "Prosecutor, you have no further witnesses. Is this correct?" she asked. Jacobson stood up and shook his head oozing confidence. Lucy had a sneaking suspicion he was plotting something.

"The prosecution rests, your honour." Lucy almost scoffed feeling that whatever he was planning was far from over, but then what could he be planning if he had no more witnesses or evidence? Perhaps she was being paranoid. The judge looked over at Elijah.

"Then the defence has the floor." Elijah stood up and Lucy got the impression he was almost stealing himself.

"I would like to call Doctor Daniel Robertson to the stand." Lucy turned to see Daniel slowly making his way down the aisle. Though he looked exactly the same as he had done when she had seen him this morning, her heart began beating just a little bit faster and her face flushed red. She wondered why she was suddenly so nervous, but then realised it was perhaps because she and Daniel were usually alone and were not usually in a room full of crowded people together. Lucy noticed that Daniel was avoiding her eye contact; she supposed maybe it was because he was trying to remain professional. Elijah approached Daniel on the witness stand, and Lucy almost felt that she could feel the tension radiating between them.

"For the record would you like to explain who you are for the court." Daniel nodded and cleared his throat.

"Yes, of course," he began, "my name is Doctor Daniel Robertson. I'm a psychiatrist at the institute where Lucy is a patient. I started working with her six months ago, at which point she was suffering from a condition called Dissociative amnesia." Lucy lowered her head feeling how stupid she had been to believe she was innocent when she couldn't even remember what had happened that night. It was like she had been a whole different person back then, one who was free to not feel the guilt of what she had done.

"Tell me Doctor," said Elijah, "why do people generally suffer from Dissociative amnesia?"

"A sudden shock, a traumatic event…for some people it leads to Post Traumatic Shock Disorder, but for some people the brain goes into a more severe form of shock where they can block things out, such as specific events." Elijah gave a quick glance at Lucy who looked back at him feeling ridiculous. The whole court could now see just how damaged she had been and still was, and she hated it with every fibre of her being.

"Did you have any reason to think Lucy was faking her condition?" enquired Elijah. Daniel looked over in Lucy's direction, but again did not make eye contact with her, it was beginning to irritate her.

"No because she was very forthcoming about other traumatic events in her life."

"Is there any reason to believe she might have just kept what happened from you that night?" said Elijah. Daniel shook his head slowly.

"No, for two reasons…" he began, "Number one…she was so sure of her innocence and couldn't understand why she was even a patient. Number two; she was so traumatised after she finally remembered, I highly doubt anyone could have faked that." This time Daniel's eyes caught Lucy's and they shared a look of recognition, but it lasted a mere second before Daniel turned his attention back to Elijah.

"So, she finally did remember what happened?" concurred Elijah. Daniel nodded.

"Yes," stated Daniel, "once Lucy remembered the incident she began to suffer from PTSD."

"In your professional opinion do you think Lucy intended to commit murder that night?" asked Elijah. Jacobson quickly jumped to his feet.

"Objection, your honour," spat Jacobson, "speculation. How can the doctor know what her intentions were that night? He wasn't even there!" Elijah sighed; Lucy couldn't blame him.

"Your honour, Doctor Robertson is a qualified professional who is capable of assessing peoples states of mind and motivations. I'm simply trying to draw on his expertise as a professional. I'm not trying to state that it is the absolute truth. All he can give is his professional opinion on the matter."

The judge looked between Jacobson and Elijah as if she could not make up her mind, which one of them was her biggest annoyance. "Objection overruled."

"So where were we before we were interrupted," said Elijah, "ah yes, in your professional opinion do you think Lucy intended to commit murder that night?" Daniel looked rather uncomfortable as he glanced at Elijah but straightened his tie poised to answer the question.

"It's my professional opinion that Lucy believed she was acting in self-defence," he stated, "she felt her life was threatened when her only source of protection was nearly taken away from her and reacted to stop it. I don't believe there was any intention of murder." Elijah nodded and then turned away. Lucy felt numb; how could this amazing man stand in that box and defend her, knowing it was his son? Was he really that estranged from the fact he was his father? Or was it that his love for Lucy clouded his judgement?

"No further questions." Elijah walked back to the desk and the judge looked at Jacobson expectantly, but he was too busy whispering something to his colleague with a big smile on his face.

"Prosecutor, would you like to cross examine the witness?" asked the Judge impatiently. Jacobson stood up looking a little sheepish.

"Yes, your honour. I would very much like to cross examine the witness." He strutted towards the witness stand, turning to look at the jury as he went. "Doctor Robertson," he began, "I have a lot of respect for psychiatrists, I think the work you guys do is beyond compare." Daniel looked seemingly unimpressed by Jacobson's compliment and Lucy could not help wondering if he was slightly biased based on what Lucy had told him.

"Thank you for the flattery," retorted Daniel, "but is there a question in there?" A loud laugh descended in the courtroom at this, and Lucy could not help joining in; trust Daniel to be a smart arse! The judge looked unimpressed by the chaos that was now happening in her courtroom and banged her gavel down immediately.

“Order! Order!” she observed firmly, “Prosecutor, please cross examine the witness instead of just paying him compliments.” Lucy caught Daniel’s eye, and she noticed his eyes sparkling in amusement, but he dared not smile.

“Yes, your honour. Dr Robertson what was it that caused Miss Borogas to remember that night?” Lucy felt her stomach sink as she suddenly realised why Jacobson had been smiling. He obviously knew the truth about Remy and who she was; it would have been fairly easy to look it up on the public records. She saw Daniel grimace slightly before he answered the question, as he too realised what was about happen.

“She was attacked by another patient,” he said cautiously. Lucy knew he was trying to keep his answers short and to the point to avoid being caught out. Somehow though she knew it might not be enough, because she had a horrible feeling Jacobson was about to launch a full-on verbal assault.

“Attacked how?” asked Jacobson Daniel straightened his tie and did not make eye contact with Jacobson as he spoke.

“They held a knife to her throat,” he replied quietly. Jacobson looked at the jury with a shocked expression on his face, but Lucy knew this was all for show. He had known about all of it before he began his questioning; it’s why he had been smiling.

“Wow, that’s pretty poor security for a mental institute. Why did they attack her? Did she provoke them?” Lucy held her breath; if he told them the real reason Charlotte had attacked her then it could have serious consequences for the whole trial.

“Not as far as I am aware,” said Daniel. Lucy almost sighed in relief, but she also felt badly that Daniel was lying on the stand for her. She knew how much it must cost him to betray his integrity in such a way.

“Doctor Robertson isn’t it true the attacker was your own daughter?” asked Jacobson. Daniel’s mouth dropped opened as he struggled to form an answer. Eventually after a few moments of silence he lowered his head to the floor as he spoke.

"Yes, but I had no idea that she would attack Lucy," explained Daniel regretfully, "My daughter is a psychologist. The board of directors and I were led to believe that she was conducting research, she was very convincing. There has been an investigation into all of this in the institute, I'd be happy for them to send you the report." Lucy's heart went out to him because she thought he had done exceptionally well in giving such a good answer despite the circumstances.

"No, no that's fine I believe you. I'm sure you're all doing your best to make sure it doesn't happen again. Still, that must have put you in a difficult position as Lucy's psychiatrist?" Daniel looked slightly uncomfortable but nodded slowly.

"Yes, of course," replied Daniel, "A new psychiatrist was discussed but it was felt that Lucy had made a lot of progress as my patient so…" He trailed off feeling a little lost for words.

"Why do you think she made a lot of progress with you as opposed to her other psychiatrists?" asked Jacobson curiously. Suddenly Lucy realised what was happening, she grabbed Elijah's arm and urged him to do something, anything to stop the trial. Elijah looked at her in confusion wondering what she was getting at.

"Erm…I'm good at my job," replied Daniel sheepishly. Jacobson smiled and nodded at Daniel, then turned to face the judge.

"I bet you are!" he replied sinisterly, "your honour, I'd like this expert witness testimony to be struck from the record." Daniel's mouth dropped open in confusion. Lucy felt the courtroom swim around her, she wanted to stand up and scream, do anything to stop what was about to happen next, but her legs felt like jelly, and she could not stand.

"On what grounds?" asked the judge curiously. Jacobson looked like a cat who had got the cream.

"On the grounds that he is having a romantic relationship with his patient Miss Boragas here," he stated. Lucy froze as Daniel looked towards her in shock, she shook her head slightly to indicate that he should lie; do anything but tell the truth. However, Lucy knew that he wouldn't because he'd already told her as much.

"Is there any truth to this claim, doctor?" asked the judge, looking at him sternly. Daniel took one last glance at Lucy who looked at him fearfully before he turned back to the judge.

"Yes," said Daniel honestly, "unfortunately your honour it's true." The whole courtroom gasped, and Lucy felt silent tears falling from her cheeks. She wished more than anything he would have lied, because now his career would be over. It was one more thing she would have to feel guilty about, on top of everything else. Elijah leaned back in his chair and gazed at the ceiling for a moment. Lucy knew he must be thoroughly fed up with the turn of events. The judge looked far from impressed as she gazed at Daniel debating to what she could say to such a confession. Finally, she seemed to come to a decision and looked toward the jury.

"In that case, jury you are to strike Doctor Robertson's testimony from the record and," she said sternly, "Doctor Robertson the American Psychiatrist Association will have to be informed of this, as well as the institute." Lucy did not attempt to conceal the tears that were falling freely from her eyes now.

"I understand your honour," said Daniel sadly, "thank you." Daniel slowly made his way off the stand and Elijah stood up.

"In light of this new development your honour," he began, "we'd like to request a recess until tomorrow morning." The judge nodded in approval, almost looking relieved.

"Yes, I think that would be extremely sensible given the circumstances. The court is adjourned until tomorrow at 1pm to give us all time to reflect." She looked pointedly at Lucy as she said this, and Lucy could do nothing but sit there with her head lowered, feeling utterly ashamed.

As soon as the judge had left the courtroom, Lucy jumped up from her seat and fled the courtroom, leaving Elijah to gather his things. She walked into the corridor followed by two-armed security guards, turned, and saw Daniel looking rather forlorn at the other end of the corridor. She walked towards him slowly with a pained expression on her face.

“I’m not sure I want to face the journalists just yet,” said Daniel. He was trying to make it out to be a joke, but Lucy could sense the nerves behind his facade. Without warning she jumped into his arms and started to sob on his shoulder, Daniel took a quick look at the armed security guards before holding her tightly. He knew there was no point in being careful now, especially when things were looking so bleak for them both anyway.

“I am so sorry,” Lucy muttered into his chest, “I can say it was me, I can…” She trailed off as she could barely form coherent words.

“Lucy, it’s ok,” Said Daniel emotionally, “that’s not important right now.” Lucy looked up at him with tear filled eyes.

“Not important, how can you say that?” she sobbed, “You will lose your job.” Daniel grimaced and shook his head.

“It’s not just my job,” he affirmed, “they’ll revoke my license, but Lucy I am the one who should be apologising to you. This will have completely destroyed your case.” He looked almost on the verge of tears.

“I don’t care,” stated Lucy, “I always knew I was heading to jail or worse. You could have got away from all this.” She started to sob all over again and Daniel lifted her face gently to meet his.

“I didn’t…don’t want to get away from all this,” he uttered. Then he kissed her, disregarding the fact they were in public. Suddenly they both heard Elijah cough loudly near them and broke apart. Daniel let go of Lucy and walked towards Elijah, so they were standing face to face.

“Did you tell them?” asked Daniel. Elijah held up his hands and slowly shook his head.

“No, I promise you I didn’t,” he replied bitterly. Daniel studied him for a few moments and then nodded.

"I believe you," he confirmed, "you'd at least be truthful about it." Elijah looked at Daniel coldly.

"Nice to see you still respect our friendship a little." Daniel grimaced at his statement and Lucy looked at the floor; she was as much to blame for all of this.

"I'm sorry, Elijah," said Daniel sincerely. Elijah sighed and shoved his hands in his suit pockets.

"I appreciate that, I just need time," said Elijah, "this is complicated enough, but despite how I feel about this situation, I did not tell them. Somebody else did and it will be hard to come back from this." He looked pointedly at Lucy, and she knew he was trying to prepare her for the worst. It didn't bother her as much as she thought it would have though, because she had only ever expected the worst anyway. Suddenly she remembered something, and it made her feel sicker than she already was.

"It might have been Max," stated Lucy regretfully, "he saw us…but he promised he wouldn't tell." She looked at Daniel apologetically, but he just shrugged his shoulders.

"Either way it's out there now," said Elijah, then he looked towards Daniel. "I hope you are ready to deal with the consequences of all this," he stated seriously. Daniel looked equally serious as he nodded.

"I am." Elijah put his hand on Daniel's shoulder and Lucy almost smiled at the gesture.

"Well, that's something at least. We all have sin, but the only one who can truly judge is God." Daniel nodded, then Elijah stepped back and looked at Lucy.

"I best get you back to the institute," said Elijah apologetically. Lucy looked from Elijah to Daniel.

"At the risk of taking the piss," she began, "could you give us a minute?" Daniel sniggered slightly as Elijah's mouth dropped open in annoyance.

"I must be an idiot!" he said in frustration, as he stormed off down the corridor. Daniel put a hand to the back of his head as if trying to gather his thoughts and Lucy stepped forward and wrapped her arms around him.

"I'll be here tomorrow," whispered Daniel. Lucy shook her head as she began silent sobbing once more.

"It won't be the same though," she replied sadly.

"I know," said Daniel. Then suddenly he squeezed her more tightly too him. "Promise me you'll be brave," said Daniel quietly, "that you'll still come tomorrow come what may." Lucy wanted to reply, but she couldn't see a tomorrow, not with how things were currently. Instead, she buried her head into Daniel's chest and secretly hoped that the moment would never end. Daniel gently lifted her face to meet his, desperation etched on his face. "Lucy," he said pleadingly, "I need you to promise me you'll be ok, at least until tomorrow." She could barely seem him through the tears that continued to flow from her eyes.

"I can't promise I'll be ok," replied Lucy honestly, "but I will be here. I deserve to face up to what I did." Daniel did not offer any words of comfort, instead he leaned in and kissed her slowly and softly. Suddenly they heard coughing and they broke apart thinking Elijah had come back, when in actual fact it was one of the guards gesturing that Lucy should leave. She sighed and squeezed Daniel tightly once more before letting him go.

Chapter 31: Nothing less than I Deserve

I've fucked up big time and now Lucy is probably going to go to jail for sure. I don't know how I'll be able to live with myself after this. I don't care about losing my job or my licence, it's unfortunate yes, but it's nothing less than I deserve. Lucy doesn't deserve to rot in jail because I crossed a line. I wish I could put this right somehow, but it's too late. It's fucking shit, but there is not a single thing left I can do to help her. I can only watch as she is punished for a split-second decision she made; the only decision she could have made to survive and the same decision I made so many years ago.

Chapter 32: It was you!

The next morning, Lucy woke up exceptionally early and groaned as she recalled the events of the day before. It had been a difficult night. Spending most of the night sobbing, she had finally succumbed to sleep sometime in the early hours. Her thoughts had been plagued by guilt manifesting in a series of negative thoughts that involved reliving all the choices she had made that had led her to this moment. Having no motivation to get up and venture out of her bedroom, she just lay there staring at the ceiling thinking about what Daniel would be doing right now. She knew he wouldn't be in his office as usual, that he would have been suspended the moment the institute was informed of their relationship.

About an hour later, Lucy was torn away from her dark thoughts by a knock on her door. She made no attempt to answer it, hoping that whoever it was would just leave her be. However, she had no such luck as the door opened and Elaine entered the room. Lucy sat up and looked at Elaine curiously and her heart sank as she read the expression on Elaine's face. There was no mistaking her disappointment.

"Are you ok Lucy?" asked Elaine. Lucy blinked at her, surprised at the kindness in her voice, which she knew she didn't deserve.

"Do I look ok?" she replied pointedly. Elaine did not reply but studied her carefully, shuffling around rather awkwardly. Lucy could guess the reason for her discomfort. "You know about Daniel and me, don't you?" Elaine nodded slowly.

"Everybody knows," said Elaine quietly. "Did he hurt you, Lucy?" Lucy jumped off her bed in outrage.

"What?" she stated, "No! He would never hurt me." Elaine calmly walked over to the locked cabinet and took the key out from her pocket.

"I should have seen the signs," Elaine said. Lucy put her hands on her hips and waited for Elaine to turn back from the cabinet and look at her before she spoke. Is this what everyone would think? That Daniel was the predator, and she was just some helpless girl who had gone along with his advances?

“Elaine, I’m not some poor vulnerable person. I knew exactly what I was doing. I love him!” Elaine did not respond but observed Lucy with a sympathetic glance. “He didn’t trick me, Elaine,” Lucy added, “he loves me too.” Elaine could not conceal the disgust now etched on her face as she handed Lucy her tablets.

“Oh Lucy!” she said emotionally. Lucy snatched the tablets from her then folded her arms in defiance. This woman had no right to tell her who could love her or who she could love.

“Even monsters crave to be loved!” spat Lucy angrily. Elaine’s face now changed to a softer expression as she handed Lucy the water bottle. Lucy put the tablets in her mouth and swallowed them with the water. She then opened her mouth and waggled her tongue around.

“You’re not a monster, Lucy,” offered Elaine reassuringly, as she locked the medicine cabinet. Lucy rolled her eyes feeling annoyed; why was everyone so willing to believe she was the victim and Daniel was the monster? She was the one who had killed someone, she deserved all the blame!

“No?” retorted Lucy, “I killed someone, Elaine! I took my knife and I plunged it through someone’s heart, which made them bleed out and die on a cold hard floor.” Elaine gasped and looked shocked at Lucy’s confession. Lucy then lowered her head in shame. “I didn’t mean it, it was an accident, but it’s the action that makes me a monster. That makes people look at me like I’m a monster. Intent…what I meant to do… has nothing to do with it, not to most people. Daniel was the first person to ask why. Everyone else just treated me like I was diseased, corrupted…he was the one who actually took the time to get to know me.” Elaine sighed and placed her hand on Lucy’s shoulder. Lucy looked at it curiously; she was feeling rather cautious around Elaine at the moment.

“That was his job though, Lucy,” explained Elaine. Lucy shook her head quickly in disagreement.

“No, it wasn’t,” retorted Lucy in frustration, “All the other psychiatrists treated me like a murderer before they even knew if I did it or how. All of them acted like they were listening, but they were all sat there silently judging me.” Elaine withdrew her hand from Lucy’s shoulder and looked as though she wanted to say something.

“Remy…” she began, “the girl who…” Lucy cut her off.

“I already knew that Remy/ Charlotte is his daughter. He told me, he told me everything before yesterday because he cares about me, and he felt guilty about it all. Now because of me he’ll be fired.” Elaine looked pointedly at Lucy as if trying to get her to understand something she was missing.

“As much as you may love him,” she began, “as much as he loves you; that doesn’t change the fact he was your doctor.” Lucy nodded slightly; she understood that Daniel had been her doctor and in an ideal world it shouldn’t have happened, but she had never really seen him as her doctor anyway.

“And the first person who made me feel like something other than a monster. The funny thing is that when people look at you and treat you like a monster for so long, you have a hard time seeing yourself as anything else. Until someone…”

“Tells you that you’re not,” interrupted Elaine, but Lucy shook her head.

“Telling someone they’re not a monster after years of thinking they are, won’t do anything at all. Daniel did something even kinder; he held up a mirror so I could see for myself! He gave that choice back to me.” Elaine opened her mouth and closed it again as words seemed to escape her. “Has he been here to collect his things?” asked Lucy impatiently, “or to meet with the directors?” Elaine shook her head and looked at her seriously.

"Lucy he's not allowed within fifty yards of the institute now," affirmed Elaine, "he'd be arrested if he tried to come near here. Frankly, he's lucky he hasn't been already." Lucy shivered and wrapped her arms round herself; she couldn't have Daniel end up in jail because of her, even it was unlikely that it would happen.

"Don't say that!" snapped Lucy fearfully, "Look it wasn't his fault you know. I kissed him first." Elaine quickly turned away from Lucy and headed for the door.

"I don't need to know the details, thank you," said Elaine sharply.

"What happens now?" called Lucy before Elaine could open the door to leave. Elaine sighed and turned back towards her.

"Well, he's suspended of course," said Elaine, "but he'll have his licence removed; that's almost certain!" Lucy nodded as silent tears cascaded down her cheeks; not only was she going to jail, but she had ruined the career of the man she loved. Suddenly Elaine's harsh exterior melted as she came back to observe the damaged woman in front of her.

"Your mum is coming at ten this morning," said Elaine quietly. Lucy sank down to sit on the bed.

"I don't want to see her," replied Lucy. Elaine sighed wearily and shrugged her shoulders.

"Too bad," she stated, "she wants to see you." Elaine headed for the door, but Lucy called after her once more.

"He could have lied you know," stated Lucy. Elaine turned and looked at her blankly. "But he didn't." Lucy continued, "he chose to tell the truth, because he felt so guilty and because he knew it was the right thing to do." Elaine opened the door and then looked back at her pointedly.

"If he was so concerned with doing the right thing," she began, "then you two never would have happened." Elaine left, shutting the door rather loudly behind her, leaving Lucy alone with her dark thoughts. After a few moments of mulling over Elaine's harsh words, she began to get ready to meet her mum. She knew it would not be an easy meeting now that her mum would know about Daniel.

Lucy felt a strong sense of dread as she walked into the visitor's room; she had no desire to argue with her mum, but something told her that she was in for an argument either way. When she saw her mum, her sense of dread dwindled as she observed the woman sat the table. She did not look like her normal self; her hair was barely styled, her eyes with puffy and red and there was a sense of defeat that oozed out of her pores like a manifestation. Lucy guessed that perhaps her mum now realised how serious things were for her in the trial. When she reached the table, her mum jumped up as her eyes fell open her and there was a strong sense of desperation in her voice.

"Lucy," she began, "I'm so sorry!" She reached forward and embraced Lucy in a hug. Lucy blinked wondering why her mum was apologising to her when she had expected a lecture.

"It wasn't your fault," replied Lucy. Lucy's mum sighed, then moved back to the table and collapsed into her chair.

"It was!" acknowledged her mum quietly. Then she looked up at Lucy with tear filled eyes of emotion. "I told them about you and Doctor Robertson," she whispered. Lucy's mouth dropped open as she quickly took a chair in front of her mum.

"It was you?" gasped Lucy, "What? How did you…"

"I'm your mum," she interrupted, "I suspected something was going between you two that first time I met him. It wasn't until I saw you kissing in the corridor yesterday, through the glass of the visitor's centre…I'd come to wish you luck before the trial. Well, I told the director because I was worried about you, they must have told the court. I didn't realise that it would screw up your trial." Lucy felt numb at her mother's confession; she knew she should be relieved because she now had someone else to blame, but the truth was she was sick of blaming other people for her choices.

“Why didn’t you talk to me about it?” asked Lucy curiously. Lucy’s mum studied her carefully; she seemed to be confused that Lucy had not reacted negatively to her confession.

“I panicked,” she admitted, “he’s your doctor Lucy, it’s not right!” Lucy sighed and leaned back in her chair; how could she make other people understand?

“It’s not like he forced himself on me or anything. I love him! And it’s not because he’s my doctor. I don’t have some sick doctor patient- fantasy going on!” Lucy’s mum looked rather uncomfortable as she fidgeted in her chair.

“I’m not saying he forced you,” confirmed her mum, “it’s just…”

“He loves me,” interrupted Lucy, “he’s the only person who was there for me when I felt like a monster, unlovable! Do you know what that feels like? To feel that you are ugly, worthless, that nobody could ever love you? Don’t you get it? He made me feel loved, even when I didn’t think I was worth loving.” Her mum’s face fell, and Lucy could tell she was wondering if she had lived up to her role as a mother, but she did not have the energy to reassure her.

“You’ve never been unlovable,” affirmed her mum. Lucy merely shrugged her shoulders.

“It’s how I felt.”

“I never even knew you got attacked,” said her mum sadly, “That’s what made you remember isn’t it?” Lucy avoided her mum’s eye contact; it seemed ridiculous now that she hadn’t confided that detail to her.

“Yes,” she sighed.

“And it was the doctor’s daughter?” enquired her mum.

“Yes,” confirmed Lucy, “but she used him as much as she used me.” Lucy’s mum looked at her sympathetically and Lucy knew what she was thinking; that Lucy was deluded, or her love was misplaced somehow. It made Lucy angry, because her and Daniel were the only real thing she was sure of right now.

“Lucy it’s just…” began her mum. Lucy quickly jumped forward and leaned on the table.

“You can’t help who you fall in love with,” argued Lucy. Lucy’s mum nodded slowly.

“No, but we all have a choice in how we act on it.” Lucy sighed.

“Daniel makes me happy,” explained Lucy earnestly. “I make him happy. How can that be wrong?” Lucy’s mum looked torn at Lucy’s frank statement.

“I don’t know, but it is. He was in a position of authority over you!” Suddenly Lucy slammed her fists down on the table and an angry expression emerged on her face.

“Nobody has authority over me!” she snapped, “not you, not Daniel, not anybody…I made this decision!!” Lucy’s mum sighed and leaned back in her chair, seemingly defeated.

“I’m sorry it’s had a bad effect on your trial. More sorry than you can ever know.” Lucy sighed and slumped down in her chair in defeat.

“I’m not even bothered so much about that. I kind of thought I’d go to jail, I deserve to go to jail, but now Daniel is going to be fired and that’s my fault too…” Lucy’s mum studied her carefully and Lucy began to feel self-conscious at her discerning gaze.

“Are you incredibly angry with me?” she whispered quietly. Lucy did not respond straight away, as she paused to consider the question. Was she angry with her mum? She was possibly a little disappointed that her mum had chosen to report it instead of speaking to her first, but anger? It suddenly dawned on Lucy that she had spent most of her life being angry and sad; it was exhausting, and she no longer felt a salve to it as she once had. Was it merely as simple as making a choice?

“No, I don’t have the energy for it and frankly it’s a waste of time,” affirmed Lucy, “Daniel knew everyone would find out eventually, he was even thinking of turning himself in. I just wished it hadn’t come out in front of the court…the press…” She trailed off and shuddered as she wondered how bad things might be for Daniel right now.

“I’ll visit you every week in jail,” said her mum. She grabbed Lucy’s hand and squeezed it as if trying to prove the truth of her words. “I’ll move to the US if I have to,” she continued. Lucy smiled and squeezed her mum’s hand, knowing that it probably wouldn’t happen, but she knew her mum needed to know she believed it.

After the meeting with her mum, Lucy headed back to her bedroom unable to face talking to anyone else in the institute. She briefly thought about Max and how she had been so quick to assume it was him who had betrayed her trust. Lucy wondered if she should seek him out, but she just didn’t have the energy. She was already emotionally exhausted, and she still had the trial to come this afternoon. Once inside her bedroom, she looked around the four grey walls and for a fleeting moment, actually wondered if she might miss them when she was in jail.

Lucy looked at her watch and sighed, it was only 11am. The day was going so slow, and she couldn’t bare it, but she had promised Daniel that she would try her best to carry on. Deciding a nap may do her some good, she got into bed, figuring that she couldn’t feel guilty or overthink if she was asleep. As she began to drift off, Elijah’s words came back to her like a haunting melody; ‘The only one who can truly judge is God’. Lucy suddenly found that falling asleep was rather difficult. because she could not help but wonder how she might be judged for the darkest choice she had made. She knew she would give anything to go back and change it and she hoped that God, if he did exist, knew it too.

Chapter 33: What if I'd have Walked away…

I am freezing and I'm hungry. I have resorted to begging people for money, but I don't care. I have no dignity left. I think it is nearly Christmas because there are lights up, but I could be wrong…Christmas might have already happened. I walk past a group of teenagers laughing, I envy them, I can't remember the last time I laughed. I turn the corner and find myself facing a dark alleyway, I wonder if it is safe, but then I remember that nowhere is safe when you live on the streets, so I begin to venture down it keeping my eyes out for half eaten food that has been left on the floor or in any bins. On the opposite side of the alley, I see a man wearing a duffel coat with curly black hair; I'm not sure if he is homeless like me. He is smiling at me and summoning up my courage I begin to approach him. "Please sir," I say, "Have you got any spare change?" He looks me up and down the way that a lion looks at their prey and it makes me feel very uncomfortable.

"I might have," he says charmingly, "but what would you do to earn it?" I roll my eyes at him and turn to walk away, but then he grabs me by the arm. "I didn't realise we were finished negotiating," he says nastily. I pulled my arm out of his grasp and try not to show him how frightened I am.

"There's nothing to negotiate," I snap fiercely, but he just laughs at me as if I am somehow amusing.

"Come on darling, let's keep each other warm," he states, and I cringe. I know I am pretty much desperate, but not enough to curl up with a stranger. I reach into my inside pocket and wrap my hand around the cool sharp knife that I stole from a takeaway kitchen last week. I know stealing is wrong, but I've lived on the streets for 6 months now and if it's one thing I know how to do, it's survive.

"I'm leaving," I say menacingly "Don't you dare follow me." Though he can't see the knife he can see I have my hand on something inside my jacket pocket and holds his hands up in surrender.

"Alright then darling," he says, "some other time then." I think the matter is closed and then suddenly he jumps forward to grab me and

I scream. We wrestle as I struggle to get away from him, eventually I kick him in the shin, and he loosens his grip on me. I run as fast as I can down the dark alley way and back to the main street.

As I run into the main street I turn to see if the man is following me and then all of a sudden run straight into another man who is well built with a big bushy beard. “You look lost,” I hear a voice say, “Allow me to help; I won’t hurt you.” I scowl and struggle to get away from his embrace; his promise means nothing to me; I don’t trust anybody.

“LET ME GO!” I scream.

“Hey, calm down lady,” he says firmly, “I’m trying to help you.” My head is whirling; I just want to feel safe, and I dare not believe him. Then suddenly he put his hand on my shoulder and I freeze. Everybody wants something from me, yet they’re not prepared to give me the only thing I crave. Remembering the knife I stole earlier; I quickly retrieve it from the inside of my jacket pocket and point it at him. I don’t want to hurt him; I just want to be left alone. “Hey,” he says, “Woah there! No need for that.” He takes a step back and I almost sigh in relief. As he is talking, he begins to move towards me and my grip on the knife gets stronger. Finally, he is right in front of me, and I am petrified, what does he want from me? Why is he helping me? “Give me the knife,” he says firmly, “you are not going to hurt anyone.” I sneer at him wondering how he thinks he can tell me what to do? But then suddenly I wonder to myself who the hell do I think I am? I am standing here holding a knife, pointing it at him. What am I going to do? Stab him! Still cautious I hold one hand up and lower the knife to the floor.

“Somebody tried to hurt me back there,” I say imploringly, I need him to know that I’m not a bad person.

“That’s ok,” he says, “you’re safe now.” Then he holds out his arms and I cannot help but almost run into them. As he embraces me, I feel safe for the first time in a long time.

Predicted Verdict: Not Guilty

Chapter 34: The Final Verdict

Lucy took a deep breath as she stepped out of the car to the overwhelming screams and flashes of waiting photographers. Once more, she was alone, bar the two security guards that escorted her into the courthouse. Thinking that Elijah must be really pissed about the whole situation, she walked down the corridor and the first person she spotted was Daniel waiting at the other end.

Lucy looked at the guards who were escorting her and then decided she didn't care. Without giving them any warning, she ran down the corridor and straight into Daniel's waiting arms. Daniel said nothing, he just held her tight against him. Lucy turned her head slightly and saw in amusement that the guards were watching her and Daniel with an awkward expression on their face. She could tell they had no idea what they should do in that situation.

"Elijah didn't turn up again," said Lucy quietly.

"He'll be here," said Daniel. Then he froze and looked down the corridor behind her. Lucy turned puzzled to see what was causing him to react in such a way, when she saw her mother shake her head and hurry into the courtroom. Daniel looked at her with a pained expression.

"She already knows," said Lucy, "I'm so sorry. I found out it was her that reported us." Daniel's mouth dropped open slightly surprised but then he shrugged his shoulders.

"If it hadn't been your mum, it would have been someone else. I think it would have come out eventually either way." Lucy looked deeply into his eyes trying to gauge how he was feeling about this colossal mess.

"I did this to you," she admitted, "I'm the reason you got fired; that you'll probably have your license removed." Daniel shook his head and ran his hand through her hair.

"Lucy," he began, "I did this to me. It was my choice; not yours. I chose my happiness above all else." Lucy shook her head and smiled slightly.

"That's not true," she affirmed, "you chose my happiness too." Daniel's eyes bore into hers until eventually he sighed and looked down at the floor.

"I know," he admitted, "but now look at where it's got you." Lucy leaned back and placed her hands around his neck so that he had no choice, but to look at her. She was through with other people making excuses for her own actions.

"I got myself here," she stated, "I should have walked away, but then I suppose we wouldn't have met then." Daniel opened his mouth to speak and then suddenly let go of Lucy, pushing her slightly to the side of him. Lucy looked around in confusion until she saw Elijah making his way down the corridor towards them with a determined look on his face.

"Lucy," he stated. Lucy nodded at him.

"Elijah, I thought you weren't coming," admitted Lucy, "after all that happened; well I wouldn't have blamed you." Elijah flicked his hands out as if this situation didn't bother him in the slightest.

"Water under the bridge," he explained. "You'll never believe what I might have found. I'm waiting on something, an informant, but I can't tell you everything just in case they don't show. I don't want to get your hopes up, but if they show I think I can get you off." Lucy's mouth dropped open; it seemed impossible given the circumstances. She looked at Daniel who also looked somewhat confused.

"Where are they?" asked Daniel, looking around hopefully.

"I don't know," confirmed Elijah, "let's hope they show." They all made their way towards the courtroom together, Daniel grasped Lucy's hand in his as they walked feeling the disapproval of the security guards watching them. Once they walked through the courtroom doors, Lucy let go of Daniel's hand and he smiled at her reassuringly. She found it odd that just him smiling like that could give her a small glimmer of hope, even in the darkest time.

Once Elijah and Lucy had taken their seats, Lucy was about to ask him who the mysterious witness was, when the bailiff stood at the front and told them to rise. Once they were on the feet, the judge walked in and took her seat calling the court back into session.

“I understand that all that is remaining is the closing statement,” she affirmed, “unless anybody has anything further to add?” Jacobson was suddenly on his feet and Lucy glared at him inquisitively wondering what other stunt he was about to pull.

“Actually your honour,” he said, “The prosecution would like to invite Miss Boragas back to the stand.” The judge nodded and looked towards Lucy expectantly. Lucy blinked; he’d already questioned her. Why an earth would he want to do so again unless he had new evidence? Elijah tapped her on the shoulder and gestured that she should comply. So, with a sinking feeling in her stomach and a heavy feeling in her heart, Lucy stood up and made her way back towards the witness stand. Once she had taken the oath, once again refusing to swear on the bible, Jacobson approached the stand and smiled at her. It was a smile that Lucy did not return.

“Miss Boragas when you were last on the stand, you spoke of regret of your actions, and I get that, I do,” he began, “but what became abundantly clear is that you’d had a very difficult past; rejected by your birth mum, addicted to drugs, then left homeless. You said it had made you consumed by anger and rage. I just have one simple question left I’d like for you to answer today. Would you have stabbed Mr Pembrokeshire if you had not been so upset or angry that night?” Lucy knew that she could lie, should lie to have any hope of staying out of jail, but it was by lying about her pain, hiding it...that had led her to this very moment, and she didn’t want to make the same mistakes of her past.

“I don’t know,” she admitted. Jacobson smiled in triumph and began to walk away from the witness stand, but Lucy knew this was her final chance to say her piece and she would not let him or anyone else take it away from her. “Humans are social beings,” began Lucy.

Jacobson turned around and observed her curiously. "We react off each other, that's a psychological fact. To what extent did other people play a part in my mental state, my emotional wellbeing...everything I am as a person...I can't say. I'm not here to speak for those people. I'm here to speak for myself and to take responsibility for my actions." Jacobson crossed his arms and watched her smiling as if Lucy were a spectacle that he found entertaining. "I keep thinking about that night," continued Lucy, "about every bad experience that led me to it. Wondering if just one thing could have been different would it have changed the outcome. Would I have acted any differently…" Jacobson opened his mouth to speak, but Lucy glared at him, daring him to interrupt her.

"All we can do in a moment is react in a way we feel is right at the time, even if later it turns out we were wrong. I didn't ask to be approached, I wanted to be left alone because I was terrified and feared for my life," confessed Lucy boldly. "I did what I could to defend myself, and if I have to go to jail for fighting for my right to survive then so be it, but you nor anyone else will convince me that my truth isn't the truth, that what I felt wasn't really how I was feeling, that you would have done any differently…you weren't there; you don't know!" Lucy let out a shaky breath as she looked around the courtroom, her eyes caught Daniel's and he was looking at her with a gaze of sheer admiration. A gaze that Lucy couldn't begin to fathom but accepted gratefully. Jacobson opened and closed his mouth like a goldfish struggling to find the words to say in rebuff to Lucy's statement, but how could he? She had basically said that she was firm in her truth, and nothing could shake her from it.

"Are we done here?" asked Lucy sweetly. A small wave of quiet laughter filled the courtroom, and the judge banged her gavel.

"Miss Boragas, you will remember your place in this courtroom," she stated. Then as she looked at Jacobson with distain, she added, "And prosecutor you will remember yours, do you have any more questions for the accused?" Jacobson scowled at Lucy slightly, and then remembered himself, but Lucy was passed caring about what he thought of her. If she was going to jail, she was going to make sure that people such as Mitch Jacobson knew it was not because of them.

“Just one more question Miss Boragas,” said Jacobson, through gritted teeth, “At what point did you and Doctor Robertson start having a romantic relationship?” Lucy glared at him, she had clearly been wrong that he was unable to provoke any more reactions from her, but she’d be damned if she was going to answer that question and contribute to the evidence brought against him for the medical board.

“That’s none of your business,” snarled Lucy. An eery silence descended around the courtroom. Jacobson held up his hands as he looked at the jury. The judge looked down at Jacobson sceptically. “I fail to see how that is relevant to this case?” she asked.

“Your honour,” began Jacobson, “I’m just trying to establish whether their relationship began before she remembered what happened that night?” The judge nodded then turned to Lucy.

“You will answer the question Miss Boragas,” she instructed. Lucy chanced a glance at Daniel who looked pained but gave her a small nod. She took it to mean that he wouldn’t blame her for talking about it.

“It literally started a week ago,” admitted Lucy, “It was me who instigated it and it was because I was feeling emotional about this trial…killing someone…everything. As horrific as it all sounds, it’s nice to have at least one person in this world who doesn’t think of me or treat me like the monster I believe myself to be.” Lucy caught Daniel’s gaze and he tiled his head, as he looked at her, feeling mixed emotions of love, sympathy, and defeat. Lucy was suddenly aware that the atmosphere in the courtroom had shifted significantly. It wasn’t that they thought she was innocent, it was that they now seemed less willing to condemn her. This was in stark contrast to Jacobson, who practically danced back towards his seat.

“No further questions,” he stated happily.

“If that’s all the witnesses and evidence presented,” began the judge “I’d like to invite the Prosecutor and Defender to submit closing statements.” Jacobson was halfway on his feet when Elijah shot up out of his chair, looked around and set his eyes on the judge.

“Your honour,” he began, “I am waiting on new evidence from a new source. I’d like to ask if another recess is possible.” The judge quickly shook her head as she peered at him sternly over her glasses.

“Motion denied,” she said firmly, “you have had weeks, months councillor to get your evidence together. We will not be held to ransom. Prosecutor your closing statement please.” Jacobson shot a smug smile in Elijah’s direction, as Elijah sat back down in his seat looking utterly defeated.

“Thank you, your honour,” began Jacobson, “given what the court found yesterday in that the person who is providing care for this young woman took advantage of his position in the treatment he was providing…” Lucy could not contain herself; she would not allow him to speak so ill of Daniel when he didn’t have a clue what he was talking about.

“THAT’S BULLSHIT!!” she shouted. Elijah put a hand to his face thoroughly fed up with all the drama. The judge looking thoroughly appalled, banged her gavel.

“I will not have language like that in my court room,” she warned, “you speak up again like that Miss Boragas and I will have you removed from my court.” Lucy slumped back in her chair and folded her arms; she just couldn’t bring herself to care about this whole charade anymore. Let them throw her in jail, but she would not go down without a fight.

“Where was I?” said Jacobson thoughtfully, “Ahh that’s right. Given the fact that Lucy’s treatment that she has been receiving for the past six months is unreliable, how can we be sure of anything she says? I would ask the jury to look at the facts. She was seen stabbing the victim, he was seen trying to help her, she had a knife, he was defenceless. Not to mentioned she was carrying a concealed weapon, something which is in fact illegal in the good old State of Florida anyway. Surely the evidence speaks for itself, and on the evidence, the only conclusion you should have is, guilty.” Jacobson straightened his tie, oozing confidence as he headed back to his seat. Right before he sat down, he looked over at Lucy and if looks could kill he would have been on the floor stone cold dead on the courtroom floor. Elijah gave Lucy a pained expression before he stood up and made his way to the front.

"Have you ever been scared for your life?" began Elijah, "It does something to a person. Most of us in here come from a life of privilege where we have never had to use our survival instinct to ensure we stay alive. Miss Boragas' mental health had deteriorated, she was living on the streets, terrified for her life. How many of us can put ourselves in her position." Lucy thought it was an extremely strange closing statement, until she suddenly realised, he was stalling for time. Looking around the courtroom, she wondered who his source was and why they were so important to her case.

"Miss Boragas has made it quite clear that she wants to take responsibility for her actions," continued Elijah, "but has it been established without a doubt, the intent of her actions? Can anyone prove without a shadow of a doubt that…" He trailed off glancing towards the courtroom door which had just been opened and Lucy along with half the courtroom turned to see what he was looking at.

A man with a long coat and neatly combed hair began making his way down the aisle. Lucy gazed at him curiously wondering what significance he held. Suddenly Lucy gasped as she realised that he was vaguely familiar to her. He had changed a lot over the years, cutting his hair short and it had been extremely dark when they had last met, but there was no mistaking the piercing eyes that had filled her with terror. It was the man who had tried to attack her in the street that night! The man who had caused her to run in terror towards a terrible decision. Was he Elijah's evidence? If he was, would he openly admit to attacking Lucy that night? The judge who seemed equally confused stood up and studied the man carefully.

"You there," she stated sharply. "What is the meaning of this?" The man cringed looking around the room apologetically while holding his hands up. In one hand he held a cardboard folder and Lucy wondered what was in it.

"I'm sorry your honour," said the man politely. "I've got some papers for Mr James here." Lucy was more confused than ever, the man standing in the middle of the courtroom aisle was extremely different to the one she had confronted many years ago, but then she remembered that people change and hopefully so had she. Elijah walked towards the man in full view of the court. Everyone in the courtroom was silent as they anxiously observed the unexpected interruption. The man held out the folder to Elijah who nodded graciously and took it from his grasp. Elijah walked backed towards the front of the court as the man stayed put in the courtroom aisle looking uncomfortable, not sure if he should still be there or not.

Once back at the front of the court, Elijah opened the folder and quickly flicked through the papers in front of him. The courtroom watched with anticipation to see what new discovery this may be. Lucy looked around and caught Daniel's eye; he looked back at her curiously and shrugged his shoulders to indicate that he did not have a clue what was happening either.

"Your honour," began Elijah, "this is the evidence I have been waiting for that will call this whole case into question. I'd like for you to take a look at it if that would be ok." The judge took a moment to gather her thoughts before shrugging her shoulders and shaking her head wearily.

"Since this courtroom is already resembling a circus of sorts, I'll allow it," she proclaimed, "you may bring it forward." She reached out to take the folder from Elijah and began leafing through it. Elijah glanced at Lucy, nodded, and gave her a reassuring smile. This only served to confuse Lucy more. The atmosphere was tense as everyone waited to see what the folder contained or whether the man still standing in the aisle would be asked to testify. As the judge was looking over the papers in front of her, suddenly her mouth fell open in shock, she removed her glasses and put her hand to her head despairingly. Then remembering herself, she quickly placed her glasses back on her face and observed the courtroom, before standing up. Lucy bemused by this sudden change of events stood up also, along with the rest of the courtroom, wondering what an earth the papers could contain.

"In all my twenty years of being in this courtroom," she began anxiously, "never has a situation like this presented itself." She paused and looked over at Lucy shooting her a pure look of sympathy. Lucy in confusion wondered whether it was possibly a lot worse than she could have imagined, but how could it be worse? "I am dismissing this entire case and releasing Miss Boragas with immediate effect," stated the judge, "on account that the murder victim Alex Pembrokeshire has been found alive." Lucy felt the court room swim around her as the gravity of the judge's words sunk in; she had not killed him? Had she killed anybody? The last thing she saw was Daniel running toward her with a look of shock etched on his face before she collapsed on to the courtroom floor.

Epilogue

This close, I was this fucking close to destroying that bitch's life. Just like she destroyed mine and then right at the last minute it all fell apart. All because one man couldn't keep his mouth shut. Now everyone knows I'm alive which presents its own set of problems for me, but first things first...I'm going to take care of Lucy Boragas once and for all!

To be concluded...

# *Acknowledgements*

This book wouldn’t have happened without a few key people as it takes an army to help a book come together.

The first mention must go to my editor Natalie who gives me great feedback, even when I don’t like it or don’t understand it at first. Also, my secondary editor and advanced reader Pauline for her help with this book and my first one too.

The next mention must go to my friend Seth, for acting as an unofficial legal consult for this book. It’s hard trying to find all the answers on the American legal system when you’re actually a UK citizen living in England.

To my American friends Ricky and Nicoletta, who have supported my journey with their encouragement and kindness.

To my best friend Kath, who bit by bit has probably heard the whole of this book, as and when I have written it due to my excitement to share and get her feedback.

www.ingramcontent.com/pod-product-compliance
Ingram Content Group UK Ltd.
Pitfield, Milton Keynes, MK11 3LW, UK
UKHW021036270726
13967UKWH00013B/2815